A LITTLE LIKE

ROMEO

To my husband, Derek. You're better than Romeo

Chapter 1

You shouldn't want to kiss your nemesis.

Well, at least one of your nemeses. How many enemies can one almost twenty-two-year-old woman have, you might ask? An entire family, including all past and future generations, because family loyalty and all.

I practically snort-laugh whenever I hear the cliché that time heals all wounds. Whoever said that never met Viggo Olsen and my grandfather— Philip Jacobson, affectionately known as Farfar. Each man brings back the fury of the Viking invasions with their own touch of Norse cunning and strategy. The problem with all this Northman rivalry is a matter interwoven within secret crannies of my heart. You see, the Olsens not only own a bakery like my family, but I'm utterly in love with Axel Olsen, Viggo's grandson. Take my word for it, Axel is what dreams are made of. This problem I have is dire.

I should mention he has no idea I will disavow my heritage for a taste of those perfect lips. All true. As far as I know, Axel is completely oblivious to my secret. I hide my heart well.

Honestly, if my family apostasy is ever unearthed then I will be cut off, my name stripped from branches of the family tree, and my Farfar will see to it all my Swedish DNA is surgically removed from my cells. And I'm not being dramatic.

Other than that little thing, my family is great. Especially at Christmastime.

Slinging my canvas messenger bag over my shoulder, I stomp down the walk, the snow soaks my wool socks with each step. Already my fingertips are numb, and I only debussed ten minutes ago. Breathing deeply, I ignore the nip of winter air and inhale until my chest expands to the brink. Aromas unique to *my* street during the holidays fill my lungs. I am convinced nothing will ever rival the holly wreaths, the carolers on the corners, and the twinkling fairy lights along the shrubs and shops. People bustle about with gift bags in tow, and some with my favorite sight of all: pastry boxes imprinted with the Swedish flag. Doubtless filled to the brim with buttery cookies, lingonberry marmalade, and Swedish ginger treats, pepparkakor.

Home is nearly perfect at Christmas, but it also digs up the same question I've asked all my life. What happened between the two bakers of Lindström, Minnesota? This year is different. I *want* to know. My grandmother's final, secret words to me are the spark that ignites my hunt for the truth.

A gyrating bell from a rather peppy Santa nearly takes out my front teeth. I've stood still too long, and grunt a quick pardon before scurrying down the walk.

Everything from the streetlamps to the snow smells like butter and cinnamon. I pause at my family stoop and study the two festive bakeries. My family owns *Hanna's Swedish Pastries* and the Olsens own *Clara's Chokolade Café*. From the outside both shops are cheerful, each with a mirroring bay window filled with sweets. Each with a wooden door and iron hinges. If you weren't already a local, you'd never know turmoil existed in the foundation of such delightful bakeries.

From top to bottom, boughs of real holly with red and green lights deck the frames and windowsills of *Clara's*. A spruce advent wreath is in the window. Four white candles are nestled in the live branches surrounded by red ribbon. Already two of the candles are lit, and though I will never admit it to Farfar, I look forward to the next two Sundays when the Olsen family gathers to light another candle—and by light, I mean flip a switch. Viggo conceded six years ago to using false candles once the fire marshal threatened to close his shop after he nearly burned down half the street.

Before she died, Clara Olsen, Viggo's wife, always winked at me. I have a sneaking suspicion if not for the feud, Clara would have let me try a few of her famous cream cheese turnovers. She passed away nearly three years ago, and to the shock of the entire state Farfar delivered a bouquet of daisies to the funeral home. It only adds to the mystery. But since Clara died before my sweet grandmother, maybe Farmor sent the flowers. I will never know. Farfar, even Mom and Dad, never talk about the Olsen family. *Ever*.

3

Silver bells jingle on *Clara's* door. I've dawdled too long, and am now at risk of causing the third world war.

Clara's door is ajar, and old Viggo shuffles out, knobby cane in hand to flip the open sign to closed. I don't blink, but as if Viggo can smell my Jacobson blood his pale eyes drift across the street, piercing me like an arrow to its target.

His eyes narrow. I risk being disowned, but with the smells, the people, the songs, I wave. Bulky, childish mittens and all. I like mittens— we all have flaws.

"Happy Lucia, Mr. Olsen!" I say. Find common ground, something Scandinavians can relate to—the Santa Lucia holiday. Paintings of the young girl with braids curled around her ears and a holly crown of candles on her head hang in every window of *Clara's* and *Hanna's* But as I offer my olive branch, my voice is hardly more than a soft peep. Viggo still hears.

The old man tightens his lips until they disappear in the folds of his wrinkles. He snaps off in Danish. From what I gather by my limited linguistics, Viggo insults me for stealing Lucia's day from Denmark. Then some kind of curse against the entire Swedish nation. He goes on until another voice breaks through the tirade.

"Grandpa? Oh, there you are. Hey, it's freezing out here, come inside."

Axel.

In the back of my throat my heart bulges. And then…my mittens! I fling my kindergarten hands behind my back and stare, like an idiot, I just ogle. Some girls have ogling pinned to an artform; batting luscious lashes, puckering full red lips. Let me put it out there straight—my dark hair is wet and stringy; my lips haven't seen lipstick in two months; and one wool sock is tugged up and over my pant leg. I am not an ogling artist.

Axel steps onto the porch and takes Viggo's elbow. His honey hair, his whimsical eyes that look like diamonds. I didn't expect to see him. Foolish to think I could safely arrive in grunge-chic.

Go inside. Why am I not moving? By some neurological phenomenon, the connection from my brain to my feet severs. Axel nods in my direction, no smile on his lips—his perfect lips—but playfulness lives in his pale eyes. I bite my bottom lip and a genuine fear of drool overwhelms me.

Axel's voice sounds flat, but I'm pretty sure I see him wink. Like Clara.

"Brita," he says.

That's all, just my name. But I can't feel my tongue.

Axel starts to usher old Viggo back inside as the door to *Hanna's* bursts open.

"Brita! My lilla älskling, I was beginning to—" My grandfather's jovial face falls, his pleasant Swedish accent changes with rough, brisk words. His eyes home in on Viggo, who now swats Axel's arm to face his foe. "Viggo, hide your grisly face away, you'll frighten my granddaughter."

"Farfar, that isn't..." But my voice drowns beneath the frosty response.

"Ah, Philip, how much did it take to bribe your children to come? I'm surprised to see any at your door this year. You twit!"

My grandfather chortles with a kind of growl he saves special for Viggo. He grips his own cane, waving it in the air. "Jealousy is all I hear, you old relic. You leeching, cheating—"

"Okay, let's just go inside, Farfar," I whisper, forgetting about my mittens. With a sharp glance, I silently plead with Axel to do the same.

Because he is simply brilliant, Axel takes the hint and crooks a gentle arm around Viggo's shoulders, nudging the old man toward the warmth of his shop.

"You are nothing but a dense *trold*!" Viggo shouts over his shoulder.

Speaking in native tongue is never a good sign. Escalation is imminent. Even passersby on the street begin to belly-up to the show. My grandfather's jaw drops, a flash of malice crosses over his smoky eyes, and he takes a powerful step into the snow.

Axel moves faster, offering me a dark, flustered expression that creases two lines over his brow. He is swift, and has Viggo locked behind their bakery door in another heartbeat.

"Old *feg*!" Farfar shouts into the night, drawing a few curious glances from new shoppers. Those who know of the relationship chuckle and go about their business.

I want to melt into the snow and pretend for a moment that I come from a normal, neighborly family.

When my heart is back in my chest, I link elbows with my grandfather. "Come inside, Farfar. Viggo can't hear you anymore. Come on now, let it be. I made spritz!"

Victory. He whips his eyes toward me, a smirk on his thin lips. "What recipe?"

I roll my eyes, and stomp my boots before we step onto the threaded entry rug. "Farmor's recipe. I couldn't do Christmas without a bit of her."

"Beautiful girl," he says, patting my cheek.

Time heals all wounds? In my experience time makes stubborn men more sour, causes pleasant people to do the strangest things, and forbids all grandchildren of those sour men from mingling with the enemy—no matter how breathlessly attractive one might be.

Chapter 2

When the cuckoo clock in the hallway sings the official closing time of the bakery, I dare pull back the white linen curtains on the bay window. *Clara's* front light shuts off before the clock finishes chiming. Axel isn't there. I guess part of me hoped he might be looking for me, but then why would he? I'm a Jacobson, he's an Olsen. My private thoughts alone will send my grandfather to the grave.

Tracing the beautiful Linnea blossoms stained onto the bakery window, I sigh and shove one of my aunt's almond thumbprint cookies into my mouth. Ah, the sweets, each one is enough to convince me to stay in Lindström and give up dreams of being a literature extraordinaire, entirely.

I snag a second cookie, honestly tell me who can have only one cookie? The house seems quieter than usual.

"Caughtcha!"

Spoke too soon. Two sharp fingers dig into my sides, my blood heats as if waking from a nightmare. I fumble against the bulky shoulders of Oscar, my loving nuisance of a cousin, and fight to keep my cookie in hand, then swat the oaf in the gut.

"Oscar! I told you to stop doing that."

"You know the freshman fifteen applies to seniors, Brit. Better watch it." He pats my stomach.

A retort tickles my tongue, but my Aunt Inez stalks into the room, her narrow nose coated in a layer of white flour. "Oscar, hush," she says. "You could do with a little self-control too. It'll be you next year and I think Brita's the last one in this room who needs to worry about junk in the trunk."

"Mom don't try to be hip," Oscar says.

Inez snickers and pinches the back of my arm. "Seriously," she says and nudges a plate of snickerdoodles into my hands. "Eat up, girly, I see your ribs."

Lamppost, string bean, skeletor. I mean, I've heard all the nicknames. I'm bony, flat in areas you don't want flatness, and everyone around me always thinks I forget because they tell me all the time. I shove a cookie into my mouth until my aunt smiles and wraps her thick arms around me. I love the smell of her hair; spicy with a spritz of rose, almost as if she mixes her famous cinnamon rolls in a flower bed. On top of being too thin, I look nothing like anyone in my family. The beautiful icy blond hair of Oscar and Inez is far from my bitter coffee color. My dad even has honey golden hair and sea blue eyes. A Jacobson trademark. My family matches

9

every Scandinavian stereotype like they wrote the book. Except me. Nothing about me screams, *Sweden forever*!

I take after my mom, but she isn't Swedish. Mom billows in Italian beauty. After she married my dad, I am told my grandmother searched high and low through genealogical records for any hope the blood of their future grandchildren could be saved. My parents' first Christmas together, Farmor framed the detailed findings of my mother's *minuscule* connection to Sweden somewhere back in the twelfth century. The frame still hangs on the wall beneath their wedding photo.

Speaking of which, I nod at the picture and ask, "Why does Farfar keep that up?"

Inez shrugs as she wipes off a layer of flour from the countertop. "Divorce is hard, even for the rest of the family. I guess he likes to remember better days."

"I guess," I say, and start to help her clean up the shop.

How many kids can say they grew up in a bakery? I don't know, but I can, and it isn't an ordinary bakery. Long ago I determined the shop is a living organism, part of all of us and our customers. Always filled with funny dialects, a lot of Swedish cursing hidden behind polite smiles. Tourists enjoy a few words, but they don't need to know what we're saying. I love the place, but I guess Mom didn't share the same affection. Not that I blame her. I'm sure helping inventory a busy shop, raising me while my dad worked and socialized at the law office sort wore her to bare bones.

The bakery is in the front of the house. A few round tables decorate the shop, with the glass display cabinets filled to the brim with mouthwatering, diet-pulverizing sweets. My room is upstairs, Farfar sleeps downstairs near the shop, and Dad sleeps in the attic. That might sound awful, but the attic is the best part of the house. Mom had it remodeled and decorated before the divorce, so now it looks like a penthouse suite with a little modern flare unique to my mother.

Mom left for Michigan two years ago. I'd already been underway at school, and I wanted to be near Lindström while Farmor was sick. As much as I love the bakery, and Lindström, and all the constant reminders that the Swedish people are superior in every facet of existence, I miss my mom. At Christmastime, more than ever. My mouth tastes bitter thinking how Mom will spend the holidays snuggled up to Todd.

Listen, I'm an adult and all, but the new boyfriend sure slipped into our lives quickly.

I guess he's okay, sometimes he tries to father me with college advice and stuff. Weird, I know. I'll be cliché and say, if Mom's happy, then I'm happy, but come on, every kid says that through gritted teeth.

"Brita! Look at me!" A high, perfectly adorable voice shakes me from thoughts of Todd with his hands all over my mother. Gross, first of all, and second Agnes is the ultimate sweet distraction.

I clap my hands and beam at my six-year-old cousin. Buried in a white robe she tries to spin, but stumbles a bit. Even still, she's careful not to mess her curls out of the traditional holly bough crown Inez topped with battery-powered candles.

"You make a perfect Lucia," I say.

11

Agnes grins, two teeth missing from the front. The splints on her legs are expertly hidden, and her taut, curled hand keeps catching on the long sleeves. But I hardly notice her limp. Agnes equals pure joy.

Santa Lucia day is a beloved tradition in the Jacobson house. Even after immigrating from Sweden, Farfar insisted on keeping it alive in our home despite most of their neighbors conforming to America. I think we use it as simply another excuse to eat more food.

"Grandpa said I get to plug in the tree this year, and I even helped Mom frost the cookies!"

I am the only one who uses the Swedish terms for my grandparents. Farfar, for being my father's father, and of course Farmor, for my father's mother. Oscar always calls Farfar *Grandpa*, or *Papa* when he was little. Agnes simply follows her big brother's example. But for me Farfar stuck and I will keep it.

I pinch Agnes on her freckled nose. "Stop it right now, Aggie. You stop growing up."

She squeals, a pitchy sound, the kind that rattles in the ears. Oscar groans.

I slug his shoulder. "Payback for pinching me," I tell him. "You know I can make her laugh the loudest."

Oscar offers a gesture that relies heavily on his middle finger, but hurries away when Agnes exclaims quite delightedly that she has mighty plans to tattle on her brother straightaway.

We are hurried to the table when Farfar and Oscar's dad, Karl finally returns from fixing a frozen pipe. Uncle Karl is the only other person in the family with a darker complexion and sandy brown hair. We tagged ourselves as the misfits.

There is an empty chair at the table, and when we're halfway through our chicken and spuds, I almost think Farfar won't notice.

I'm wrong.

"Brita, my girl, where is your father?" Farfar says. "I thought he was picking you up from the bus station."

"Oh, he did," I lie, sort of creepy how easily I come up with it too. "He just ran to the office for a bit. He'll be here."

Oscar catches my eye; his lips pull into a frown. He's quick enough to hear my fib, but I won't ruin the night, not with Agnes twirling and humming at the tree.

"Ack, he better hurry," Farfar mutters, his accent comes thicker the deeper he speaks.

"Pops, remember Nils keeps busy doing all the bakery legal work for free and it takes away from his regular clients, so give him a break, yeah?" Inez says.

"I raised you and Nils to respect our traditions. I will hire a new attorney for the shop if it causes him to miss Lucia.

Inez rolls her eyes. I snort a little. Farfar can't afford another lawyer and we all know it.

"I'll keep a plate warm for him," Inez says.

With a few more jabs at my father's long work hours, we stack the plates, and the celebrating of Lucia finally begins.

***

"Brita, would you mind taking out the trash? I have to get Agnes up to bed," Karl whispers. Little Agnes sleeps soundly on his shoulder while Inez eases the splints from her thin legs.

"You don't even need to ask," I say.

Outside, the winter winds nip at my ears like a thousand bee stings. The dumpster is already bursting out the top from the busy bakery days. Glancing across the street just to be certain no one can see, I clamber up on top of the bin. Careful not to slip, I start stomping the mess down. Without a little help, trash will overflow before garbage day.

Across the street, *Clara's* is dark as pitch, but I look up toward the top floor apartment in the building next door where the Olsens made their home. There is a warm light through the pulled shades. Is Viggo still awake? Or is that Axel's room? How would I know? I've never stepped foot inside the Olsen's apartment. The only way I even know the apartment number is an accidental mail delivery.

I start to climb off the trash, but pause. Hushed voices come slow and steady from the front of the house.

"Good work today. Sorry for keeping you late. You have a knack for this."

"I appreciate the opportunity, and the trouble it could cause." A firm reply follows.

I suck in a sharp breath. The first voice is my father, home late enough I can't lie for him again, but the second one—I can't breathe. My legs turn into dead stumps sinking in the countless bags of garbage. That voice. My heart evaporates into mist right there in my chest. The gray can wobbles, but I quickly steady myself.

Keep it together, Brita.

Axel. My father is speaking to Axel. I mean, he's the only one who could possess such a silky, *delicious*, baritone. I hate to say it, but at this point I must eavesdrop, and I do so, thinking myself rather sly, rather cunning. I lean just a touch, hoping to catch a little more of this most unusual conversation.

"Tomorrow at noon, then?" my father asks.

With what I imagine as expert balance, I place one foot on the lip of the can, the other shoe lost in plastic filth. Desperate to hear the response of what will happen at noon, I don't notice the tipping, and by the time I do, it's too late.

Everything crumbles so quickly. First, I am listening for the reply, then the can that is supposed to be my trusty anchor succumbs to my awkward stance and spills me and the bags of garbage all over the icy walk. I skin my elbow, and a trash bag, smelling grossly of rotting bananas, smashes in the center of my face. Coughing and gagging, I shove the cloying plastic off my face and pray no one notices.

Kind of funny how I thought I might be so lucky.

"Brita?" My dad heaves me up from my trash bag bed. "Sweetheart, what are you doing out here?"

When I find my footing, I keep my eyes focused on the brown loafers I borrowed from Farfar. My hair drapes over my eyes and smells disgustingly sweet. My face feels hot. I swat away snow, dirt, bits of lettuce, and look at my dad.

"Trash duty. I...slipped on ice."

Someone chuckles, softly. This. Is. Not. Happening. Axel is still here! I need to face him sooner or later. From this day forth, Santa Lucia will always be known as the day Brita Jacobson became Trash Girl to Axel Olsen.

Dad helps gather the fallen bags as I slowly lift my eyes to face my fate. I stumble again, this time truly on ice, and my breath hitches when two hands steady me. He smells like pine needles on a spring day. I *love* pine needles. Like a psychopath I sniff his shirt; I can because my face is pressed against his chest. My eyes widen with surprise, lashes touch my brows. Even in the darkness I see how the royal blue of his eyes breaks through the obsidian night. His hair is combed neatly; darker than I remember. A brownish blond, and he has trim layer of scruff on his face.

But I am not sniffing Axel.

"Jonas?"

Jonas Olsen. Axel's twin brother.

Oh, I guess I should've mentioned there are two Olsen grandsons. Well, three actually. They have a younger brother, Bastien.

Jonas flicks his brows. His hands are on my elbows. I've always believed you can gauge a guy's strength by his hands. There is a shudder

16

in my stomach. If I took a wager, I'd guess Jonas is strong. And then I realize I'm still clinging to his waist. What is wrong with me?

Trying not to groan and show my hot cheeks I push away, slip on ice again, and my face nuzzles his *neck*!

When I finally find my feet and take a safe step back, Jonas straightens his suit coat, and clears his throat. In all my life I've spoken a handful of words to Jonas. Even with our families being at enemy status, Axel found the nerve to flirt with me in high school. Jonas said very little. To anyone.

"Are you all right?" he asks.

Clearing my throat, I flip into enemy mode. "I'm fine. Thank you." I smell *really* bad.

"Jonas is home for the holidays too," Dad says.

"Yes, I can see. How long is your break?" I ask, maybe a little pompously.

Jonas smirks. "As long as yours."

"Brita, Jonas goes to the University of Minnesota too," Dad says. *Is he embarrassed?*

My lips part, my pulse throbs between my ears. "I didn't know. How would I know that, Dad?"

"You've probably never seen me because I'm usually in the business buildings," Jonas responds. "Well, I better get going." Is the curl on his lips for my ignorance, or the fact that I have a plastic straw in my hair? Either way I want to disappear. "Thank you, Mister Jacobson. Goodnight Brita. Watch out for the ice."

17

My eyes narrow at Jonas's tight smile and I quickly tear the straw from my hair. Well, he is agitating.

Whirling on my father, my hands fly to my hips, the same way my mother stands when she is frustrated. "What was that?"

"Oh, come on Brit," Dad says, closing his eyes and rubbing his temples. "You aren't playing into the feud, are you?"

"What are you doing with Jonas Olsen that would keep you from Santa Lucia dinner, and I might add, from picking up your only child?"

Dad's shoulders slump, his eyes weary, but his playful smile already brings my forgiveness. I allow him to pull me into a tight hug. "I missed you kid," he says. "And I do apologize for making you take the bus. We had a bit of an emergency this morning with a client. I couldn't get away today. You could always buy a car, you know."

"How about I pay for textbooks first. Fair warning, Farfar is about to disown you," I say as I follow him up the side porch steps.

"I'm sure he is."

My father opens the door, holding it for me, but I don't budge. "Dad, what are you doing with Jonas?"

"Nothing to get an ulcer over."

"Okay, then I can tell Farfar?"

"No," Dad answers sharply.

And just like that I cross my arms in a smug victory.

Dad sighs. "Brit, you know how Farfar is, and this isn't a big deal. Jonas wants an internship next summer and the firm has a competitive program, so he took the initiative today to ask if he could work a bit over the break—without pay, I might add. It wasn't my decision. Edwin made the final choice, but to be honest, he made the right one. I wouldn't have given the kid a chance simply to spare your grandfather, but Jonas is impressive with finance law. Even without experience."

"Finance law?"

"I think I've failed you," he says and nudges me inside. "It's human courtesy to speak to neighbors, you know. You really didn't know that Jonas is a pre-law student?"

"Jonas doesn't talk to a lot of people. I know Axel is going into physical therapy, so not knowing Jonas is clearly not my fault. Still, why did he come to you?"

Dad chuckles, but the sound doesn't hold much humor. "I'm a lawyer last I checked, and he wants hands-on experience for law school applications. He's just trying to get a head start on his future."

"I'm guessing you want me to keep your secret from everyone?" I finally step out of the night; a wall of hot air strikes my face when Dad closes the door behind us.

"Yeah, I hope things can stay between you and me, however after watching that impressive interaction out there, I have something to speak with you about. I think you'll like the idea."

"Impressive, huh? You're right, I think Jonas will be asking me to marry him by tomorrow."

Dad slugs my shoulder like he always does and hangs up his jacket. We work our way into the kitchen where I hand him the plate of carbs. My stomach churns like a hurricane as we pick at cookies and pie crust, but I don't let it show.

This is weird. My dad is mingling with the enemy too. I'm not alone, except Dad isn't in love with the enemy. I am.

Chapter 3

Although darkness enrobes the morning, the fresh snowfall casts a blue glow outside on the street, and I can easily make out Farfar's curled frown as he sips his tea. My dad joins us for the obscenely early breakfast since he missed dinner. He turns a page in the Sports section of the paper, his eyes flicking to Farfar.

"Pops, are you going to scowl at me all morning?" Dad asks. He neatly folds the paper onto the table.

"I do no such thing," says Farfar.

Oh no. I hold my breath. The man is going into his proper-talk mode. It's what Farfar always does when he wants to lay on the guilt-trip extra thickly.

He barrels on, accent pronounced, nose in the air. "It matters not to me whether my children attend the vibrant traditions of their heritage."

Another sip of tea—eyes still on Dad. "It matters not that your mother, may she rest in peace, gave up years of her life teaching you children the splendor of the Homeland." Sip. Glare. "I have no ill will against you, Nils. You are a grown man. How you spend your nights is of little concern for me."

Oscar slurps a spoonful of oatmeal, but his two dimples dig deep into his cheeks as he suppresses a smile. I sigh and clear my throat when Dad's cheeks start shading the same color as the raspberry jelly.

Playing the part of my father's hero, I toss out my best distraction. "Farfar, you're still wanting me to make the breads today, right?" And just like that, Farfar breaks his dagger eyes and smiles.

"Yes, love. Inez has an entire batch of cinnamon rolls and pepparkakor to make. Popular sweets this time of year. And Oscar, my boy, I'm so thankful you've come to help your mother."

"Sure, Grandpa," Oscar mutters as he slops his spoon around the bowl. Inez flicks the back of his ear and burns Oscar with an icy stare. He clears his throat. "I mean, I'm really happy to be here. I love to help in the bakery…teaches me…hard work and all."

I snicker into my cocoa while Oscar stammers through a prepared speech I've heard Aunt Inez drill into his teenage brain for years. The cuckoo chimes five in the morning, I can guess where Oscar would rather be than preparing to open a bakery.

"Then I will prepare the creams for the fillings," Farfar says with a quick clap of his hands.

"Ah, Pops, maybe you should greet the customers. I promised the creams to Agnes—you know she enjoys licking the spoon when it's all done," Inez says.

"Can she stand for so long?" Dad asks.

"Of course she can, Nils," snaps Farfar. "Where does our blood come from?"

"Dad…" My father closes his eyes.

"Vikings, that's where," Farfar goes on. "Agnes will stand just fine."

"Therapy has been helping, she's good," Inez says. She whispers something through her teeth, I don't hear it, but Dad must because he nods. As the children of a stubborn man like Farfar, Dad and Inez are always muttering secrets.

I do know that Agnes isn't doing the creams, but Inez knows (as we all do) that Farfar will stand all day if she doesn't make something up. Farfar will be seventy-three in five months and he still tries to behave as if he is as spry as Oscar and me. Probably to stick it to Viggo, who passed all bakery and café duties to Elias and Sigrid, the twins' parents. I know my dad went to school with Elias and Sigrid, but it seems, by their indifference, it is entirely possible they have never uttered a word to each other. All the more reason Dad's secret apprentice comes as such a shock.

I shake my head, scooping out the final three marshmallows from my mug and melting them on my tongue like sugary clouds. Everything about the feud seems so ridiculous this early in the morning. I think about what Dad asked me last night. Then I think about Jonas and the way he laughed at me and my dance with the trash can. That makes me think of Axel and

23

how his twin probably recited my shame all night long. I can picture them both laughing until their sides burst. Finally, all my rambling thoughts bring me to my grandmother's letter. Our little secret.

I layer the butter on thick and shove half a croissant into my mouth while Farfar and Dad start arguing again. This feud and family nonsense is too much to take on myself. Farmor placed her hope in the wrong person.

"Brita, apart from your bakery mornings, what else do you plan to do during your break?" Farfar asks, pouring more hot water into his mug. Dad holds the paper again. I notice how the edges tremble in his firm grip, a clear sign that he will work away his frustrations late into the night again.

"Oh, I plan to work a bit. You know, help make up for where my scholarship doesn't fund," I say slowly.

Farfar lifts one of his bushy eyebrows. "Work? Where did you find such a temporary job? Oh, unless you've…Brita have you decided to stay home for the final months? I've been told those online courses are quite popular, yes?"

"No, Pops. I hired Brita," my dad says. "She's going to edit our depositions and reports."

"What?" Farfar asks.

"She's an English major, Pop. I think it would look good on a resume."

"Well, that sounds terribly boring," Inez says, though she smiles. "No offense, Brita. I'm glad there are people like you who love to fix words, but I tell you what, I would rather pluck out all my leg hairs."

Oscar scrubs his eyes. "Nice visual, Mom."

24

"Well, as long as it doesn't interfere with the bakery, I think that's a wise financial decision," Farfar says.

"Glad you approve," Dad scoffs.

Farfar may not have noticed the sarcasm, but Dad layers it on thicker than my butter.

I nod, though I choose not to say anything else. In truth, I'm excited to use what I've been studying in school. Dad is right, having an actual job will help with a resume when I graduate. But there remains one awkward downside to the arrangement we discussed last night.

"You can't say anything about Jonas. Not to anyone," Dad said once I agreed to work for the Anderson-Collins Law Firm.

"What's going to happen when Aunt Inez shows up?"

"Because she always comes to my office? Name the last time."

"Maybe she'll randomly decide to take you to lunch or something. Or what if I edit a project from Jonas and Farfar sees it? Why do we have to always keep these secrets, Dad? For crying out loud, what happened with the Olsens?"

I may have gotten a little dramatic, but it was late, and I ate too much pie.

"Just promise, Brita. It might cause trouble for Jonas too, and you know what this would do to your Farfar."

"Fine," I grunted. "But then you need to be home Christmas Eve *and* Christmas, and I mean home. Not on the laptop, not writing reports, not on the phone, or I'm going to go stay with Mom."

25

"Are you threatening me with parent picking?" Dad asked, his lawyer shoes laced up. He'd negotiated, debated, and tried to find a loophole in my contract. Then soon remembered I am his child, and learned all my skills from him. I won.

"How is your mother?" he asked after concession. "Is she still dating…"

The conversation then moved into a weird realm I'm not ready to replay this early in the morning.

"Well my loves," Farfar says. His knees crack, and his back stays arched a little too long when he stands from his seat. "It's time to get started on the day. We have a public to feed."

I wipe a blob of butter from the corner of my mouth. Inez instructs Oscar to clear the table—he of course protests. A bold move. Inez is not one I would challenge, and soon enough, Oscar clears the plates.

"You're leaving already? It's not even six-thirty." I say to Dad and help Oscar with the juice glasses.

"Yeah, I thought I'd get an early start. We're still dealing with that hiccup from yesterday. See you around noon?"

"Well there's a bus that leaves at eleven forty-five, so I might be—"

"No, just go to the gas station. Your ride will come meet you there." Dad sips his orange juice before I take his glass. My jaw drops.

"Dad, are you kidding me?" I lower my voice to make certain Oscar won't hear. "That is not part of the deal."

"Oh, I made it part of the deal. I've got a feeling you're going to enjoy your ride. And I've got near perfect instincts, so there's that. See you at noon, Brit." He smiles, taps my nose, and turns out the door.

I stand in the dining room, my palms sweaty, my heart thumps in the pit of my stomach. Am I understanding this right? Yes, of course I am, Dad was too pleased with himself for it to mean anything else. In a few hours I'll ride twenty minutes to Dad's office with Jonas Olsen. Not Axel Olsen. No, his brooding, crabby twin. This is not the way to cozy up with the Olsen family before Axel begs me to become Mrs. Brita Olsen. Not at all.

Chapter 4

Joy to the World echoes in my ears as I hug my body to block out the cold. The speakers at the station are crackly and the rendition by Whitney Houston seems to mock my sour mood the longer the song plays. Day shoppers and commuters pass by me, some wave but most are too engrossed by their phones or purchases to notice anything else. Nothing feels very joyous in the moment.

I stand on the corner, fight the chill that bites through my coat, and grip a gas-station hot chocolate while guilt wraps around my stomach. Farfar pleasantly bade me farewell when I clocked out of the bakery and rushed off with all my secrets tucked beneath the surface. I lift my chin and remind myself all my remorse is ridiculous. We are both just normal college students using whatever means at our disposal to further our futures. Dad is right, now isn't the time to dwell on the feud.

And on a brighter thought, this might be my shot at finally breaking down the barbed-wire fences keeping me from Axel. No one said going the back way to his heart isn't a good option. I can impress the twin brother; Jonas and I will get to know each other. We'll be civil.

My hair still smells like flour and salt, but at least the tresses fall straight. Despite my reservations on getting to the office, I do want to impress my dad's colleagues. A letter of recommendation will go a long way with a publishing house someday. I sip the cocoa, a bit surprised gas station hot chocolate has a silky taste, but when a black sedan pulls up close, the final gulp misses my mouth and flows down the front of my coat like a brown river.

Batting at the dripping chocolate, I glare through the passenger window. The insults on the tip of my tongue are soon lost when he meets my harrowing gaze.

"You're jumpy," Jonas says, flatly.

An actual huff escapes my throat when I toss my cup into the trash. Taking a deep breath, I secure my messenger bag, and step into the car. *Jonas Olsen's car.*

Farfar will set flame to the pies if he finds out.

Jonas moves a file folder stuffed with papers from my seat and tosses it in the back. Scruff from last night has been shaved this morning; now Jonas looks even more like Axel. The twins have distinct differences though. Axel's eyes are like a summer sky, Jonas's are like the deepest part of the ocean. Axel has full lips which add to his distinguished smile. Jonas has the full lips, but they are always set firmly in displeasure. Axel is broad and strong, Jonas is made of leaner tone. His navy suit makes him

29

look, I don't know, lawyerly, while last night Axel looked perfect in sweatpants.

"You could have pulled up in front of me instead of trying to run me over from behind. Then I wouldn't be so jumpy," I say as he pulls away from the gas station.

I think he almost laughs. "Valid point," he says.

Clutching my bag to my chest, I stare out the window. Jonas stays quiet and I believe we can do this. We'll drive to Dad's office without awkward small talk. What would I say anyway? Okay, I haven't said many things to Axel either, but talking to him seems easy if I ever get the nerve.

For example, in high school Axel talked to me a few times, away from the watchful eyes of our grandparents. I played softball with one of his old girlfriends, and he came to a few games. I think he shouted "Nice catch" once. Sometimes Axel acknowledged me in the halls; flirty, confident, and wonderful. I suppose that is part of my infatuation. The 'wanting something you know you can't have thing'. I couldn't have him in high school, the man always had a significant other. And I can't have him at all because of his last name. He is a unicorn.

I don't like to think those thoughts too much, sometimes they make my desires sound shallow, and I want a *real* connection with Axel.

Funny how my memories of Jonas are wholly different. Jonas, the focused, quiet, and uninterested-in-flirting twin. Not much has changed.

I dig into my bag after a few silent minutes and open my well-loved textbook. I breathe in the ink and paper smell, a smile that can't be helped

30

paints my face. Soon I am back in Venice. I can practically smell the musty cobblestones.

Lost in the plots and betrayal I hardly hear Jonas interrupt. "*Othello*? You know school is out, right? Or is that just some light reading?"

So, forget the silent drive. "I'm trying to decide on my senior capstone project. Shakespeare is one of the choices, but for your information I do enjoy reading his works. They're fascinating."

"Sure, especially that one. I love the way misunderstanding and assumptions bring death. Stirring Sunday read."

I'm not sure what shocks me more. Jonas speaking to me, albeit mocking me, or that he knows *Othello*.

"You've read this?" I ask shaking the book next to my face.

Jonas shrugs. "You can't escape high school without a literature class. I only knew about *Romeo and Juliet*—which I refused to ever read again— and I thought I'd be safe with one about a bit of jealousy. I think Shakespeare was a total killjoy."

My jaw drops and I quickly come to the defense of my William. "So, you've written off the most brilliant playwright in history because of two stories? Both are clearly labeled tragedies, by the way," I say. "He wrote comedies too. Ever heard of *Taming of the Shrew*? *Much Ado About Nothing*? I mean, you can't deny the man was a brilliant storyteller, a romantic really. Even if some of his plays were tragic, the complexity of it all is stirring, and inspiring and…"

I halt my rant when Jonas chuckles, and I discover his smile is different than Axel's. Shier, but enough to show his teeth and brighten his eyes. I don't like the way it makes stomach tighten.

He holds up one hand. "Okay, I get it. You have a thing for Shakespeare. I would still argue he had a passion for the depressing."

"Arguing my love of Shakespeare, how very pre-law of you." I tuck dear William back into my bag.

Jonas shakes his head, the smile hides behind his indifferent expression once again. "I'm not going to be in courtrooms, you know. I like the business side of things, like finance, maybe even patent law someday."

"Hmm," I respond and lean my head against the window again. In truth, I want to learn more, but can't break the innate instinct to be aloof around an Olsen, or maybe I am still shell-shocked an Olsen told me personal goals.

"And you?" he asks when we pass through two more streetlights.

"What?"

"What are you planning to do with English? Read Shakespeare in coffee shops with a little black beret?"

"Very funny." I make sure he catches my significant eye-roll.

"Are you intentionally avoiding the question, or is it that you don't want to say them to me?" Jonas's eyes have a way of shadowing or brightening depending on the tone of his voice.

I don't answer at first. He studies me and I think I sort of like it, and then that sort of freaks me out. The dark blue of his eyes leaves me unexpectedly wanting to know what he's thinking. Strange.

I swallow hard after a pause and shake my head. "I'm not avoiding the question. Honestly, I haven't told anyone what I plan to do except for my mom."

Jonas stops at a red light. His brow furrows for at least three heartbeats. "Why? Is it some big secret?"

"No," I insist. "Just something that doesn't involve inheriting a bakery."

Jonas nods, but his shoulders curve forward a bit, almost like an invisible weight presses down. "Now, *that* I can understand," he says. "Well, don't worry. I promise your secret will not leave this car."

I smile. A bit of the discomfort between us melts away—only a bit. "Fine. I want to work for a publishing house as an acquisitions editor someday."

"You want to read books for a living?"

"It's so much more than reading books. Finding that *gem*, you know?"

There is a reason I only mention this to my mother. When I think about it, speak about it, something happens. I lose my mind. Unable to cease a blast of literary passion. Mom tells me I go starry eyed with a stupid smile.

And now, Jonas Olsen earns the honor of my whimsy. "The idea of taking something in a raw form and helping polish it until it's a masterpiece. To be the one someone trusts with their creation—it's very

33

vulnerable, I would imagine, putting such a personal piece of your soul out there. Books are a window to the soul, that's what my Farmor always said. I totally believe it though."

Jonas grins, somewhere between a real smile and smirk.

My caprice fades as I sit straight in my seat again. "But, it's not a realistic goal."

"Why not?"

"I think my aunt expects me to come back and help her out in the bakery when Oscar goes to college. I can't tell you how many times I've heard my Farfar say how sensible I am to choose a career that can be done 'at home' so I can help run the business." I pause. I've been rambling. "Sorry, you don't need to be dumped on."

Jonas pulls into the law firm's parking lot by the time I've finished vomiting out my fervor. *Wow, time went quickly.*

His jaw tightens, he reaches into the backseat for his bag. I eye him with a layer of caution and unbuckle my seatbelt. I think I can safely assume Jonas sees me as a literature lunatic at this point.

Halfway out of the car, he speaks. "I think it's really awesome how passionate you are about your degree. Not many people find that. For what it's worth, I think you should do what you want to do. Don't get me wrong, I'm not downplaying the pressures of family, I get it. Still, you should go for it. Can I be honest?" He doesn't wait for me to respond before barreling on. "I wasn't really looking forward to this whole working together thing. I think it's stupid that I'm keeping this a secret from my family. But maybe it won't be so bad. After all these years, one of my neighbors turns out to be interesting."

Jonas stuffs the file folders in a sleek brown bag. His shy smile passes over his mouth briefly before he heads to the building. I stand dumbfounded for a few moments. From the time I woke that morning, I too, dreaded my time with Jonas Olsen. But the car ride teetered on enjoyable.

My cheeks flush as I imagine that just maybe, Jonas might speak of my awesome passion to his twin brother. One can hope.

Chapter 5

The day before Christmas Eve the law firm bustles in preparation for the holidays. By now, I find a normalcy around Jonas. We chat surface talk on our rides to the firm, and hardly see each other during the day. Then I drive home with my dad. Okay, I admit Jonas isn't so bad, though I still know very little about him. I gather he isn't too keen allowing people see through his fitted suits and courteous grins.

At the office, I work in a small cubical adjacent to the copier and if the law firm needed to invest in anything, it is a new copier. On my first day I was certain the back wall was being demolished. Jonas, on the other hand, works with the paralegals. The fancy side of the office, as I call the spaces next to a constant snack cart. The wheeled cart has coffee, cocoa, and juice. And muffins! I don't know who keeps the cart stocked, but they do a marvelous job. I'm not bitter, but the desks where Jonas works are topped with new PCs and have chairs with lumbar support. In my dad's defense, he did give me a decent chair, but being the only person in the office without any legal drive or knowledge banishes me to exile.

My routine of few encounters with the Olsen enemy has become so normal that my heart leaps into my ears when Jonas taps my shoulder just after the lunch.

"Whoa," he says with a laugh. I straighten my frilly blouse and tuck my hair behind my ear. He leans against my cubicle. "I didn't mean to interrupt your daydream."

"I wasn't daydreaming," I insist. "I was working. You're like a ninja." Jonas lifts one brow, the corners of his mouth hardly budge, but I've learned by now he smiles on the inside. At least that's what I tell myself. He just stands there, a black leather folder in his hands. Jonas has stripped his suit jacket due to the heater blasting uncommonly hot today, and his sleeves are rolled up, showing off a fancy antique watch. I rock a bit in my chair, waiting. "Um, is there something I can do for you?"

"Oh..." He taps the top of the folder. "Yeah, I need you to look over this. It's my first report. Your dad wanted it to have a pass through you before he turns it in to Mr. Collins."

"Talk about daydreaming. That wasn't so hard to say." I reach for the file, but Jonas clutches it tighter. "I'm going to need to see the writing if you want me to edit it. That's kind of how it works."

"Yeah," he says. Is he blushing? Jonas glances at the ground—still holding the folder.

I lean over my knees; my voice drops to a dramatic whisper. "I'm getting the sense you don't really want me to see it."

"No, that's not it at all," he says, handing over the file. Yet, still he stands there, his eyes tracking the report when I take the leather in hand.

"Either you really like me, or you're really possessive about this folder," I say, then click my tongue and pretend to inspect the sides. "Not that I blame you. Real leather." I make an 'okay' symbol with my fingers. "Quality stuff."

The sharp ridges of his cheeks flush crimson. "Laugh it up," he says, but his shoulders aren't so stiff anymore. "I'm not much of a writer, okay, but I've been working on it since day one. And, well—just know that I'm not much of a writer."

"I got it," I say with a laugh. "Don't worry, I won't tease you too much. I mean, you are an Olsen—"

"Jonas!" A familiar voice calls from around the thin walls of my cubical.

Jonas looks up, then smiles wider than I've seen before. I roll my chair out and groan. Logan Snyder. A former classmate. Crass and crude, and he lives for the Jacobson and Olsen rivalry.

"Hey Logan," Jonas says, allowing Logan to pull him into a loud, backslapping man-embrace. Logan hasn't changed much. I've seen him twice since he graduated with the twins, but he still has that annoying, arrogant half-smile as though he is the greatest gift to the world. Logan's raven hair has grown out, and wings over his ears. A shadow of whiskers coats his chin, and he's dressed in khaki shorts and a blue T-shirt. Two days before Christmas. In Minnesota. Is he trying to prove something to the cold?

"Are you ready?" Logan asks.

"Almost, just turning in my paperwork," Jonas replies, and nods in my direction.

My neck flushes with heat. I can feel my pale cheeks turning rosy pink as Logan's aggravating gaze locks onto my desk.

"Brita Jacobson. What are you doing in a place like this? Careful, wouldn't want anyone to see you speaking with Jonas. What would your grandpa say?"

"So good to see you, Logan," I mutter, my voice drips with sarcasm. "If you'll see the staff directory, I think you'll find this is my father's law office. But your hilarious comments are always so appreciated."

Logan laughs and slaps the top of my cubical wall as though he's never been so entertained. "Always the same sass, Brita. I've missed that."

"I'm sure you have." I turn my attention back to the stack of tax grant proposals for businesses in the area. Not the most riveting piece I've ever edited, but as I keep saying, this is a notch in a resume.

Thankfully, Logan turns back to Jonas. "You're going to wear that?"

"I'm going to change when we get there," Jonas says.

"Come on you guys." A second voice—a voice I know all too well—whispers by my desk.

I roll my seat back. No, I'm not ready for this. Not at a law office. Not with so many people around. Not next to Jonas. But that thought leaves me wondering why I care what Jonas thinks.

Axel stalks toward the back of the offices. His white teeth gleam in the afternoon light. Slow motion takes hold. I hear sappy music, an out-of-nowhere-breeze ruffles his hair. He winks. Curse that wink. Somewhere in the recesses of my daydreaming mind I know that I'm staring, gaping really, but Axel's beautiful qualities deserve admiration.

"Brita, nice of you to let my brother hang around here." Axel is speaking.

Talk, Brita! I'm certain if people knew the truth of my feelings then they would find me a silly, ridiculous woman with an over-the-top crush. But I'm also certain those people have never seen Axel. He's funny, charming, delicious. Have I mentioned his smile?

"Uh, yeah no problem," I say, fiddling with the yellow post-it notes on my desk. The shame of my repulsive reply stabs along my back. My voice is hardly louder than a whisper. Taking a deep breath, I remind myself what Farfar always said. Where do we come from? Vikings! *Be a Viking, Brita.* "How are you enjoying your break, Axel?"

Axel leans on his forearms over my cubical wall. Everyone else disappears. I cross my leg without thinking and put the end of my pen between my teeth before I realize it is the actual pen point and I've stabbed my tongue with blue ink.

The ground shifts when the Vikings roll in their graves.

"It's been great," he says. "I was going to do a clinical with a physical therapist in New Jersey, but he had a family emergency. So, home it is." His black T-shirt beneath his suave jacket pulls tightly over his broad shoulders. He nudges his brother's shoulder. "I didn't know Jonas would

40

be such a stiff and work all through the break, but I have to admit it's kind of fun keeping his little secret."

"Come on, we're going to be late," Logan whines, and punches Axel in the shoulder. I'd like to punch Logan's nose.

I look at Jonas. He watches me. Those royal blue eyes bounce between me and his brother. One corner of his mouth flicks up, another expression I've never seen before. Whatever it means he is spinning my head and I don't like it.

"I'll meet you in the car, I just have to grab something," Jonas says.

"Hurry," Axel adds before turning back to me. "See you around, Brita. Let me know if Jonas gives you a hard time."

"Okay," I gurgle. Not chuckle, not giggle. I gurgle.

Logan jumps up and slaps the doorframe before he and Axel disappear out of the office. I release a long, pent breath. My chair whirls around with enough force I need to grip the armrests. Jonas leans forward, caging me between his arms. His face has never been this close, and that smirk reveals a new mischievous side I kind of like.

"You have a little secret, Brita Jacobson."

"I have no idea what you're talking about," I say, scooting my chair back.

"Oh, I think you do. How long?"

"Jonas, get out of here. Go do whatever it is you're going to do."

"It's just basketball. How long, Brita?"

41

I huff, something I do often around Jonas. "How long, what?"

"How long have you had a thing for my brother?"

"A thing? Really, Jonas, are we still in junior high?"

Jonas rests one hip on my desk. My breath hitches again when he leans closer. An unusual sensation, having a tingle of nerves around Jonas. Something unfamiliar and unexpected. The crazy thing? I like it. A lot.

"No, we're not in junior high," he says. "So answer the question."

"We're not talking about this," I say. I take the file folder and try to stand, but his hand rests on my forearm. What is happening? A pleasant burn warms my skin under his touch.

"Oh, we are talking about this," he says. "Come on, I'm not going to tell anyone."

"Sure, let me just spill everything to you because we're so close."

Jonas removes his hand and returns to his shy grin. "Okay, good point."

"Why thank you counselor." I have no shortage of lawyer jokes.

"How about I tell you something about me that's personal as a sign of good faith," His brow furrows, and the shade of blue in his eyes deepens. He's serious.

"It has to be big then," I tease. "Like your deepest fear."

Jonas shakes his head. "No, we aren't at that point yet." He turns my chair, so I'm facing him again. "But I've got a good start. If my grandpa ever hears about this, then I'll be disowned. You will never repeat this—got it?"

I can't help but smile. Crossing my heart, I hold up one hand. "I swear."

"Okay." Jonas lowers his voice. "Every Santa Lucia Day I pay my parents' neighbor girl to go and buy those ginger cookies from your family's bakery. There, now you know."

I study him. Jonas keeps his arms crossed over his chest; his expression unchanged. "You're serious?"

"I can't help it. I love them. We make something similar, but I love those cookies," he says. "You understand more than anyone what that means. I just told you a big thing. So, your turn."

Jonas isn't playing, and I have the sneaking suspicion he's not leaving until I add something. Closing my eyes, I tangle my fingers into bony knots. "I may find Axel…interesting."

"Now who's acting like we're in junior high?"

"Okay, I am attracted to your brother, is that what you want to hear?"

"Yes, because we're twins, so what does that say?"

"Ugh, I don't like you."

"Nope, but maybe Axel."

I laugh and pinch his arm. "Fine, I like Axel. Happy?"

"Yes." Jonas's smile fades slightly. "But you don't think anything can happen because—"

"Because our families are sworn enemies, yes. That does pose a bit of a problem." I tap my pen along the edge of my desk, an embarrassing burn swells behind my eyes. "Don't you ever get tired of it, Jonas? I mean, I don't even know why Farfar and your grandpa hate each other. No one talks about it—it's just what is. You should be able to come into a bakery and get cookies without sending a surrogate. I should..."

"You should be able to care about who you care about," he finishes for me. We sit in a welcome silence for a moment, then Jonas backs out of my cubicle. "You know what, you're right Brita. I'm going to help you out."

"No, no, no," I beg. "Don't say anything, please."

"Don't worry. I'm just going to mention some of your less-annoying qualities and encourage Axel. Whatever happens will happen. I won't mention our conversation to anyone, I promise."

I question if I can trust him. Words won't form, so I keep tapping my pen. Those confessions came too easily, and I'm a little unnerved.

Jonas slings his leather bag over his shoulder and steps out of my cubicle. "Well, I'm going to go. I won't break my promise. Merry Christmas, and I guess I'll see you in a couple days."

Dad is keeping *his* promise to spend all Christmas Eve and Christmas Day at home. I heard him speaking with Edwin, the Anderson in the Anderson-Collins Law Firm. Our holiday starts tomorrow.

"Merry Christmas," I say.

Jonas disappears behind the cubicle wall with a small wave.

I startle when he hurriedly pokes his head around the corner again. "Hey, you know what's kind of funny? I was just thinking, this whole situation with Axel, it's kind of perfect for someone like you."

"What? How is it perfect?"

"Well, because of your love affair with Shakespeare. If you think about it, Axel is a little like Romeo, and you're a little like Juliet."

I cross my arms. "Well, I'm not one for death and sorrow, but if we're the stars then who does that make you? Mercutio?"

He shakes his head. "No, he dies too. I'll be the Friar. Just a decent guy trying to do the best by everyone."

"You know, for hating *Romeo and Juliet* so much, you know a lot about it."

"Must have burned a hole in my brain. Merry Christmas."

I scoff when Jonas stalks out of the office. His words replay through my head like a broken reel of film. A romantic notion, Romeo and Juliet. Except for the tragic ending of course, that part is definitely out of the picture. Brushing my hair behind my ears again, I smile, roll my lip over my teeth. Pulling Jonas's folder toward me, I open to the first page.

Chapter 6

Christmas Eve and Christmas morning are special in the Jacobson home. Dad keeps his word, though there are times I see him peer at his watch or tap his knee as if he knows how much work is mounting while he idly sing songs and eats braided sweet bread.

The house is packed Christmas Eve. Farfar's brother and his wife stop in to celebrate. Uncle Gunnar is pleasant, though in the early stages of dementia. But still sharp as a tack during a round of poker Karl and Oscar insist on starting. Gunnar left with two batches of spritz and an entire case of cupcakes.

Uncle Karl's sister came up from Duluth. She is single and dotes on Oscar and Agnes—and me. She gifts me a complete collection of Jane Austen's works. Thrilled doesn't describe how excited I am to dig in. Agnes squeals most of the night in pleasure, especially when presents are passed around. Only Santa Clause gifts are opened on Christmas morning.

I don't know who started that rule, but as a kid I loved opening half my gifts the night before. Now, it is ten times as entertaining watching Agnes limp back and forth from the tree to her designated place on the couch, opening her Christmas Eve treasures, and dreaming of what might come the next morning.

As enjoyable as Christmas Eve is, the peace of Christmas morning is even better. I sip some of Farmor's special peppermint tea in the new china teacup Inez gave me. I love teacups, so does my aunt. I gave her the same gift, a cup with beautiful ivy vines along the edge and a handle curled like a delicate leaf.

Farmor made the tea every Christmas and it seems wrong not to make it this year. I stare out the window thinking of my grandmother. Missing her.

My cell phone buzzes on the table. I smile away the melancholy, answering the video call. "Merry Christmas, Mom!"

"Sweetie! Merry Christmas. Thank you for the scarf! Seriously, Brita it's beautiful. I miss you." My mother's smiling face breaks through the screen. She holds her own mug of something—I hope Farmor's tea. She smiles and her eyes crinkle in the corners, but I think it adds a bit of cheer to her face.

"I miss you too. I'm glad you liked it. I got the tickets! Mom, seriously? We're going?"

Mom smiles. "I thought you deserved something amazing. It's kind of a huge celebration all rolled in one. Christmas, your birthday, graduation. It'll be a blast, just us girls."

47

"Thank you. I've always wanted to go to New York, and Broadway! I can't wait."

"I'm glad you liked it," she says.

"How was your morning?" I ask. Her house is dark, but I can see a few flickers of candles behind her. Mom has a thing for scented candles.

"Cold and quiet," she says.

"Todd isn't there?" I don't want her to be alone. I would rather her be here, filling our house with her plumeria perfume. No one would mind.

"He's coming later. His mother is in a retirement home nearby and he went to visit with her. We're going to his brother's house for dinner. How has your break been? I still think I need to steal you away for a few days before you go back to school."

"I would love to, but I'm working with Dad, remember?"

"Right, how could I ever forget the super-secret?" Mom giggles, but my smile drops, and I quickly glance over my shoulder. No one is there to hear.

"Mom, careful." I tried to keep my promise with Dad, but this is my mother—I tell her almost everything. Except about Axel. Even so, I suspect Mom knows. She can sniff out things like that.

"Brit, relax. I think it's a great thing you're doing, and your dad's right, it will look great on a resume. I just find it a little entertaining that the guy next door, I'll call him that, is there too. I'm even more surprised your dad allowed it."

"Edwin Anderson approved it actually."

48

"Well, it's all very dramatic," she says, still smiling. I know she's teasing, but I agree. The feud is dramatic, and today in particular I feel weary of the Jacobson-Olsen war. My mother takes a sip of her mug and adjusts the angle of the phone. I can see gentle snow falling outside her bay window. "Brit, you should take this time to get all the secrets of the enemy."

"He's actually a nice guy," I say. By the way my cheeks heat I'm sure are the same shade as the holly berries over the mantle.

Mom notices and lifts a brow. "Is he now?"

"Mother," I sigh. "I just mean it's not like we're ready to duel or anything. He's just trying to secure an internship like any normal, motivated—"

"Kind of sexy…"

"—pre-law student. I'm going to pretend I didn't hear that."

Mom smiles, her eyes doing that cheery scrunch again. "Okay, I'll stop. Honestly, I think it's great. I married into that feud, but never understood it. And if I'm being honest, I'm not sure your grandmother cared much for it either. I mentioned that once to your dad, but he didn't agree."

One hundred percent, I agree with Mom. I know Farmor's secret distaste for the feud. My thoughts drift back to her letter stuffed inside my purse. I carry it everywhere.

"Didn't agree with what? I can't believe I would ever argue with anything," Dad's voice interrupts.

Mom laughs. I'm glad it isn't the same unfeeling tone they kept with each other the last year of my high school experience. Those are the days I first noticed something might be off with my parents' marriage.

"Merry Christmas, Nils," Mom says politely.

"Merry Christmas, Judy. You could have joined us, you know. No reason to be alone during the holidays."

"*Dad*," I warn. He knows about Todd. My parents are crazy and held a family meeting over the new relationship. I'm going to go out on a limb and say that was the cringiest dinner we've ever had as a family.

"That's a nice offer," Mom says—a little stiffer. "I do miss Inez's sugar cookies. I'm glad to see you home, Nils. Christmas was always such a busy time for you."

I close my eyes, praying this will stay mellow.

"Well, Brita is home and can hold her own in a rebuttal. I'm not sure where she gets that from," Dad says, flicking my bun.

"I have no idea." Mom finally frees a lighter laugh. "Well, you two, I hope you have a wonderful day. Brita, call me later? I want to hear all about your plans for your final semester! I can't believe you're graduating. When did this happen, Nils?"

Dad shrugs and clicks his tongue. "I don't know, but I don't like it."

"You two stop," I tease and nudge Dad's elbow.

"Well, Merry Christmas, love you." Mom blows a kiss. "I'll see you next month!"

Dad snacks on some of the cinnamon rolls from breakfast when we disconnect. I stare at him while he gazes out the window. "Dad? You good?"

"I'm fine," he says and points at my blank phone screen. "You should be thrilled we can talk with each other now."

"I am, but I imagine it isn't easy sometimes."

Dad kisses the top of my head. "It's not, but you don't need to worry about it, okay? That's a pretty great gift you got from your mom. I think you'll have a good time."

"It'll be a lot of fun. I love the watch too. You guys spoiled me this year," I say, holding up my wrist to display the rose-gold Apple watch.

"Oh, I had ulterior motives. Now I can track you when you go back to school."

We laugh easily and are soon overtaken by the others in the house. I often wonder why Inez and Karl don't move in. They are rarely at their house two blocks away. Dad once offered to find an apartment, but I also know the Jacobsons do what the Jacobsons do. Change is never easy in this house.

When night shadows the streets, and the soft glow of the twinkling white lights burst like stars along the shops I stare out my window. Yes, I look at *Clara's*, and just as the Olsen brigade makes their exit into the cold from their bakery. Sigrid Olsen leads the way with Bastien. The kid has grown into a lanky bean pole through the last year, and towers over his mother. Sigrid seems nice enough. When we came close enough to lock eyes once, I discovered her eyes look like mist after an ocean storm.

Sigrid types away on her phone, and not far behind her Elias follows before they turn into the front door of the neighboring apartment building.

I don't know Elias. I wonder if he gave Axel his playfulness, or Jonas his shy kindness. I smile to the window thinking of how Jonas's brow furrows whenever he grins. I braid and unbraid the ends of my hair, puzzled at myself. I study Axel—not in a creepy way—because of my infatuation, but when had I started knowing things about Jonas?

I draw in a breath when I see Axel. He follows his father, with Logan. I'm curious why Logan is there on Christmas like I have a right to know. Jonas waits by the door of the bakery with his grandfather as Viggo locks up. Then Jonas links his elbow with his grandfather's arm when they trudge through the snow to the apartment building. Sigrid stands at the door and takes Viggo the rest of the way.

I feel sad. For the first time that day something shifts all wrong. The Olsens are a normal family just like us. In the moment I can understand Farmor's frustration. Digging through my black purse I find her letter. Already the envelope is yellowed and creased from my incessant opening. Glancing once more to the street before planning to read the note for the umpteenth time, my breath rips straight from my lungs. Never has the darkness of my room been so welcome.

Jonas readies to step inside the apartment building, but he stops, and glances across the street. He looks at my bakery. He looks at *me*. Well, okay he can't see me. A familiar need to know what thoughts are running through his mind overwhelms me until my stomach hurts.

Then I wonder why the idea of Jonas looking my way sends my head into a spin.

***

The next morning, I wake extra early to help get ready for the after-Christmas sales in the bakery. It is nearly eleven-thirty by the time I find my way to the gas station corner. The black sedan waits near a pump. I grip the small gift bag filled to the brim with ginger pepparkakor to give Jonas. He won't need to pay for his little spy anymore.

Without a thought I slip into the car, untangle my bag from over my shoulder, and buckle up. "Sorry, I'm a little slower today. Busy morning. How was your…"

All my speaking skills fade like the faint breeze when I look up. Jonas is not in command of the car.

"Axel, hi," I mutter. My heart makes a run for it and pounds somewhere deep in my ears.

"Hey, Brita," Axel says. His perfect white smile sends a splay of heat through my stomach. "I hope you don't mind, Jonas had to go in a little earlier, but needed something done on his car. We switched and I offered to drive you. I have to run some errands for the shop, so I figured it would be pretty perfect."

"That's great," I whisper and lean my head back against the seat. My mind is devoid of clever comments, so I opt for short acceptable responses.

"What's all that?" Axel asks.

My skull must've been empty because I simply stare at him as he pulls into traffic. Axel lifts a brow. *Be still!* He is smiling at me. I know the smile belonged to me because, simply put, there is no one else in the car.

53

"Brita?"

I love the way he says my name. Until I realize he keeps saying it. *Pay attention!*

"What? Sorry, I kind of dazed off."

Axel laughs. He's flawless. "I asked you why you brought all those cookies," he says. "Or is that lunch?"

I blush, fire spreads through my face. "No, I…well, I actually brought them as a thank you to your brother for driving me all the time." A lie, but I promised I wouldn't tell anyone about Jonas's secret, right?

Axel reaches his hand into the bag. "Well, then he won't mind if I get a taste of what I've been missing all these years."

What did that mean? My heart races, pumping all my blood at the base of my skull. *Stop it, Brita.* His comment means nothing. Just that he's never had our cookies.

"These are amazing," he says, sincerely. Even eating he is perfect. "Now I'm even happier I came this morning."

"Stick around, I'm full of secrets," I say. Listen, no one said I had a knack for flirting, I don't, but I am glad to try.

"I hope so."

His voice sounds lower, and his bright eyes watch me for a moment longer before he turns his focus back on the road.

I flush, and I don't even care if he sees the pink color the tips of my ears. This is more than I hoped. Axel is better than I hoped. I have a feeling this is going to be a great day.

Chapter 7

Conversation with Axel comes remarkably easy. After a few rusty beginnings, I'm amazed how naturally we fall into a back and forth. Axel tells me all about his interests in athletics and his desire to work in Physical Therapy. It sounds perfect. But he doesn't only talk about himself. No. Axel wants to know about me!

I pick my words carefully this time. Unlike with Jonas, I practice restraint and keep it cool. I'm enjoying myself so much that I almost forget this is likely all arranged by his brother.

The way Axel's eyes brighten, and his pupils dilate when we talk, some psychologists would say that means he's enjoying himself as much as me.

I talk about literature, how I enjoy reading between the lines and diving into what the authors may have thought when penning the words. How the history of the written word fascinates me, and how there are more and more viable career choices with literature degrees than most people understand. I tell myself he's impressed, but I'm not sure. He grins the entire trip to the office and leaves me feeling light.

By the time Axel pulls into the parking lot, at least ten pepparkakor cookies are gone, but I make sure to save about another ten for Jonas. Axel puts the car into park and turns to face me in his seat. I half expected a drop and roll, but he wants to stay, like he doesn't want the moment to end. The burn returns to my cheeks as I gather my things.

"Thanks for the ride, you really didn't need to. I can take the bus or come into work with my dad if Jonas can't drive me again."

"I wanted to," Axel says. "I can't believe we've never done this before now. Seems sort of like a waste, doesn't it?"

"Yeah, it sort of does." He has no idea how much I really believe that.

Axel taps the steering wheel, the small muscles in his jaw pulse for few breaths. Turning back in my direction, he flashes one of those melt-in-your-seat smiles and leans a little closer. "I know this might sound crazy, and I know it could cause some problems, but would you like to do this again? Maybe we could get dinner sometime before you head back to school."

This must be Jonas's doing. There is no way my lack of natural flirtatious ability has secured a real date with Axel.

Before I ruin the euphoria by overthinking, I nod. Not too eagerly, of course. "That would be—" What word should I use? "—fun."

"Great. Can I get your number and I'll give you a call?"

My voice is held hostage while I surrender my phone. He adds his name and when he hands it back to me, our fingers brush. I imagine the feeling equates to a round of Fourth of July fireworks bursting along each one of my cells. When I back out of the car, it takes all my concentration to wave and stay upright. Axel leaves me gawking like a simpleton in the snow-packed parking lot as he pulls back into the rush of lunch hour commuters. Only a group of paralegals returning from their lunch break snaps me out of my fog, and back to the reality that I still have a job to do.

Inside, I find Jonas right away. His back is turned to me, he smacks the side of the copier as I lean against the machine.

"Hey," he says. "You made it in. I was going to let you know I had to come in early, but I don't have your number and would probably be shot by dough bullets if I stepped foot in your shop."

I shake my head and laugh, but never deny his face in the café would start a riot. "You could have called my dad."

Jonas furrows his brow and glances sheepishly at the copier. "I could have done that, yes."

"It's okay. I had a feeling you were going to pull something like this after our last conversation."

"Nope," he says. "I did a lot less than you think. I had grand plans to describe you in detail to Axel, all about how you were the long-awaited love he's never realized—"

"Stop," I say, shoving his shoulder.

Jonas beams a milder smile than his brother, and slams the side of the copier again. "Honestly, on Christmas Eve all I said was that you're pretty

58

fun to work with. I was talking more to myself when I mentioned I couldn't drive us today. Axel came up with the idea to give you a ride. He had to take my car in for an alignment to do this, so honestly I think I got the most out of the deal."

I laugh, then double tap the copy button when Jonas looks ready to take an axe to the machine. I enjoy his exasperation too much when the light bar flares to life and scans back and forth, the machine humming.

"Come on," I say with irony. "You can't tell me that *right* after I admit I like your brother he just asks me out all on his own."

"He asked you out?" Jonas asks, his ocean-blue eyes locking fiercely with mine. "No, ma'am. I never even went into the realm of going out. I thought I'd need to build slowly, break through some preconceived notions, you know? Sounds like maybe Axel has been keeping his own secret."

I narrow my eyes, studying Jonas for a moment. He does look different from Axel. His face narrower, but it suits the rest of his trim shape. He keeps his hair a little longer, but the way it wisps over his ears doesn't look juvenile like Logan's. Jonas lets his facial hair grow out more than Axel. The trim, light brush of scruff makes him look older. But I like it.

I should tell him, but I move on. "I'm not sure if I believe you. Either way, I'm glad you haven't found me totally detestable so you could say I'm okay to work with."

"I said you were *fun* to work with."

"Even better. How was your Christmas?"

59

Jonas shrugs. "I ate way too much and spent most of my time getting slaughtered in basketball by Ax and Logan."

"Logan stayed with your family?" I know he did, but admitting I spied on the Olsens last night might cause me to lose my 'fun to work with' status.

"Yeah, his parents decided to go to Hawaii for the holiday and made it clear it would benefit their relationship to go alone. At least that's how Logan put it. He's not in school right now so my mom invited him over. How was your Christmas?"

"Almost perfect," I say, and quickly wish I picked better words.

Jonas is too quick to miss the tone. "Almost?"

I wave him away, but he settles in, unmoving. "It's nothing, this was the first year in my entire life that I haven't seen my mom on Christmas. And it's our first year without my Farmor."

Jonas's face falls into his reserved expression. "I didn't even realize...I'm sorry. It's always hard the first Christmas after a death. My grandma died in October so Christmas that year sucked."

"I remember when she died," I say softly.

"I didn't even think about the divorce and holidays," he says, almost as though he is chastising himself. "Bet it isn't easy for you or your dad. Are you going to see your mom before going back to school?"

"No, but it's fine. We're going to New York in January and I can hardly wait. Oh, before I forget, here," I say, trying to steer the conversation away from my family woes. "I brought these for you."

Jonas opens the gift bag, and I vow to bring a hundred more cookies if I'm promised that same smile each time.

"Marry me," he says, bringing out one of my snorty laughs; I don't even have time to hide it. "This is by far the best Christmas gift."

"Good, and I'll think a bit on your proposal," I say. "I had more, but Axel may have helped himself to some." And me. "I just wanted to say thank you for being willing to drive me every day. I'm glad we've gotten to know each other. Who knows, we might even end the feud."

Jonas meets my gaze. I don't understand the intensity of his stare, but he's frozen me in my place.

"Thanks, Brita," he says, his voice a low rumble. "I hope you're right." We watch each other for about two solid seconds before he holds up the bag, a mischievous scowl on his face. "Although, you started a new war by letting my brother eat my cookies. I won't forget."

Jonas tucks the bag under his arm, takes his copies, and dramatically takes a bite of the ginger morsel before stalking to the classier side. I mutter a lame response under my breath and take my seat. This morning I plan to work on Jonas's report. I thought to work on it the nights of Christmas Eve and Christmas, but Dad reminded me he wasn't working so I wasn't allowed to either.

I pull out my phone and set it next to the folder, and my stomach wrenches as though a strong fist wraps around my insides. There on my screen is a text message. A thrilling, dreamy text message from someone newly labeled *Brita's Date.*

Hey, just wanted to say I'm looking forward to dinner. I'm glad J had to work early. Talk to you later.

I keep my lip rolled over my teeth so long, all my lip gloss smears all over my tongue. Yes, today is going to be a great day.

Chapter 8

Saturday morning shopping with Oscar always brings a decent amount of entertainment. My cousin is well known around Lindström with the opposite sex. More than once I am shooed away so he can work his charm. I gather groceries while Oscar casually leans against the shelves, some blushing girl giggles at everything he says.

I rest on my elbows on the cart handlebar and scroll through my phone. When the latest pit stop from Oscar takes longer than normal, I set to wandering. This girl is a raven-haired beauty, and Oscar genuinely seems interested. I already know exactly how I will tease him on our drive home.

Three aisles over, I click on a voicemail message from Jane, my roommate at school. "Hey Girl," she says, her Canadian accent thicker after spending a few weeks at home. "I'm ready for the new semester. Just checking in on your holiday. Also, I got a call from the apartment management. They've got all new keys and locks. It will all be ready four days before classes start. I think I'm going to get there as soon as I can. I just wanted to check and see when you were heading back. Anyway, miss you, love ya! LAST SEMESTER!"

She finishes by screaming into the phone. I laugh. Jane is vibrant and hilarious. For four years we've spent countless hours studying, pining over cute college guys, and working toward our futures. I'm keeping my fingers crossed she snags a job in the Midwest like she wants. I'd miss her too much if she became some computer genius on the west coast or back in Canada.

I move on to the texts. I've already read them at least a hundred times. Axel texted me last night and we went back and forth for an hour. It started as securing plans for tonight. Ah, tonight. We are going out, and I can hardly wait. Truth be told, normally I hate texting. I never use emojis, so my messages have caused numerous misunderstandings that I didn't even know could happen from a simple text. But texting Axel is different.

I read a few of my favorites, aimlessly wandering the aisles around Oscar.

Axel: I'm having a hard time not meeting up tonight. I could sneak out.

Like we're in high school?

Axel: The way things are we need to stoop to high school levels. But it makes it edgier to keep a secret, don't you think? That's why I can't wait until tomorrow.

Some secrets are more fun than others. I think the wait makes it even better.

Axel: Fine. I'll wait. Right now, this is my favorite secret to keep.

My heart pounds reading those words again, even with my stupid reply that took me exactly seven minutes to compose.

Mine too.

"Brita, there you are. Ready?" Oscar asks behind me. He holds a bottle of orange soda and a bag of donuts.

I cock my head. "You know we own a bakery?"

"Sometimes I just want a plain donut," he says.

"Are you sure you're done chatting up the girls?"

"You are kind of lame, you know," Oscar mutters.

I don't realize how mammoth Aunt Inez's shopping list is until we're checking out. I think the cashier breaks a sweat by the time we're done.

We pay quickly, then hidden behind heaps of bags, we make our way to the parking lot. The three bundles of paper towels block my view, or I would have noticed people in my way. I should know better than to let Oscar lead the way.

"Whoa, watch it."

I pull back on the cart and peer around the mess. "Oh, I'm sorry, I didn't—"

I lose my words and my fingertips go numb. Logan looks down his nose at us, but he isn't alone.

Elias Olsen stands at his side, a bitter scowl paints his face. Bastien is next to his father and eyes Oscar, though I detect a hint of admiration from the sophomore to the senior. Oscar told me Bastien made the basketball team—maybe they like each other as teammates. But behind them all are Jonas and Axel.

The twins have opposite expressions. Axel smiles, almost as if the tension entertains him. Jonas looks like he might be sick. Jonas and I talk so easily on our car rides and at the office, but in public we fall back into quiet, tense nods or glances. I hate it.

"Might want to watch out where you're going, Brita," Logan says. "One might think you were getting aggressive."

I can't believe it. For most of my life I've been blessed to avoid the anger and harsh words shared through bitterness between Viggo and Farfar, but now I am standing in the middle of a gaping, dirty, puddle of it.

"Really, Logan?" I start, but Oscar takes over.

"Hey, we didn't see you. Relax a bit," Oscar snaps.

There it is. The same wretched resentment from my side!

Maybe Inez and Karl hate the Olsens more than I know and have polluted my cousin. The way Oscar glares at Elias, then Logan, then the twins is disheartening. The only person who escapes his wrath is Bastien.

I appreciate my parents for never encouraging me to take up arms. Although, they never discouraged it, we simply never talked about the Olsens unless necessary.

"Logan don't be an idiot," Jonas says, and I feel as though I could kiss him. He nudges his dad in the arm. "Let's go. Forget it." He tries to urge them all forward.

Logan glances at my cousin, his eyes dark and sullen. "Hey, Elias maybe you ought to tell Coach Marks his team captain bad mouthed you."

Elias doesn't say anything, but it looks like he might. He simply narrows his eyes at Oscar. Bastien looks at the ground, uncomfortable. I see him nudge his father.

"Okay, Logan stop." That comes from Jonas and now I am two seconds away from kissing him right on the mouth. He's the only one showing some brains. "Dad, come on. Brita, Oscar." He nods curtly, taking the first initiative to walk away.

"Come on," Bastien repeats to his father.

Hate isn't the right word for this situation, I utterly *loathe* this whole thing. Am I the only one who notices how stupid this feud is, and the impact it has on the youngest among us? I think of Agnes. She is a pure spirit; she loves everyone, but how upsetting it is to think of someone in the Olsen family mocking her for her cerebral palsy. I can't think so little of them, but what if they did? Would they harm her tender heart?

When the others leave, Axel walks next to me and winks. I wish to ignore the unsettling stress like him. Through it all he's relaxed. My stomach whips in harsh waves.

"See you later," he whispers by my cheek, so quietly I hardly hear him.

Oscar doesn't notice, he still glares at the backs of Elias and Logan. I watch Axel follow his family, my nerves and anticipation break apart the knots from the near explosion. Tonight, we can relax. I'll get to know him as a separate entity from his family name. He will know me for who I am, not only as a Jacobson. I take a deep breath.

Maybe I'm dreaming. If anything, this moment proves kindness, civility, and maybe even love between our families is a fairy tale from a children's book.

***

"Well don't you look nice," Farfar says when I prance down the steps later that night.

My brown ankle boots fit snugly over my favorite faded jeans. I went back and forth between a lacy top, or my sweater. The black oversized sweater won out. I love the way it drapes over my thin frame giving the illusion I have a few more curves than I do. The hair is a different situation. To some being born with natural curls is a blessing. That might be true, if naturally curly hair ever did the same thing twice. I spent an hour blowing out my waves until the locks fell over my shoulders like a frizzy mop. But that will need to work.

"Where are you off to?" Inez asks.

"Just out with some old friends from high school." Did I mention my stomach is in knots, and has been all afternoon as I prepared to deliver that very deliberate lie? "We're going to go out to dinner before I head back next week."

"That sounds nice. You are cooped up too much, älskling," Farfar says, flicking yesterday's newspaper wider, his eyes never leave the black and white text.

"Do you need the car?" Dad asks. He's looking at me weird.

Shaking my head, I drift toward the front door. "Nope, we're meeting down the street at the gas station."

True. Axel found it only added to the suspense of the night to keep going to the place where all this new interaction with the Olsen brothers began.

"Well, keep in touch. There's a storm moving in. I don't like the idea of you out there at night."

"Oh, for heaven's sake Nils," Inez says. "She's almost twenty-two."

"I agree with Nils," Farfar mutters. Of course, he does.

"I'll be fine. We're just going to dinner. Would you like to come chaperone, Dad?"

He scoffs and crosses his arms over his chest, but I kind of think he's considering the idea.

Agnes bumbles into the room, coloring book in hand. "Bye, Brita. You look weird," she says and points to my pale-rose lips.

I chuckle and squeeze her tightly, but she winces. "What's wrong kiddo?"

Agnes points to the brace on her left leg. "It scratches."

69

"We'll fix it munchkin," Inez says. "Now, let Brita go out. She needs a life."

"Wow, I feel so loved," I say. "I'll be back, don't wait up," I add with a scrunch to my nose. Dad doesn't seem to appreciate my sarcasm.

My first step into the frigid air doesn't settle with the guilt in the pit of my stomach. But the closer I come to the fluorescent lights of the gas station, the faster the guilt transforms into excitement.

Axel is waiting by the time I arrive. He leans against the passenger side of a blue coupe. A few paces off, I take a moment to absorb all of him. His brown jacket fits his strong arms with near perfection. I like the way his short blond hair shows off the defined shape of his face, but my favorite piece of the Axel canvas is the way his eyes always brighten when he looks at me.

"You made it. You look beautiful," he says, his white teeth shining through the blue night. Axel moves away from the door and holds it open.

"Thank you," I say, my voice cracking a bit with a new wash of nerves.

My insides do somersaults when Axel finds his way into the driver's seat. He rubs his hands for a moment, reviving the blood flow from the frigid air and looks at me. "Ready?"

I nod, and resist the urge to bite my lower lip. When the car moves, Axel drops one hand and then like a dream, he takes mine. I can die a happy woman. Cliché but oh so true. I've had eyes for Axel and his brilliant wit, his handsome face, his…everything, since age seventeen. Nothing compares to this headfirst plummet into something unknown.

70

Axel takes us to a hole-in-the-wall Italian restaurant. Like his car, the space feels close, personal. The dark sets the mood, a warmth spreads in my gut. Nerves tingle along my spine, but then ease when the waiter brings us a basket of bread and we fall into lighthearted talk.

To my surprise, in the back a small stage is set up behind moth-eaten black curtains. Halfway into my lasagna the curtains pull back and a young woman with a middle-aged man step out to sporadic applause. They are dressed as if they were lost on the way to a renaissance fair.

The man clears his throat loudly, and Axel peers at me over the rim of his water glass. Something is happening.

"But soft! What light through yonder window breaks?" the man says in a mediocre British accent.

My mouth drops, and I smile as the two performers play through the entire orchard scene of Shakespeare's *Romeo and Juliet*. There are a few blunders, and at times the gasping passion and method acting as they profess undying love is a little hard to swallow. Still at the end of the scene I pound my hands together with such vigor that I'm teetering close to calling for an encore.

The curtains close and the lights brighten a little more. I'm sure Axel will tease me, but when I face him, he simply wears a satisfied grin. He's thoughtful, but entertained.

"Did Jonas tell you?" I ask.

"Tell me what?" He seems genuinely confused. "Jonas hasn't said anything to me. I didn't even tell him we were going out tonight, although he said you did."

"In my defense I wondered if it had been your brother who'd told you to take me out," I say, but catch myself before I confess Jonas knows about my years-long crush.

Axel shrugs. "I don't know why Jonas would tell me to ask you out. After we came to your dad's office the other day, when I saw you—I don't know, I realized I'd been letting what other people think stop me from something great. I mentioned that I thought you looked amazing when we left. Believe it or not, it was Logan who suggested we do this."

I raise an eyebrow. "Logan?" Thinking back to the grocery store that morning, I can think of zero reasons why Logan would ever suggest Axel and I spend time together. "That's hard to believe."

"I know he's rough around the edges, but he's a good friend. He thinks we might hit it off."

"And what do you think?"

Axel props one elbow on the table and flashes one of his smiles that means he is up to something. One of my favorite smiles. "You understand the circumstances aren't really…normal." Where is this going? I cover the anxious beats of my heart with a toss of my hair over my shoulder. He studies my face for a moment longer. "But so far, I think I couldn't care less what anyone else says. This might be the best secret I've ever kept."

He leans his shoulder against my arm, leaving an imprint of heat where we touch. I fumble with my words for a moment as I analyze what he means. If I understand him right, then the feud bothers Axel as much as it does me. This is the moment, the time I might be the person my grandmother asked me to be. With Axel's help maybe we can bring the change our families need. Clearing my throat, I sip some water and stare down at the ratty stage.

"So, how did you know about my love of Shakespeare if Jonas didn't tell you?"

Axel takes a long drink of his water before drawing his face inches from mine. I can smell his masculine scent and like a trap it draws me in until I am completely captured. "Logan again. He told me this place did performances on the weekends. I knew you were an English major, so I took a gamble that you'd enjoy a little bit of Shakespeare."

I remind myself to put aside my frustrations with Logan and thank the man. Scooting a little closer an insatiable desire to feel his hand on mine again fills my insides with warmth. I don't have to wait long. Like a natural reflex Axel curls his fingers around my hand, turning my palm over in his and tracing my lifeline with his thumb. A shiver shoots up my arm until it reaches my head and creates a pleasant fog in my brain.

"You were very right," I whisper.

Axel smiles, then leans closer. Was this happening? I swallow, trying to clear the path for my airway to start passing air again.

"I'm glad we did this, Brita," Axel says. His lips are so close, only a few more inches. My heart pounds like a war drum in my ears.

"Me too," I breathe out.

Axel's hand comes to the side of my face, and I lean into his warmth. You know in movies when couples kiss and sweet music plays all around as if heaven stamps approval on their love? I can check off the same thing from my bucket list.

With a perfect balance of steadiness and anticipation, Axel draws my lips to his. Right there in the back booth of the restaurant. From the stage a new scene is setting up, and over a pair of rumbling speakers plays the peaceful sonnet of a harp. I've kissed three guys in my life. Well, four if you count Lionel Hendricks in first grade, but I don't. Yet in that moment all my training is lost. Axel's palm cups behind my head, I tremble when his fingers tangle through my hair. Those perfect lips I've dreamed about move seamlessly against mine. I'm embarrassed that he knows what he's doing ten times more than I do, but I don't want him to stop. I lean against him; his hand traces the curve of my waist. Maybe we kiss for thirty seconds, or ten minutes, I don't care. I've finally gotten my first addicting taste.

Chapter 9

Jonas will only drive me to the office on Thursday now, when Axel works at *Clara's*. Every other day is spent in the blue coupe, my fingers laced with Axel's. Driving with him is the only thing that makes the upcoming separation bearable. One more day remains before I bid farewell to Lindström and return to school.

My campus isn't far from home, but tonight Axel heads to Wisconsin. Since he is in the first year of his therapy program, I have a feeling when classes start he will become a memory. I don't know when we'll talk, or see each other. Of course, he promises when we're both home for weekends we'll get together, but I'm a grown up; I know what the final semester of a year looks like at school. And I'm also not blind enough to realize that Axel seems less concerned about the separation than me.

When nights come, if he is aloof about leaving, those thoughts seem far away when he kisses me. The final week is spent together, every night building on the one before. I am falling headfirst into something. I'm not sure what yet, but I like it.

"You look tired."

I startle and drop my pen.

Jonas smiles, lifts a brow and leans against my cubical wall.

"And you wear glasses," I mumble.

I think his cheeks color a bit when he pulls off the stylish eyeglasses. "Yep, cursed with the worst eyes in the family," he says. "I ran out of contact solution, so of course Axel and Bass are living it up at home with the dweeb, nerd, you name it, remarks. After living with them, I can take whatever you've got."

"I was just thinking you look good in them, but I can see it's a sensitive subject for you."

I laugh and rock in my chair, a habit that happens when I'm nervous. And usually around Jonas. He's not wearing a suit today, but he looks handsome in his navy polo shirt and dark jeans. Today is our final Friday at the Anderson-Collins law firm, and thankfully the firm set a New Year's resolution to institute casual Fridays. I'm not debonair like Jonas, but Jane always tells me green makes my eyes pop and so a green tunic it is.

"So, I wanted to check on that report. Have you had a chance to run through it?" Jonas asks, a hint of anxiety in his tone. "I need to turn it in before we go today."

"Oh, yeah," I say. I rummage through the top drawer and return his black leather folder. "Sorry it took so long, but Martin gave me two full grant applications to run through last minute. It's all done."

"Was it awful?"

For the first time since really talking to Jonas, he seems unsure about something. The last three weeks I've grown to admire his confidence and innate drive to work. Dad even mentioned he thinks Jonas will make a fine attorney. Yet I've been given control for a moment. And if I had a more sinister bone, I might twist his nerves more. He's stepped into my realm of know-how. I do love seeing a bit of vulnerability from strait-laced Jonas Olsen.

Because he knows I am obsessed with words I even cackle, wickedly. "I sense fear, Mister Olsen."

"Have I told you how dorky you are?"

"No, would you please?"

Jonas drags his fingers through his hair, a tell that he's uncomfortable, but not enough to leave.

Mylanta, when did I start to know so much about this guy? I slump down in my chair. "Alright, I won't make you sweat anymore, but I need to be honest.

He nods and scratches his chin. "I hope you are."

I lean forward, steeple my fingers in front of my lips just to add a touch of theatrics. He looks at me like I've pulled a knife on him. "Jonas," I say sternly. "If you wanted to switch majors, you would find a viable career in writing."

"Don't tease me. I need to get better, I know."

"I'm not teasing," I insist, standing so I can look him in the eye. "Your report was the first legal jargon mess I've actually enjoyed reading. You have a way with words. There may have been a few punctuation sins, but I mean it. You did really well."

Jonas's smile is different than Axel's, I already know that. I revel in his impishness, but I won't admit to anyone but myself that I find the same enjoyment in Jonas's. He has a genuine look to his smile, trusting and gentle. He frees it only when he is truly pleased, or happy. When he's nervous, his lips press together, or he messes with his hair. Agitated, Jonas gets a furrow over his nose. Okay, that's enough. My palms start to sweat when I let my thoughts of his quirks run wild.

But I am not the only one studying. Jonas watches me, his eyes bounce between mine. A buzz jolts through my insides. Clearing my throat, I take a step back until the threat of blushing passes.

"You're serious?" he asks. "You're not just trying to make me feel good?"

"Yes, I'm serious." I shove his shoulder gently. "I never thought of you as insecure before now."

"I don't like writing, and I especially don't like other people reading what I write. But if you're not just trying to make me feel better, it gives me hope. I have a writing class this semester. Obviously, I've been putting it off all these years and I swear it, if that's the class that keeps me from graduating..."

"You'll do fine. Now you get to come to my side of the campus. Do you know the professor?"

Jonas shakes his head. "I've hardly glanced at my schedule. But I needed a language class and the advisor suggested the one I picked. I believe his exact words were, 'A sleep through it and pass class'."

I wiggle my finger. "Don't think language arts is an easy 'A'. But you shouldn't worry too much, I'm not just being nice. I know you need to write a good report, so I would tell you if it's something you really needed to work on."

Jonas flips open his folder, his eyes scan the contents before he flashes me a half grin. "Well, thank you for reading it."

"No problem." Jonas rocks on his heels as if he wants to say something more. I pause long enough to give him the chance, then determine he is bound to simply stand there, so I take the initiative. "It's been interesting working together. I've actually had a good time getting to know you."

Jonas lets out a long breath, and the corners of his mouth curl up a bit. "Me too, and you even got a little something more out of the deal." I'm certain color stains my cheeks. Jonas doesn't let it slide either. "Oh, is that embarrassment, Brita Jacobson? Maybe this is the part where I ask what your intentions are with my brother."

"Okay, you can go back to work now," I say, turning my back to him.

"I'm actually wrapping up the last few things for your dad and then I'm finished. I've got a few minutes." Jonas steps into the small cubby and hops onto the edge of my desk, his legs dangle off the side. Those royal blues slice through me, but not in an intimidating way, sort of breathtaking.

"You've gone out with Axel a few times," he says. "How is it going? Everything you ever imagined?"

"We're not having this conversation."

"Why not? Thought we were friends now."

"We…are…" I stammer. "But do you really want to know what your brother does at night?"

Jonas lifts his hands in surrender. "Fair enough. What are you two going to do with school though?"

"It's called a phone, Jonas."

He chuckles, but it wasn't as light as before. "Okay, sure. Axel has played the field a lot before, but he seems to like spending time with you. Maybe you can tame his wild ways. Are you seeing him before he leaves?"

"Just for a little while. He wants to get on the road early."

It isn't a secret Axel has his fair share of ex-girlfriends, and I've been thinking of little else the last few days. I don't know who is in his graces in Wisconsin, but I'm not going to be *that* girl. I refuse to be the possessive, clingy one. I might want to be, but I won't.

"Well, I guess time will tell," he says.

"Your confidence is underwhelming."

He hops off my desk, grinning. "Sorry. I'm sure it will be great."

"Yeah, stop being encouraging, you're not good at it."

80

Jonas shoves his hands in his pockets and starts to inch out of my cubicle. Our carefree minutes are waning before adulting will take over. "What are *your* plans for getting back to school?"

"The bus tomorrow night, Sunday set up and move in day, then classes bright and early Monday. My roommate is already back at the apartment, so I don't have too much to do. What about you?"

Jonas glances at his nemesis The Copier, and his lips together. The Jonas is Nervous About Something look. "Well," he finally starts, "I was going to see if you want to skip the bus and just ride up with me. We're going to the same place, and since we've both realized we aren't the Devil's spawn, kind of seems ridiculous having you sit on a smelly bus when I can take you."

"I don't mind the bus, for your information," I say, poking his arm. But the truth is, I really like the idea of driving with Jonas.

"Okay, ride the bus then. I will enjoy snacks and eighties music by myself."

"Wait, you said nothing about eighties music."

"Oh, yeah. The entire time."

"Jonas, you had me at eighties. I would love to road trip with you."

He drums the top of the cubicle and smiles. "Great. So, we'll meet tomorrow night at say, seven?"

"That's perfect. Thanks for the offer."

"Okay, have fun tonight," he says. "I'll see you tomorrow."

Axel's mouth is near my ear, he kisses me there. A tremble runs down my spine. I pull away and lean against the window in the front of his car. My hair is wilder than before, and Axel keeps his hand on the top of my knee. He turns in his seat, facing me, a coy grin on his face. My grandmother would blush shamelessly if she were alive to see how quickly I'd fallen into such a relationship, and with an Olsen, no less. Part of me wonders how Axel and I went from very few interactions, to magnetized lips. I suppose years of pent up tension on my part has something to do with it. Axel's reasons are still a mystery.

"So, you're riding with Jonas tomorrow?"

I smile shyly. "Yes, he was nice enough to offer."

"Maybe I've got competition with my own brother." He kisses my lips, then my jaw, cheek, lips again.

I close my eyes, try not to make any weird sighing noises, and shake my head. "I don't think you have to worry about that. It's a good thing if I'm friends with your brother, don't you think?"

Axel doesn't say anything; he is too focused on finding my mouth again. After a time, I pull back and rest my head on his shoulder. "I can try to come up to Wisconsin sometime." I bite the inside of my cheek, nervous for the response.

"Yeah," he says, his cheek on my head. "We'll figure it all out. It's your last semester, so you need to have some fun. I loved last year, now it's all serious and work in the actual therapy program. Well, I take that back. I have roommates who still know how to have a good time. You should too, though. After school then it's going to be real life, with finding jobs and all that boring stuff."

"Fun and studying don't really mesh well. I just want to get through and be done."

"Oh, you've got to go have some fun. Meet new people. I challenge you to do something crazy this semester—out of the ordinary for you. I think you'll be happy you did."

"Okay then, what about you?" I say, arching to meet his gaze. "What new thing are you going to do?"

Axel considers for a moment, then shrugs. "I don't know, yet. Maybe I'll find a new study group every week. My roommates and I did that one semester, we met so many people."

I can't nail down why these suggestions feel a little different than what I think a boyfriend should tell his girlfriend. Wait. Is that what we are? We go out. Talk on the phone, text late. We certainly aren't afraid to touch. What else is there that qualifies a relationship? The idea sends a spark of heat through my stomach.

"Are you coming back for the summer?" I ask, hopeful.

Axel glances at me his smile fades a bit. "I guess it depends on clinical rotations—like an internship basically. I have to get so many hours."

I wrap my arms around his waist. "It just feels like life is changing, and this is just it."

"Hey, we have fun, so when we see each other we'll just pick up where we left off. I don't have any plans to make any drastic changes soon, do you?" I quickly shake my head. "See, nothing to worry about then."

We sit in silence for several minutes. I trace my fingertips along his palm. One of his hands tips my chin up toward his face. "I hate to say it, but it's time for me to go."

This moment has been coming, I'm ready. Not really. I can't shake the gloomy thought that things will change. The unease is most likely from the distance, the newness of the relationship, and my tendency to overthink. But then Axel cups his hand around my face, my skin tingles beneath his touch. I grip his wrist, wishing we could stay like this all night.

"Drive safely. Will you call me, or text me, or whatever works for you?" I whisper.

Axel answers by kissing me. Hard, and the kind of kiss that leaves me limp and at his mercy. He brushes my hair out of my face for the millionth time and smiles his beautiful, charismatic smile.

"I'll talk to you soon," he says right next to my ear when he pulls me into a tight hug. "This has been awesome, Brita."

I flush and bury my face into his shoulder. "I would have to agree," I say. "Okay, I'm going now, or I'll never leave."

"Remember," he says through the open window. "Do something crazy."

"Only since you asked," I tease.

"Okay. Don't let Jonas bug you."

"I'll try. Talk to you soon?"

Axel nods, takes my hand and kisses the top. I want to fling my arms around his neck and never let go. But I step away and wave like a woman bidding farewell to her love who is heading to war. The icy wind, the billowing snow, and my frozen fingertips are the bleak reminder that summer, when we might both be back here again, is astronomically too far away.

Chapter 10

Agnes sits next to me on the couch as we giggle and snap selfies together. I am named the best frowner, while Agnes blows my silly faces out of the water. Her left hand trembles as she exerts all her concentration to grip my cell phone. It takes every bit of self-control not to help her scroll through the photos. I know she needs to work her muscles. Axel took a slight interest in Agnes's motor control, and mentioned a few kids he'd observed during school clinics. We didn't get far into talk about cerebral palsy and kids before the conversation drifted to other things that didn't involve much talking.

I've received one text since he left. The one I asked for; letting me know he made it back to school. He asked me to call him when I get back. He cares.

"Hey dweeb, feel special that I'm missing Amy Matheson's party to hang out with you," Oscar grumbles when he slumps onto the couch.

"Oh, please. I'm leaving at seven, what party starts before seven on a Saturday night?"

"That's mean, Oskie. I'm going to miss you Brita. You always leave," Agnes pouts.

I squeeze her small shoulders. "I always come back, and just make sure you're on the calls every Sunday, okay? Oh, and flick Oscar's ear once a day for me."

Agnes squeals and tries to get her brother's ear. Oscar teases a bit, dodging and ducking from her little fingers, but like a good big brother, soon Agnes grapples her thin arm around his neck and snags a good solid flick.

"Alright, everyone get in here," Farfar calls. "One last family dinner."

"You all act like I'm dying," I say. "I'm going to be an hour away."

The table is set nearly as grandly as Christmas dinner. Karl helps Inez with a heavy baking dish filled with a savory roast, followed by a heaping bowl of Karl's famous mashed potatoes. Farfar beams when we all take our places. Dad sneaks in just in time for grace. Farfar harrumphs disapproval for his tardiness, but my dad only gives my hand a squeeze.

Oscar is still digging into the potato bowl for thirds when I groan and pat my stomach. "I think I ate enough for my first week at school. Thank you," I say and take Farfar's wrinkled hand in mine. "I'm going to miss you, but May will be here soon enough."

"It will be wonderful having you back here. I know Inez is looking forward to your help in the shop again," Farfar says, sipping his water. "It brings me such joy to see our family working what we built with our own two hands. Now, I am blessed to see you all leading the bakery so beautifully."

"Are you wanting to run the bakery, Brita?" Oscar asks through an enormous gravy-soaked bite of potatoes. "I thought you would actually use your degree."

"Of course she's coming back," Farfar says before I can reply.

I pick at my leftover bits of roll wishing a sink hole would open in the floorboards and swallow me up.

"Have you asked her, Pops?" Dad says, but he'll always have my back.

"Brita has always wanted to work in the shop, right?" Inez asks.

Everyone is counting on my return, no one more than my aunt. "My degree is versatile," I say softly. I'm weak and spineless. Harsh, but I deserve it. A glaring opportunity to spout off what I want, and I crumble.

That's right," Farfar says. "She can run the bakery and work with English on—what did you call it—telecoming?"

"Telecommuting, Pops. Some careers can be done from home," says Inez.

"Very sensible," Farfar offers with such pride. I feel my skin turning green. "Brita, you've always been so thoughtful to this family. You have worked hard these years at school and will do greater things with *Hanna's* than I could ever imagine. We are all so proud of you, so we wanted to give you a little gift."

Dad dips under the table and holds a wrapped package.

I smile, forgetting for a moment in a few months I will be forced to choose between partnering in my family's bakery or chasing a dream career. "You didn't need to get me anything."

"You deserve it," my dad says. "Your mom chipped in too."

With new excitement, I tear into the brown wrapping paper. I'm stunned silent. A brand new, top-of-the-line, fully loaded, college-graduate-style laptop. Through all scholarly years, I've used the computer lab stocked wall to wall with outdated, testy computers. I run a gentle hand over the box as if it might shatter if I press too hard.

"This is amazing," I whisper.

"She hasn't seen the best part!" Agnes shouts.

"What's the best part?"

"Open it!" She clutches her curled hand in front of her mouth, as if trying to stifle another squeal.

The box is open. I slide out the sleek black computer and with uncanny speed the machine fires up. On the screen was a smiling picture of my family, beaming at me at the front door of the bakery. Oscar is making a face; Agnes's head is thrown back in laughter. Karl is kissing Inez's cheek, Dad smiles the way he always does, and Farfar truly looks like he has every treasure in the world.

"I love it you guys. I love it so much," I say, fearful I might break down in tears.

"I knew she would," Farfar says. "We will miss you, älskling. Nils, you should drive her. Don't you want to drive her?"

"Farfar, I'm fine," I insist. Dad seems ready to agree for a second. As much as I love my father, I'm looking forward to my drive with Jonas. We've found an easy companionship over the last three weeks. I'm not too proud to admit I enjoy his company. And I hope if I am with Jonas, it might fill the void of missing Axel. "Really, I like to go back and get settled on my own. I get my independence from you remember."

Farfar smiles and nods. "I won't argue that." He glances at his watch. "Well, I suppose you should get your things. It's nearly time for your bus."

"I can wait with you at the stop," Dad says.

"Really, please. I'd rather just say goodbye at the house if it's all right with you all."

"Like a band aid," Karl says.

"Sure, something like that." This happens every semester. When summer ends it gets worse. I am loved and needed. It feels good. I only wish I could be honest.

Ever since my mom and dad began having problems, I kept so many things inside so as not to add to the conflict. Now, the habit has morphed into hiding things. Not my most appealing personality trait, and I wish I could be an open book with the people who love me. Like about who I'm driving with; about Axel; about a career in the literary field. I've spun my own web of omission, and soon it will burst. I'll be the only one to blame.

***

"Bye, sweetheart," Dad says outside. He pulls me into a tight hug. "It was so nice having you at the office these last few weeks. Have a great semester."

90

I breathe deeply. After the divorce, Dad buried himself in his work. True enough, I've cherished seeing so much more of my old dad this season too.

"See you later. Don't gain those fifteen pounds, there's still time you know, so you'd better watch it," Oscar says.

"Don't screw up the championships," I reply. He slugs me and runs back inside to escape the frigid night.

I notice the black sedan across the street, its headlights are on and the car is running. Uh, does Jonas expect me to stroll over and get in the car. Look, I want to end the feud, but I'm not ready to be that bold yet. Then I hear the cheery bell ding and the door to *Clara's* opens.

Farfar stiffens on his way to wrap his arms around me, his eyes shoot across the street. Elias, Jonas and Viggo trudge outside. Jonas carries a duffle bag and catches our staring eyes in the night. He looks as uncomfortable as I feel.

I hear Jonas's voice. He pleads with his grandfather, who hobbles around the car with his own frustrated expression burning beneath the streetlamps.

"Philip, if I hear of you spreading nonsense that my grandsons shop at *your* café, you will not recover when I get through with you, you twit!"

"Farfar, please don't." My own appeals are swiftly ignored.

Inez links her arm with Karl. They turn back into the house, taking Agnes with them.

Dad insists the family go back inside, but Farfar doesn't listen and moves around him.

"I would never say such a thing," my grandfather says. "If I saw any sign of the likes of you in my shop I would lock up for the night and consider the day a failure."

"Pops come on," Dad says.

"Please," I add.

He doesn't listen. "Now, why don't you send that boy off and leave us in peace. Any more words from your foul mouth will cause my ears to bleed."

Jonas meets my eye. I want to scream; he looks like he might. But instead he ducks into his car and slowly pulls away from the madness. I dream of the safety of that car. Where a neutral line is drawn, where maybe, for a moment, an Olsen and a Jacobson can pretend there is nothing but friendship between the two names.

I watch Elias urge Viggo back toward *Clara's*, but to my surprise he calls across the street to my dad.

"Nils, my father was out of line starting this, but you might work a little harder keeping the kids out of this. We don't go after your girl."

We're not kids, but I feel small in the thick of this. Besides, Elias hadn't been exactly friendly at the grocery store last week. If only he knew how much his family means to me. How much his two boys are a part of *my* life now.

"Elias let's just end this here. I'm trying to say goodbye to my daughter," Dad says, with a level of civility that brings a sense of pride to my heart.

Perhaps Elias has a head on his shoulders. He says nothing more, but gruffly nods his agreement and goes back inside.

"You shouldn't have backed down," Farfar says to my dad.

"He should have, Farfar," I snap. Wow. I spoke up. "I love you and I love it here, but someday it would be nice to see the Olsen family without starting a war. Now, I need to get going. Please, don't overwork yourself, Farfar. Dad, I'll call you later, okay?"

Farfar grumbles over my shoulder when I hug him, but he smiles when we pull away. Dad gets another hug, and my feet are already freezing when I start the trek to the gas station.

I'm looking so forward to Jonas's warm car that I don't even have a chance to worry about my deception.

When I make it to the station his car is locked.

"Hey, Brita." He sneaks up behind me, a plastic bag in one hand and a tray of hot chocolates in the other.

"Hi. Here, let me take that," I say and take the tray out of his hands. "You didn't need to get me anything."

"It's freezing, yes I did." Jonas clicks his key fob and pops his trunk. Tossing the snacks on the driver's seat, he takes my bag. I don't wait before I get settled in the front.

Somberness, with a hint of feeling sorry for myself sours my mood and by the time Jonas takes his place behind the wheel, there is a grim presence in the car.

"What's going on with you? Everything okay?"

I grip the hot chocolate and stare out the window. "Were you back there just now?" I snap. "I can't do it anymore, Jonas. I'm positive my grandfather would kill you if he knew you were driving me right now. I don't want to be stuck in the middle of this anymore. I can't be the person to change it."

Jonas lets me rant as he pulls into traffic. I take a deep breath after a moment and watch his jaw tighten, but his lips aren't pressed together, his brow isn't furrowed. He's simply listening.

His voice is soft when he answers, and I feel calmer right away. "Who says you have to be the one to change it, Brita? When did other people's grudges become your responsibility?"

I need someone like him right now, a listener and friend. A grin kisses the corner of my mouth. I want to tell him about Farmor's letter, but something stops me. Not now, not tonight. I don't want the reminder.

I take a swig of my cocoa. He put Irish cream in the chocolate and I almost moan at the first taste. "Forget it. It's not up to me, I guess. I'm sorry, I was upset about something else, and then to see our families go at it again, but I'll be a better road tripper now."

"What else had you upset?" Jonas asks.

"Oh, you don't want to hear about that," I say, and reach for the radio. Eighties time.

An audible gasp passes over my lips, and I'm not sure what embarrasses me more; the gasp or Jonas's intensity when he looks at me. My eyes trail down to my hand. Jonas has blocked my reach for the radio, his fingers still lightly on top of mine, and he shakes his head.

"I do want to hear about it," he says. "We're friends, right? I want to know if you want to tell me."

I'm floored. I keep my feelings close. Yet, in the dark of this car with gummies, chocolate bars, greasy chips and cocoa between us, I somehow feel safe. There arrives a new kind of relief in trusting someone other than my family. Someone who genuinely cares. I know Jonas is sincere, the warmth of it rushes through me the same as the cocoa. With Jonas I never need to impress, so naturally he's earned the honest, gritty truth of Brita Jacobson. With Axel, I guess I have more reservations. Seems backward.

"Okay," I begin. "Does your family expect you to help run *Clara's* someday?"

Jonas considers my words then slowly nods. "That's sort of why I took an interest in business and finance. I want to be able to help my family like your dad helps yours. I found some old records of a scammer that nearly took the bakery right out from beneath my grandparents about thirty years ago. Since I'm a terrible baker—I'll just get that right out there—I'd like to help protect the business from anything like that again. I don't know if I'll ever be a full-time face of the bakery. But it's a part of me, you know?"

"I do know," I say. "My grandfather believes I'm going to come straight home after graduation and be full-time in the bakery, and work from home if I *want* to use my degree. There was a perfect time tonight to tell everyone the truth about what I want to do, and I froze. Even led them

95

to believe that I wanted to run things at home. *Hanna's* will always be a part of me, and I always want to be a part of the bakery. But I have other dreams too." I cover my face with my hands and release a strange little growl. "I've made a mess of things, I think. What am I so afraid of?"

"Hey," Jonas says. "Cut yourself some slack. It's hard to fess up to things when you know it's going to bring some kind of disappointment. For example, you and I both know I *do* shop in your family's bakery. Yep, my grandpa found the bag from those cookies you brought me in the trash. So that shouting match tonight—my fault. I mean, without questioning any of us, my grandpa went straight to the idea of your family, I don't know, planting evidence. Did you see me fess up? I'm tired of it all too, but don't think you're some coward because you want to please your family. I do it too."

We sit in a comfortable silence for a long time before Jonas goes on. "Brita, I'm the last person who can give you advice on your family since I don't know them at all. But I can tell they care about you. They want you to be happy. Don't tell them if you're not ready, but you can, and you should. You have a really great dream and I would guess they would want to be a part of it." Jonas pauses, his eyes glaze a bit as though he were lost in a distant thought. "Life shouldn't be about keeping honest feelings inside. It's hard, but I hope you'll be able to tell them someday. I hope we both can. You deserve to be happy."

I offer him a watery smile in return. A heavy load is swept away. The longer he talks, the less the upsets of the evening weigh on my shoulders. "Thanks, really that means a lot." Clearing my throat, and slipping my hair behind my ears I wiggle my eyebrows. "Okay, enough with the heavy stuff. Are you ready for this?"

My fingers dance around the radio dial like a gunslinger in the Old West. Jonas laughs and flips down the sun visor. "Oh, if you're serious about this you can't depend on the radio." He pinches a CD between his fingers and slides it into the slot in the dashboard. "I've got all we need right here."

I laugh loudly. "You even have a CD."

"Of course, can't use Bluetooth or fancy stuff when you're listening to eighties. Wish I had a cassette, to be honest."

The car fills with all keyboards and electric sounds. "I tip my hat to you, sir," I tease, bowing my head. "You are the most prepared for the best road trip in history."

Jonas bangs his head back and forth and taps the steering wheel. We laugh and belt out the lyrics. The chaos and bitterness of the night dims like a bad dream. Made possible through terrible pitch and too much junk food.

Chapter 11

"You know, I feel cheated," I say when Jonas turns down my street. My apartment building is old, but has huge kitchens. Small flurries of crystal snowflakes start to fall, and I have a gummy worm hangover.

Jonas turns the volume down on the final blast of Toto's *Africa*. "Cheated about what?"

"All these years I've known you and I never knew you were so…fun."

Jonas scoffs and rubs away some of the fog on the windshield. "Thanks, I guess."

"No, I'm serious. Axel was always the loud one, the one who was constantly surrounded by people. The life of the party type—"

"Please, keep talking. I'm feeling better about myself with every word," he says.

"I'm sorry." I flop back against the seat. "I'm not saying this right. What I'm trying to tell you is that I wish I would have gotten to know you a long time ago. Maybe I played into the feud without realizing it. Oh, turn here," I add quickly.

He obeys, then glances at me. "I've always been a little more reserved, I guess. But as you said, I have Axel for a brother. He does enough socializing for the both of us. I don't…open up to people easily."

Turning into the parking lot, Jonas pulls alongside the curb. His jaw drops. "Is this where you live?" I nod, and free my seatbelt, but hurry and scoop a handful of M & M's. "Are you telling me, all these years…"

"What? Jonas, do you live here too?" I shout, and a little M & M juice drizzles over my lip.

He laughs hard and runs a thumb over my chin as though it is something he does all the time. "Nope. But I'm glad I got to see all that chocolate dribble down your face."

With a quick punch to his shoulder, I open the door, sucking in a painful breath when the bitter air robs me of oxygen.

"Brita!" A squeal from the front door the lower apartment shatters the silence of the building. Jane darts across the snowy lawn, bee lining it straight for us. She's dressed in a long sweater that hits her athletic legs just above her knees, layered with a puffy-blue ski coat. Her short hair is tousled and dyed a cinnamon color. Jane is never without color on her lips. Tonight's number is a sultry burgundy. She often tells me there are few hardships in life that a little lipstick can't fix.

99

I hardly have time to set my laptop back on the seat, when she flings her arms around my neck. "Hi," I gasp. "Janey, it's only been three weeks."

"I know," she says, keeping a strong grip on my shoulders. "But this is the last time we'll be starting a semester together. Brita, the *last time*. Oh, who is this?"

Jane eyes Jonas with a sly stare. Jonas offers a wave and his shy smile before he dips into the trunk to fetch my bags.

"This is Jonas. He lives near me back home."

"Huh, you two are neighbors and this is the first time we're meeting?" Jane shoots out her hand and Jonas offers an obligatory handshake. "I'm Jane. Is this your first semester or something?"

"Good to meet you," Jonas says. "And no, if all goes like I hope I'll be graduating this semester."

"Interesting," Jane says, a penciled brow arches as she looks to me. "You must not be close neighbors then."

"There are some unique circumstances…" I start.

"Wait! No, Brita, *is this*…" Her gummy smile shines bright. "Jonas, what's your last name?"

He looks at me with tight lips. I draw my gaze to the snow. So, I might have mentioned a few things about his family. But an intense neighbor feud is a conversation starter, add in the way all generations are supposed to spurn the other, well Jane was filled in long ago.

"Olsen," Jonas says with less enthusiasm than he'd had a few minutes ago.

"Oh, my gosh," Jane gasps. "You've both crossed enemy lines. How romantic."

"No, Jane, don't go there," I mutter. "Jonas and I are friends. We both want to end the fighting and—"

"Brita's interested in my brother," Jonas finishes for me.

Not what I planned to say. I think more along the lines that both me and Jonas would like the childish fighting to stop.

"What!" Jane looks as though she might faint. "What happened over Christmas?"

"Thanks for that," I grumble at Jonas.

"Brita, you talk to me right now." Jane takes one of my bags.

Jonas seems rather pleased with himself.

"Can we get inside first?"

"Fine. Drinks, chocolate, and girl-talk. Hurry up. Good to meet you, Joe!"

Freeing my arm, Jane prances with my bag through the snow, her long legs remind me of a cricket as she tries to avoid too much ice in her boots. Jonas is holding his arm out, my final bag dangling from his grip. His iconic shy smile is gone, and now he stands still, rather smugly.

I snatch my bag and frown. "Now Jane will not rest until she knows every dirty detail and has a wedding planner on call."

"Dirty details? You don't really seem the type, Brita," he says, the way he looks at me I'm reminded in an instant that he is Axel's twin.

"Well, maybe you don't know me like you thought."

"I think with the drive tonight and seeing you with a little Bon Jovi told me all I really need to know." Jonas takes a step closer, his hands deep in the pockets of his black coat. He smells like the spice of a forest, that delicious pine needle scent, and an unexpected rush of nerves floods my insides. This is happening more and more around Jonas. "I'm sorry," he says. "I shouldn't have said anything about Axel, I know you guys aren't exclusive or anything."

"Who says we aren't?"

Sure, Axel and I have never defined our secret escapades, but I'll say this: if you're kissing the way we kissed, well, that changes the dating game.

Jonas's grin fades. "Are you? I didn't know. Axel just never…I guess it doesn't matter. Well, now I'm still sorry. I should have let you tell your roommate. Are you okay from here?"

"Yep," I say, popping the p.

Tensions shift between us. From the playful, hysterical drive to now— an awkward sort of dance on how to say goodbye. I'm freezing and should go inside. After all, Axel wants me to call. *Axel* is the one I've wanted for so long, yet during this short pause I discover I don't want Jonas to leave. Shaking the dubious thoughts away, I dare hug him. Arms wrapped around his neck, his warm body against mine, I relax. Then like they have minds of their own, my fingers briefly play with the ends of his hair on the back of his head. Jonas is stiff at first, then his arms hold my waist, one hand kind of strokes my spine over my coat. I shiver, and not from the cold.

The problem with this picture is that I shouldn't feel so comfortable in the arms of my sort-of boyfriend's brother. Seems it'll be up to me to make things right. After another few breaths, I tap his shoulder like a true buddy and pull back.

"Thank you for the drive. I'm glad we can be friends," I say. "Oh, and if you need any help with your writing class, you have my number and, I guess, you know where to find me."

I smile when Jonas leans against his car, his hands return to his pockets. He never brings back his shy, crooked grin, and that's a shame. "I know just who I'll ask to write all my papers." He walks around the car and slips behind the wheel. I hear him say, "I'll see you around."

"You will," I reply softly, but I don't think he hears me.

Jonas waves, and waits to pull out until I'm standing on the front stoop of my apartment. I wait by the front door, analyzing every heartbeat, every emotion, every thought clouding my brain. Then my phone buzzes, a saving grace in my moment of weakness.

Axel: Hey gorgeous! How was the drive?

Filled with Bon Jovi and gummy bears.

Axel: No! I refuse to let my brother corrupt you.

Too late. I was most definitely born in the wrong decade.

Axel: Glad you made it.

Are you ready for classes?

Axel: *Totally. Hey, I'm just heading out with the guys, if I don't respond that's why.*

I'm pretty tired. Mind if I just call you tomorrow?

Axel*: Look forward to it. Sleep tight!*

I smile and clutch my phone against my chest. Serenity is interrupted by Jane's loud grunt. She steps into the entryway, two mugs in one hand, while in the other hand she's broken out our first king-sized candy bar of the semester. I'll rephrase my previous assertion. Jane believes lipstick *and* chocolate can cure life's woes. Our tradition from day one is to donate two candy bars a week to the stash—double during finals—but this is the first time we've partaken before classes start.

"Sit your butt down," Jane says, a devilish smile spreading over her lips. "We have a lot of things to catch up on."

I take one of the mugs, breathing the sweet cinnamon smell. I've missed this—Jane is the queen at making wassail. I know what it looks like, we live way too far on the wild side in this apartment. Chocolate, wassail—no judging, but we simply can't contain ourselves. Jane and I share the common thought that we don't need frat parties at this point in our collegiate lives. Those fled our system during freshman year, and even then, I hugged the corners, wide-eyed and nervous. Thanks to Jane, tonight we have all the necessities to have a great time. Jane snaps off a piece of chocolate, crisscrosses her legs and looks at me with such anticipation it's comical.

I sigh and sit on our dingy sofa. "So, I may have left out a little detail about this family feud."

"Obviously, you never mentioned the enemy has a dreamy son—Brita, did you see that guy's eyes? How did you not drool the entire way here? But enough about him," Jane says. She waves her hand in front of her face as if physically erasing Jonas from her thoughts. "What did he mean about his brother? There are two of them?"

I snicker. "His twin, *Axel*. I don't know how it happened really. One minute Jonas and I are working together, the next minute I confess that I like his brother, and then before I know it I'm going out with Axel every night."

"So, I'm going to pretend you didn't skip like a million details just now. What do you mean you like his brother? Never, not once, have you ever mentioned this Axel."

"I've never told anyone," I admit. "It would be the equivalent of walking to the guillotine if my family found out."

"Okay, a little dramatic," Jane says.

"I wish I was being dramatic."

"Whatever. Moving on." Her voice changes into something sensual. "Tell me all the details I *really* care about."

My bags stay by the front door all night. Jane and I spend the next few hours laughing like silly girls over boys, future plans, the young, new adjunct professor for computer sciences, then loop back to Axel, even Jonas, more than once. I fall asleep on the sofa, Jane in the chair, and when I wake, gray light bleeds through our thin curtains. A new text message is

105

my phone and my stomach tightens. After all my talk about passionate feelings when Axel's hands were on me, I decide to keep the way my lips form a smile to myself about this text.

Jonas: I've been singing Africa *all night. I'm pretty sure I dreamed about the Serengeti. Just wanted to say thanks again for driving up with me. You're insane, you can shovel back candy like nobody I know, and you can't sing. It was awesome. Hope you have a great semester.*

Chapter 12

The first day is freezing, the air heavy with frigid wind. My hair whips my cheeks like icicles. Mondays and Wednesdays will be my busiest days. I need to take a biology lab. Like Jonas, I saved my worst subject for the final semester, and it takes up three hours on Monday mornings. I hate the chemical smells stuck to my clothes, but at least I finish the day in my favorite class. Advanced British Literature. How I adore reading tales from Bath and Canterbury.

Golden light from the fading day casts a beautiful glow over the snowy campus. When my phone rings, I dart back into the building and hardly feel my screen against my ear when I answer.

"Hi, Mom," I say breathlessly.

"Hi sweetie. How did the first day go?"

"Pretty good. Of course, I have mounds of projects and I'm already looking forward to summer."

She bemoans with me. I hear some commotion in the background from her end. "Oh, hang on sweetie," she says. "Todd and his brother just came in."

I wait patiently while Mom talks off the phone to her boyfriend. I grimace, but quickly adjust my feelings. Mom is happy with Todd. He really is a decent guy, but then my dad is a great guy too. The thought comes out more than immature. I know it, and I know I'll get used to their relationship. Something tells me I'm going to need to.

"Sorry, Brit," Mom says a minute later. "I was going to call you yesterday, but I figured you were busy and time got away from me. Your dad said you took the bus, why didn't you let him drive you? I think he really wanted to."

The back of my throat feels like acid is bubbling. I think of what Jonas and I talked about in the car; the pain of disappointing our families. *Be bold.* I straighten my shoulders, brave people have good posture, you know. I think I tell my mom because my parents are divorced, and the risk of her telling Farfar is minimal. Don't get me wrong, I try to convince myself that I spill the goods because I'm not spineless, but I think we all know the truth.

"Mom, I need to be honest," I say as I slide into a narrow chair bolted to the wall. "I didn't take the bus."

"Brit, did you buy a car?"

My mother is thrilled at the idea. Pretty lame that parents are trying to convince their daughter to purchase a vehicle, right? My aversions aren't so noble like I'm a crusader for the environment or anything, it's simpler than that. Debt isn't my thing when I have tuition to pay, and I guess I've gotten used to the bus.

"Brit?" she tries again when I don't answer.

"I didn't buy a car. I uh, I got a ride. From Jonas Olsen."

Silence. Expected.

"Really?" she says.

I dissect the tone in her voice. Is she upset? Indifferent? Hard to tell with students bustling around for evening classes.

"Really," I respond dumbly.

"Why lie about it, Brit?"

Fair question. "I think you can understand why I did."

"Okay, but I have to be honest, I don't like that you lied to your dad."

"Mom, tell me what you would have done." My voice breaks. Emotional? Just a bit. I haven't even confessed the biggest news yet. "I know it's ridiculous, but it isn't just from our side. Jonas didn't tell his family either. Whenever we saw each other outside of Dad's office, we had to behave as though we despised each other."

"Brita, I'm not upset you drove with Jonas. I'm not. A respectful young man drove my daughter to school, what is there to be upset about?

109

I'm concerned you feel the need to lie about it. Your dad worked with Jonas too. He liked him, right?"

"Yes, but it doesn't mean he'd like me spending time with him outside of work."

"I think you're being unfair to your dad."

Okay, well then what about Farfar…"

"Brita, are you crying? Sweetie, is this really such a big deal?"

"Yes," I say. "Mom you don't need to worry about this anymore—"

"Hey," she interrupts. "I am still a part of the family, and I love them with all I've got."

"That isn't what I meant." I sniff and I look like an idiot. "The feud is worse, but for the first time I feel like I'm caught in the middle." Now is the moment, as good as any, to tell my whole truth—at least to my mom. "Because there's more."

In a matter of thirty excruciating seconds, I spill my Pandora's Box on Axel. All about the dates and how I feel about him. There are a few sticky, kissy details I skip, but Mom catches on pretty quick. Of course, she does. It's not like she thinks we only shared ice cream cones and held hands.

When I stop to breathe, an unsettling crackle surges through our connection, but I'm spent. I've nothing more to say.

I hear her throat clear, and Todd's hushed voice in the background, but Mom doesn't say anything to him either. Finally, she ends the torment of silence. "Brita, I want you to hear me. Listening?"

"Yes," I snip, and just like that I'm fourteen all over again.

"You need to really think about how you're behaving. Brita, you're nearly twenty-two years old. We're done raising you. Not to brag, but I think we did a stellar job. Now, it's time for you to make your decisions separate from what you think this family wants. I know nothing about Axel Olsen. Is he good to you? Does he feel the same? Will either of you behave like adults and admit it to your families?"

"Ouch, Mom," I say, but she quickly silences me.

"Not finished, Brit. Sweetie, these last few years I really hoped you would find that spark of strength that's inside you. I see it, but you've always worried so much about the approval of me, your dad, Farfar— everyone. Perhaps our family dynamic played a part in that. I know the resentment flows deep. It seems the Olsen boys are much the same with their own parents and with Viggo.

"But if I could have one wish for you these last few months of school, it would be that you find your own path. You find that thing that is so uniquely made for you, Brit. When you find it, cling to it. Don't let anyone tell you what you must do, who you must be, who you must care about. That is my hope. I can't do it for you. Your dad, me, Inez, your roommate—we can't give you permission to live your life. You must find the strength to stand in your own sneakers and live for you."

Another tear. My chin quivers when I hang my head, studying the threads of the ugly, brown carpet.

"Brita, you there?"

"I'm here," I whisper.

"Sweetie, I have to go. Are you okay?"

"I'm fine. You're right. About everything."

"Okay then. We keep everything out in the open?"

"Um…" She will hate this. "Can we just keep it between us—for now?"

I feel the weight of her sigh. "Brita—"

"Please, Mom. Let me tell people after I know if anything is even going to happen with Axel, okay? What if it doesn't work out?" *Please no.* "It will only give Farfar more reason to despise the Olsens."

Another palpable pause. Mom clicks her tongue and I imagine her rubbing her forehead, eyes closed, red lips puckered. "Alright, Brita. You speak with your grandfather. But I'm not keeping it from your dad. He should know, he's your father and deserves more credit. Unless you'll tell him."

"Geez, do you and Dad talk all the time or something?"

"You're our only child, divorce or not, we're going to discuss what's going on in your life. I'll tell him not to tell Farfar, okay? If Jonas continues to drive you back and forth, you should let everyone know. Nothing criminal about getting a ride."

"Unless you're a Jacobson riding with an Olsen."

"There, that's the attitude," Mom says with sarcasm. "Okay, Brit I have to go. You promise to keep me updated on all the mom-need-to-know parts of your life? Swear it."

112

"I swear," I say.

"Good. You are brilliant, Brita. This is your time, take advantage of it. Have fun, but use it to really decide what you want from life, okay? Oh, and be smart with Axel. I don't want to see you hurt."

"Deal." I want to question her meaning of smart, but frankly I don't have the energy.

It takes another two minutes for my mom to finally hang up, despite her declarations she is dangerously late for a housing meeting for a large cabin along the lake. I wipe my cheeks, now sticky with salty tears.

"Hey, Jane," I say in my brightest, non-whimpering voice, when my phone rings immediately after Mom and I disconnect.

"Happy first day!" Jane squeals. "Hey, just letting you know I'll be in The Lab pretty late tonight. If you want to invite your blue-eyes over, I'll make sure I get home really late."

"If by blue-eyes you mean dark chocolate over almonds, then yes, stay late. Have fun." Jane always calls the computer lab 'The Lab' as though it is the only place that deserves a label on the entire campus.

"See ya," she says, drawing out the 'ya' and abandoning me in the quiet of the English building. Taking a deep breath I gather my things, including my pride, from the floor, and trudge to the bus stop.

***

Throw pillows are my delight. I love stacking, designing, and squishing between the different sizes and textures. Jane teases me that my bed is merely a display shelf for my numerous pillows. When I plop onto my bed, I can't shake my conversation with my mom. Judy Jacobson is a soft-spoken woman, she hardly raised her voice to me as a kid, but she has mastered the art of punishment by disappointment. Her words about my age and my behavior sting, and the more I think on them, the more they sting.

Mom never proffered an opinion on my relationship, only be smart. Smart about what? What is so wrong with Axel Olsen? About any Olsen?

Ripping out my phone, I send a quick message to Axel, hoping that hearing his voice will somehow make the storm in my heart disappear.

Hey, can you talk?

I stare at the plaster of my ceiling as I wait. Part of me wants to call, but if I interrupt a class or a clinic or whatever he does all day, I will dwell on my shame for the next fifty years. After twenty minutes of no response, I dig a path through my pillows and turn out my purse, spilling the insides over my mattress. Pens, band aids, lip gloss and a hoard of receipts sprawl between the pillows. This letter serves as a lighthouse on the shore in my sea of heartache. Tearing open the tattered envelope, I take extra care this time to read each word; to deduce what might cause my beloved Farmor to offer such a final appeal to me—of all people—to me.

My Brita-

Little älskling—well I must say you are not so little anymore. How I love you. I know I do not have much time left in this world. I'm not afraid, Brita. Know that I am not afraid. Although, facing one's demise does bring about a time of reflection—and if it doesn't, then to that perfect person, I would say—go sit on a pin.

I am proud of the life I have lived. Your Farfar and I have worked hard. When he came to this country, he had little more than a knapsack with his dress shoes and ten dollars to his name. But oh, how I remember falling head over heels for him when we met on that ship. I knew when I found him, that I would follow the man around the world if he asked. But we stayed in our new home, we worked, we raised a beautiful family. So, I shall say again, I am proud of the life I leave behind. You are part of that life. I am proud of you.

I hope this letter does not bring you any distress. I'm certain I will be an angel (or some days a devil) on your shoulder, and I hope you will forgive my weakness in not speaking my heart in life. I have hardly the strength at this point to lift this pen. But there are things I must say. Life is short, my dear granddaughter, and the truth is that I leave behind one true regret.

I did not right a glaring, terrible wrong.

But I have hope that you might.

Now, I have my suspicions Philip may read this before it reaches your hands. The old snoop. But I want this to be for your eyes first and foremost and I'm certain you will understand.

I submitted to bitterness long ago, Brita. I'm ashamed to say I settled, though I knew I should have stood for what I believed. I hope you will have the strength to do what I did not. Resentments do not serve anyone, and you have the heart to heal what was broken long ago between two families who once loved each other.

Misunderstandings, hatred, and grudges are like poison that infects even the most beautiful of people. I've seen power inside your soul, my

115

dear. Forgive, Brita. If I could ask one thing of you, forgive. Take the time to understand the differences of others. Sometimes when we allow the ugliness of hatred to cloud our vision we miss out on the most beautiful of sights. I hope others in our family will follow your example someday.

You are my heart, and I shall always be near you. Keep working hard in school. Love our family as you do, and as I do.

I love you always,

Farmor

P.S. I had monthly tea with Clara Olsen for all my adult life, may she rest in peace. If you haven't guessed (but you're brilliant so I'm certain you have) I'm speaking of That Family.

P.P.S. Philip! If you've read this without permission I insist you return it to Brita immediately, or I promise you my love, I will not welcome you with open arms in the next life! And quit griping about my monthly tea! I know you are.

I wipe away a tear through the laugh that always comes at the end of the letter. Farmor left the note to me in her will. Yes, she willed me the letter. Farfar eyed it curiously as I read her words in the corner of the bakery weeks after she passed. In my heart I know he hadn't read her last appeal or I had to believe the tension between the rival bakers would have eased. It hadn't in the least.

This is my burden to carry. The task of healing a feud that no one talks about, no one faces, and that stacks more anger and resentment with each sunrise. Hatred has festered like a cancer between two otherwise pleasant, personable families.

Before the holidays, I never thought the idea possible. But now, I do. Jonas, Axel, and I have proven it is possible.

Though I have little confidence in my own abilities to break through the feud, tonight I somehow find some sliver of strength to try. Mom and Farmor share similarities in their advice to me. My grandmother didn't want me to regret as she had; Mom wants me to be happy by choosing my own way.

Clutching the letter to my chest, I close my eyes and drift into a dreamless sleep.

Axel doesn't write back.

Chapter 13

Doctor Nichols is one of the most influential professors of my college career. Being his assistant for his freshman courses is a dream gig. To sit on the other side, and learn from one of the greats. Bring it on.

"So, I'll be looking to you to help me structure the papers. You know, check for writing style consistency, flow, voice, all the good stuff," Nichols says ten minutes before class is to begin. A few early birds already flock into the room. "I'll need your eye, Brita, to find those gems."

"I can't wait," I say sincerely. Tuesday will be a better day than Monday. I already told myself as much.

I drove with Jane since we both have morning classes, but will be finding my own way home after lunch. Those long days in The Lab for Jane, and all. I'm sure Young Adjunct Professor might have something to do with it too. But in other news, today is my shortest day on campus. Yes, I think Tuesday will be my best day.

Plus, Axel wrote me back this morning. He apologized for being away from his phone—blaming study group—but said he would call me later. Despite the foot of snow dropped last night, today is shaping up to be epic.

"You can take the desk here," Nichols says. "But I won't require you to always attend the class. I know it will be monotonous for you. You can work in my office. I thought you might want to come to review the syllabus and course material this week, so you have an idea what I'll be working with and what I expect from the students."

"Oh, I don't mind working here, it will be fun. The poor little things," I tease, eyeing the new students finding seats. "They have no idea what you're about to do to their minds."

He laughs and adjusts his glasses. "I won't give it away just yet, next week I make no guarantees. I wouldn't want them all dropping and running to Crichton, now would I?"

"Oh, Doctor Crichton has no problem scaring students the first week," I say, knowing both professors well. In fact, Alice Crichton is my instructor for my senior capstone project. This afternoon I plan to select my subject, but I'm stuck amongst the writings of Shakespeare, Charlotte Brontë, or William Faulkner.

"True," Nichols says, glancing at his gold wristwatch. More students filter in, jabbering to one another, some take seats in the back corner, leaving plenty of empty front seats for stragglers. "Well, it's about time to start. Glad you're here, Brita. You've got a good eye for words."

Normally I don't accept compliments with much grace, I get all flitty and red in the face, but Nichols doesn't hand out praise unless he truly means it. I'd insult the man if I argued. I smile and take my place in the corner by the doorway, ready to take in the lecture.

Until I see him rush in, three minutes before class is set to begin.

"Jonas?" I say.

Jonas whips around, his brow furrows until he registers my face. Perhaps I should try to not like his smile, but truly it isn't possible. Jonas dresses much like I would expect a senior in the final stretch to dress. His long-sleeved T-shirt is tight around his shoulders, sleeves scrunched up over his forearms showing off his antique watch. His hair still delightfully tousled. Messy hair suits him. So do the black athletic pants. I like the casual look on Jonas. There, I said it.

He glances down at his phone. "Am I in the right class? This is supposed to be a basic English class."

"Structure of English Grammar, to be exact," I say.

"So, what? You're just retaking all your old classes for fun?"

My cheeks prickle with warmth not coming from the heater when he leans against the small desk. "I would if I could. I'm the TA for the class. I thought you were taking a writing class."

Jonas's smile drops. "Don't classes like this just mean a ton of writing?"

"This is much different than creative or technical writing."

Jonas shrugs, and takes in the room one time before meeting my eyes again. "So, you're going to read everything?"

"Why, yes Mister Olsen, I will be reading your papers. You don't mind, right?" Jonas takes a deep breath, truly nervous. "Jonas, I'm teasing. Well, sort of. I *will* be reading the assignments, but come on, I've already read one of your reports. It will be as easy as that. You won't even know if it's me or Nichols."

"That report wasn't easy to hand over either," he protests.

"Well, I think you'll have to face a fear this semester," I say with my own version of a sly smile. "Unless, you want to transfer classes. I think the only other class is at seven in the morning."

"You don't scare me that easy."

"Good. I knew you'd be up for the challenge."

Jonas smiles, his eyes deepen a bit. For a moment I think he might say something more the way he inches a little closer, but Nichols calls the class to order and Jonas scrambles to find a seat.

In the front. Right in the center.

He doesn't look happy. Especially when Nichols asks everyone to state their major, and Jonas endures sporadic lawyer jokes the remainder of class. I laugh, and accept that I'm not a good friend in the moment. No mistake, I'd laugh until I turned blue if it kept his tepid smile on his face all day.

The ham and cheese melt drips down my chin. I'm embarrassed, but Jonas simply snorts and hands me a napkin. Jonas doesn't have a class until five this evening. I don't remember when we arranged to have lunch

121

together; we both left Nichols' class, started talking, and ended up in the café.

"So, are you ready to graduate?" I ask, wiping the stringy cheddar from my face.

"Yeah, but I'll be right back in school in the fall. If I'm accepted into law school, I guess. But this place has grown on me. It's been a good program."

"What made you choose to stay in Minnesota? Most of my graduating class went out of state. I'm one of the few who stayed close to home."

Jonas shrugs. "I don't know. My dad came here, I think it's a good place to get my undergraduate. What about you? Why'd you go here?"

"Well, it's far enough away that I feel like I'm living on my own, but still close enough I can go home without a problem."

Jonas agrees, and I like the way a dimple forms in the corner of his mouth. I've never noticed it before.

"Any first week complaints?" I ask.

He wipes his hands on a napkin and takes another drink before answering. "The biggest stress is applying for law schools."

"Where are you trying for, Harvard? Yale?"

Jonas answers pompously. "I'm incredibly intelligent, and those schools would be lucky to have me—"

"You know I've always admired your humility," I say.

He grins and takes a bite of his panini, properly eating the bite without chewing like a Neanderthal. "I know. But honestly, I don't think my brilliance is a good match for the ivy leagues."

"Yes, it's best if you mingle with those who can only learn from your mind."

"Common folk," he says. The tinge of crimson over his cheeks is rather endearing if I do say so myself.

"So where in the world will Jonas Olsen grace with his brilliance?"

"I've applied here, which my mom is voting for of course, a few schools on the East Coast and Midwest. I plan to apply to some in Alabama, maybe Louisiana. There's also a few highly ranked schools in the west."

"So basically, you're applying all over," I say through a smile.

"Basically."

"That's exciting," I add. "Any preference?"

"Not really," he says. "I wouldn't mind going out of state for a while. Axel enjoys Wisconsin. I've never really gone anywhere else—you know how the family business sort of ties you down."

I nod and wash down the last bite of my sandwich with a long swig of cocoa. "You still shouldn't let that stop you from going to a school you want."

Jonas stares at me for a long enough moment I can feel my heart rush a bit and I start to wonder if I've spilled something more on my chin. He rubs the back of his neck and rests over his elbows. "I think it's ironic you

123

say that." His voice changes so it sounds low and calm. "Why does everyone else get to live their dream, but you allow yourself to settle for something you don't want?"

I turn my attention out the large window. A tight bubble smolders in the center of my stomach. Crossing my arms over my chest, I give Jonas my best mind-your-own-business look. "I already have a mother, you know."

"Is that what she told you, too?"

"I live my life." I toss my hands overhead. "Why does everyone insist that I don't? If anyone should understand it's you. And honestly, we don't know each other that well to give life advice." If I could bite off my tongue I would.

Jonas lifts a brow. "Fair enough," he says. "But I feel like I know you well enough to say that you deserve to live a life you want too."

I open my mouth to retort—maybe apologize for my pout—but I stop when Jane's voice echoes across the café.

"Brita!" Jane hurries over, bumping a young couple so water splashes all over the girl's sweater. "Oh, sorry. Tight quarters," she says, her cheeks flush as she grips the back of my chair. "Brita, I've got to—" Her bright eyes find Jonas and she smiles. The attention sends him back into shy mode as he picks at his sandwich. "Brit, I half expected to see you at home by now, reading in pajamas."

"Oh, I will be in about twenty minutes." I smirk, and Jonas laughs softly.

"What about you, Joe?" she asks. "What are your evening plans?"

124

"I have a night class," he says.

"Too bad. I have a free night and Brita won't give in to a social life except on the weekends."

"Hey, I've done well with my study hard, play harder system. And my weekends are pretty stress free," I say. "You could learn a few things, Janey."

Jane laughs. She has such a beautiful smile at least two guys on the neighboring table take notice. I check Jonas to see if he is gawking too, but swallow a hiccup when our eyes meet across the table instead.

Jane pinches my shoulder. "If I haven't learned it by now, I'd say it's pretty hopeless. Jonas, I'm glad you're here," she says, leaning over his side of the table. "I've been thinking, since Brita is all into your brother, the most rational thinking would be for you and me to go out—at least a few times. What do you say to, I don't know, how is your Saturday night?"

Jonas's mouth parts and my smile is gone. I don't think anyone notices the shift in Jacobson cheeriness though.

"Uh, Saturday? Well…"

Jane scoffs, charming as ever and places her hand over the top of Jonas's. His skin looks like ripe strawberries. "Does it make you uncomfortable having the woman ask you out?"

"No," he says.

"It's okay." She winks. "You'll get used to me taking the reins."

"Jane," I mutter, nudging her in the ribs.

"What?" she asks "So, Joe, what do you say? There are a few friends getting together for some awful Chinese and a movie on Saturday. I would really love your blue eyes to be my plus one. I promise, I'll let you pay."

In my short history with Jonas, I've learned his nervous habits. I watch as he runs through them now. First, he rubs his palms over his thighs. Check. Next comes the popping of the thumb knuckles. Check and…check. He swallows, and I admit to a touch of gladness that he shows a bit of reservation. I don't like that I have the gladness because there really is no cooler girl than Jane.

Jonas scrolls through his phone calendar. "Well, I have a test that morning," he says. "But sure, that would be good."

"Awesome! Brita you're in right?"

I look across the table using a split second to study Jonas's face. He leans back in his seat and seems more comfortable with the idea.

"I don't know," I say. "I don't know how Axel would feel about it."

I sip my cocoa, intentionally avoiding Jonas's glance. We don't really talk a lot about the fact that I'm smitten with his twin.

"Come on, I'm bringing a date, but most everyone else is just going to hang out. He can't be that controlling, can he?"

"He's terribly possessive," Jonas says.

I kick his shin. "For your information, he specifically told me to go crazy this semester."

"Oh, I like that," Jane says.

"Fine, I'll go," I say. "Someone will have to keep an eye on you two."

"Hopefully." Jane's sultry voice sends a new paint of rouge over Jonas's cheeks. Jane is one of my favorite people, why wouldn't Jonas enjoy her company? The better question: why do I think I even have a say? "Pick me up around seven?" Jane tickles the back of his neck, and I know she's teasing. Jane has always been confident and loves to do this to guys.

"Okay. I'll be there," he says. His smile—the Jonas smile—sets in place. Jane earns it.

When I finally plop onto my bed after leaving Jonas, I have a strange weight on my chest like thread tugs at the sinews. I shower to relieve the tension, tie my hair high on my head, and slip on my Wile E. Coyote pajama pants. Then my phone rings.

Axel's face appears on my screen. "Hey," he says, looking perfect.

"Hi," I sink deep into my pillows. Seeing him makes it much easier to imagine Axel right next to me—like our nights in his car. I imagine the scent of his skin, clean like rain. "How are you?"

"Better now." *Uh, swoon.* "Sorry I missed your message last night. Rough first day?" Axel stands outside, it looks frigid, but he doesn't drop his smile.

"First days always are, but it's no big deal now." I don't need to rehash my mother's conversation to Axel. "Today was great. I saw Jonas this afternoon."

"Is that why it's great?" His voice is playful. Strange though, to flirt about me and his brother.

127

I laugh nervously. "He's fun, I guess. He's in an English class and I'm the T.A.?"

"I told him not to put those freshman classes off. Promise me you'll tell me how awful he is, okay. Our parents think he's a genius, so you'll really be preventing some major sibling rivalry." Axel laughs, someone outside the screen taps his shoulder. I hear girly giggling, some deep voices, but see no one, and I feel self-conscious talking around his friends.

"Well, I might disappoint you," I say. "I've read some of Jonas's writing before—he's pretty good."

"No, you don't mean that." A guy with long hair sits next to him, but talks off screen. Axel brings the phone closer when the laughter picks up. "Just build my ego a bit, okay? Lie and tell me he's the worst and he's probably going to fail."

"Fine." I chuckle. "Hey, I wanted to ask you something. So, my roommate, she asked Jonas out today and—"

"Really?" Axel asks. "Is she hot?"

"Yeah, is she hot?" asks the long-haired guy.

I click my tongue. "Not that looks are the most important, but yes. Jane is very attractive. They're going out Saturday, and they asked me to join the group. What do you think? Would you mind? It's not like it's really a date or anything, more like hanging out, I just—"

"Brita." Axel stops my rambling abruptly. "You don't need to ask me. I would expect that you are going out. It's half of the experience, right?"

"Yeah, I guess." I'm starting to spend more time analyzing everything about Axel's tone than the conversation. Should it be so easy for him to know I'm going out with other people—other men? And what does he mean that he expects I'd be going out? I remind myself that right now he is on the phone with me; I'm the one he wants to talk with tonight. I remind myself to chill.

"So, listen," he says, sitting down on a bench wherever it is they are. "I was calling to ask what you're doing next weekend. I've got a buddy of mine who applied for a clinical in St. Paul. The clinic wants to interview him, so a bunch of us are coming to crash at Jonas's place. I thought we could get together."

My heart leaps to my throat in excitement. Axel, coming here! Then it sinks. "Oh, no. Next weekend I'm going to New York with my mom."

"That's next week? I forgot. Hey, that means…is your birthday next weekend?"

"No." I don't want anyone making any bit of fuss over my birthday. "It's the second week of February, but the tickets were only available for next weekend."

"Okay, good. I'd hate to be there on your birthday without you."

The same long-haired guy dives into the screen. "Taking so long," he mutters, but he's grinning.

Biting my lip, I fight the urge to tell Axel I'll miss not seeing him. Not in front of his friends. "I can't believe the one weekend I'll be gone you're coming."

129

"I know, that's kind of lame," he agrees. "You'll have more fun with your mom. You like that kind of stuff, right?"

"No, I love that kind of stuff."

There is another voice in the background. I really can't tell if they are a man or a woman, but they draw Axel's attention for a few moments. "Hey, my study group is meeting, I've got to get going." Axel flips the screen so I can see the entire group.

"Okay, well maybe we'll talk tomorrow?" I say when Axel turns the screen back to him.

"Yeah, sure," he says. "Still bummed you won't be there next weekend."

"Me too," I say softly. I want to say more; try and plan another time we can see each other. I want to ask him so many things.

"Well, talk to you later," he says. "Sleep tight."

The phone call ends abruptly, and I feel a little embarrassed being home—alone—while Axel lives it up with friends at school. Jane has a valid point about my social life; it lives on the weekends. It's not that I don't have a life. Obviously, I'm not as outgoing as Axel, but opposites attract right? Truth told, Saturday looks more appealing by the minute. This semester will be the last, after all. I stare my ceiling fan for a long time. Axel is a dream to me. Handsome, sweet; his kisses knock me to the floor. Yet, as I replay our conversation there is a stab of unease in my stomach. I can't puzzle out why either.

My door groans as Jane pushes into my room. "Hi," she says. "I wondered if you'd be asleep."

"Hey," I say and lift my head off three pillows.

She leans against the door frame, a funny grin on her face. "I surprised you earlier today, didn't I? I should've talked to you first about asking Jonas out."

I wrinkle my nose. "Why would you need to ask me?"

Jane shrugs and sits on the edge of my bed. She starts to braid the fur on a long pillow. "I don't know. You know Jonas, I don't. It just seems like something I should've checked with you first."

"Janey, you're free to ask out Jonas as many times as you want," I say, my face disappears into the pillow abyss when I flop back.

"Good." Her voice is a little brighter. "He's probably one of the hottest guys I've made a move on, and he's nice according to you. Here's the plan—you marry the brother, and I'll get Jonas begging me to be his. We'll be sisters forever."

I laugh and lock elbows with her when she joins me in the pit of fluff.

"He is a good guy, right?" she asks after a long pause.

I close my eyes and take a deep breath. Why is this hard to talk about? It isn't because...no, it isn't because of that. Nodding, I meet Jane's eye. "Yes. Jonas is one of the good ones. He's the best."

Chapter 14

Wednesday ends and I send praises to the sky. Thursday packs in two tests—who schedules tests during the first days of school? By the time I find myself curled in front of the TV on Friday with Jane and Emma and Natalie from next door, I can't wait for a needed Saturday break.

"So, Brody, Matt, and Brody's cousin—I think his name is Tyson, he's a freshman—are all coming tomorrow," Emma says, licking melted chocolate off her thumb. "I'm declaring now, everyone keep their paws off Brody."

"Are you still after him—correction, are you still secretly pining after him although he has no clue?" Jane snickers. Natalie nods dramatically, earning her a swift shove from her roommate.

"Look, I came back this semester with the full intention of telling him the truth. If it goes bad, so what right? I have four months of shame before we all part ways. He'll probably go home to New Mexico unless he finds a good job. But if it goes well..."

"You might run off into the sunset with your true love," I say, chomping into an almond bar.

"My thoughts exactly."

"Okay, noted. I will not make a random move on Brody after four years," Jane says.

"Good. As long as we're clear," Emma chirps, smiling. "What about this guy you're bringing Janey?"

"He's Brita's neighbor—*the* neighbor."

Emma and Natalie glance at me at the same time.

"The neighbor? The oil to your water? The thorn to your rose?" Natalie gasps.

"Oh, my, stop," Emma says. "You sound like you're in one of your plays."

"Hey, coming up with prose on a whim takes talent, and I might add, that talent earned me a summer study in London." Natalie straightens her shoulders with an extra pompous expression.

"Yes, we all know." Jane pops several gummies into her mouth. "But it means nothing if you don't invite all of us over there."

"You need to earn it," Natalie says. "But forget London for a sec. Brita, tell us about the neighbor."

Okay, so I might have complained about the feud to more than just Jane. But again, it makes for interesting conversation.

"Oh, me taking him out isn't the best part," Jane answers instead. I give her a stop-talking look, but she promptly ignores me. "Brita's having a secret love affair with the twin brother."

Emma and Natalie both stop moving chocolate to their mouths.

"What?" Natalie gasps—again. "Forget tomorrow, tell us everything."

"Oh, poor Tyson," Emma says. "He was so looking forward going out with an older woman."

I laugh, knowing full well even if Axel wasn't in the picture, Freshman Tyson would have to find his older love somewhere else. We talk about Axel, the feud, a bit of Jonas, and the daring confession Emma plans to make to Brody, until midnight. Finally, Jane being the responsible one— believe it or not—admits she must wake up and make a study group. I trundle off to bed, hung over on chocolate and of course gummy bears.

I have been fortunate to forge lasting friendships at school, we enjoy doing things together. I'm excited for overcooked Chinese and a stupid action movie. Not for Jonas reasons, of course not. I'm really looking forward to watching Emma declare her love for quiet, athletic, computer genius, Brody. And it will be fun to hang out with Jonas outside of law firms and a campus café. So maybe excitement is partly for Jonas reasons.

***

Hazy clouds soak the sky when Jonas pulls up to our apartment. A storm is building, but at least the air feels a little warmer. Jane looks stunning as usual. She pulls off billowy blouses and skinny jeans better

134

than anyone I know. She's styled her hair a little wilder than usual, but I am quick to encourage her to keep the look. I, on the other hand, must settle for a ponytail. Someday I will give up trying to make my curls look like the magazines. Since my hair boasts the casual look, and I'm not really on a date, I sport school pride in a form fitting University of Minnesota sweatshirt. Much to Jane's disapproval.

Emma and Natalie chat with Brody and Matt—Freshman Tyson opted for video games with his roommates instead of coming and part of me wants to back out. Being the seventh wheel is equivalent to swallowing nails, but when Jonas comes inside I decide I need to get out and socialize.

I simply enjoy Jonas's company. And I've been saying those exact words in my head all day, so now I'm practiced enough that I can almost block any weird thoughts about his strong face, or the way the blue T-shirt makes his eyes look like sapphires.

"Hi!" Jane says pleasantly. She pecks him on the cheek, and Jonas takes it with grace. "Here, come meet everyone."

I meet his eye as Jane drags him by the wrist into the center of the room, introducing him to Brody and Matt who are both part of Jane's computer science family.

Natalie inches to my side, she sweeps her gaze across Jonas's back. "Until Jane locks him down he's free game, right?"

I roll my eyes. "The way you guys talk sometimes it's like you're hunting."

"I am, I thought you knew?" Natalie says. Her brown skin is flawless, and her dimples add a sweet charm to her face. Jonas will be an idiot if he doesn't notice her if he and Jane don't hit it off.

Matt and Brody accept Jonas into their conversation. Jonas fits in easily, despite his tendency to shift to the shy side. Brody towers over everyone, and Emma's five-foot-even frame hardly hits his bicep. He looks more like a hard-core athlete than a computer enthusiast. Matt fits the part of the geek. His sandy hair is always combed to the side and his shirt is buttoned to the last button just beneath his Adam's apple. He is handsome enough, but only wants to talk about the latest technology; he never would've listened to me rant about Shakespeare.

"Well, should we go? The movie starts at eight," Jane says.

Slowly, we caravan through the snow to the cars. Emma and Brody shove into the backseat of Jonas's car, leaving me to either squish next to them, or ride with Matt and Natalie. Natalie doesn't really give me the option. In fact, she offers me the front seat of Matt's small Honda.

They are fun though. Natalie spends most of the drive reciting lines from her upcoming performance, I think she does it to irritate Matt. By the time we reach the theater they are neck-deep in a hilarious battle on whether liberal arts or computer sciences serve the greatest contribution to society.

Brody and Emma are already in line for snacks. Natalie flashes Matt the sweetest smile and he quickly rushes away to fulfill her popcorn needs.

"Brita." Jane waves a pair of tickets in front of her face. Jonas is next to her, hands in his pockets, and I think he relaxes a bit when I stand next to them. "You guys go on in, I'll wait for everyone else to give them their tickets."

"I can wait out here," Jonas offers.

"No," Jane says, drawing her face a little closer to his. Oh, there it is—a thumb knuckle cracks. "Go on in," Jane insists. "I won't be long. Be sure to save me a seat though."

"Come on, I love the previews." Natalie tugs on my elbow. Jonas follows close and his shoulder brushes mine when we scan the theater for our seats.

I'm squished between Jonas and Natalie, and I smile when he looks at me. He seems ready to say something, but Natalie speaks up instead. "Is this strange for you guys?" she asks. "I mean, we all know about the tensions back home, but you two—I don't know, you seem to get along really well."

"What? I can't stand him," I say.

"She's awful," Jonas adds. "And she can't sing at all. I had to suffer the entire way back to school."

"Oh, I'm bad? Your pitch is what most people save for showers, behind a very locked, very sound-proofed door."

Jonas tosses a bit of popcorn at my face, bringing me to giggle childishly. Natalie smiles, a knowing smile that sends a flush to my neck like a thousand pin pricks. A sense of relief comes when Jane and the others tiptoe along the row.

Jane leans in close to Jonas, who keeps his hands on his knees or folded over his chest. Once the meat of the movie is well underway, I start to drift further away from Jonas and Jane, feeling more and more out of place. It really isn't my kind of show, yet I will take the guns and explosions over watching sly hand brushes with Jonas or my best friend nuzzling her body against his. I wonder if Jonas enjoys the way she's linked her arm in his, then I wish Axel were here. I could lean my head on his shoulder, or hold his hand after we both reach for the popcorn. Even as I think of Axel, I keep stealing glances from the corner of my eye whenever Jane or Jonas shifts in their seats.

"Jane really loved that last scene," Jonas says when we all squeeze around a cramped table in the corner of the restaurant.

"What's not to love." She fans her face and mouths, *So hot*. They laugh together.

I'm glad they seem to be hitting it off.

Then Jonas looks at me. "What did you think?"

"It was intense, but predictable," I say, struggling with my chopsticks.

"Come on, it wasn't that predictable," Jonas replies. He's a pro at chopsticks, by the way.

"The technology was completely fabricated and unrealistic," Matt says as he opens a fortune cookie, but then tosses the fortune onto the table.

"You think everything is like that," Jane says. "It was meant to be futuristic, Matty."

138

"It's entertaining. Isn't that the entire purpose of a movie?" Jonas asks, watching me attempt to jab at my chicken.

"See, Jonas knows how to enjoy an evening, Matthew." Jane runs her hand over Jonas's arm, then turns to her own fortune.

"Oh, my...come on, haven't you used chopsticks before?" Jonas laughs and moves his bowl out of the way. I've dropped the same piece of chicken three times.

"Hey, I have many talents, and I'm not too concerned chopstick holding isn't one of them," I say. And all at once my head is swimming when Jonas wraps his hand around mine. *Oh, Mylanta.* He's never been this close before.

I've lost track of how we ended up this way. The warmth from his hand sends strange chills up my arm, neither cold nor hot. Jonas pauses too. His jaw pulses when he guides my fingers to pinch the sticks over the lump of saucy meat.

His voice sounds rough. "It's easy. You just have to find the grip."

Jane gnaws on the end of one of her sticks, a brow raises. She watches us. Jonas clears his throat and releases my hand. My skin feels cold when he scoots back to his place.

The tingle on my hand leftover from his touch is all wrong. I don't say much the rest of the evening. Sure, I tease and laugh, but something about sitting close to Jonas has blanketed me in a strange, unfamiliar wave of jitters. Jonas drives Jane and me home, my head still hazy. I don't even remember that Emma plans to declare her love for Brody.

With a quick wave over my shoulder I rush into my bedroom. I am smitten with Axel, he makes my stomach flutter and oh, when he kisses me…

But this is something else.

A fleeting moment when Jonas Olsen, the wrong brother, has by all accounts taken my breath away. I want to cry, and smile, and laugh, and shriek.

When Jane knocks on my door, I jump. She's doing her signature lean against my door frame.

"So, did you have fun?" she asks with a smile.

"I did, it was good to get out. How was your date?"

"He's a gem. A perfect gentleman. Did I mention he's sexy?" I force a chuckle. "But…"

"But what?" Interest and a need to know every thought in her hilarious brain cracks my voice.

Jane looks away almost wistfully for several heartbeats. "I'm not sure we fit, you know? I think I'd overwhelm the poor guy. I don't know, it was fun but at the end there I didn't get the vibe."

"I guess. Maybe you should go out again, one on one."

"I think I'll just welcome him into my friend circle. Although, I had a thought. Hear me out. If it doesn't pan out with his brother, I think you and Jonas might fit pretty well."

I offer a nervous chuckle. "No, I don't think so. Jonas is so…you know, just not really…we wouldn't be good together. Too different."

Jane yawns as she removes her gold hoop earrings. "Whatever you say. It was just a thought. You would know better than me."

She blows me a kiss and goes into her room across the hall. Hugging my favorite pillow, I sink against my buried headboard. I imagine what Dad might say if he knew—and Farfar! What am I doing? Living in a fantasy where there is golden, sweet blood between my family and the Olsens. How easily I have forgotten. Jonas and I drove together under a guise, a lie. Axel remains a complete secret. All of this will always be a secret unless I finally find the courage to speak up, but the thought still causes my heart to thump heavy in the back of my throat. I close my eyes, not surprised when a single, hot tear squeezes out the side.

Brita Jacobson, what are you doing with the Olsen brothers?

Chapter 15

My eyes start to water, and I try to snuff the loud laugh threatening to burst. Axel goes on, his voice playful and expressive as he recounts the story. An older gentleman spent the morning in the student therapy clinic convinced one of the girls in Axel's class was his lost love. Bits are kind of sweet and sad as Axel tells me the numerous ways the guy proposed. But the way he tells it, I can't keep laughter inside.

"That's hilarious," I say, and stop in front of the classroom door.

"I know, it was pretty awesome," he says.

So, Axel called me, by the way. Yep, he called just to share a funny story. Take that weekend confusion.

"You really like what you're doing, don't you?" I say, a little more serious.

"Yeah, I do," he agrees. "It fits me."

I don't know why that means so much, maybe it is my own passion for my studies. But I feel happy that Axel is happy. That must mean *something*.

"I'm about to class," I mutter outside Nichols's door. "*The* English class."

"Oh, tell Jonas to get ready for us this weekend and tell him he's failing. You promised you'd build my ego."

I giggle again and sound ridiculous, but sometimes dumb laughter slips out. "I'll do my best. Talk to you later."

With Axel on my mind, I sneak into the class right before it begins. A low rumble in my stomach doesn't belong, but I brush it away. Nothing is going to mess with my morning.

***

Fifty minutes later my stomach still gurgles, but I find a bit of distraction and satisfaction side-eyeing Jonas as he fiddles with the paperclip on the corner of his report. He waits behind a girl with coke-bottle glasses until his turn in line comes up. With pinched lips, he drops the papers on the small desk Nichols gave me, and rocks a bit on his heels.

"You know, all my other classes hand everything in online," he says. "I haven't printed out an assignment in at least two years."

I smile and add his paper to the pile on the corner of my desk. "That's Nichols for you. He likes things to be personal. He will require me to use the red pen, no highlighting, just good-old fashioned red-pen editing."

"Well, don't think too little of me after you read it."

"Jonas, you are so funny about your work. You'll be just fine." The way he looks at me, I wonder if it isn't so much that someone else will read his assignment, I wonder more if it is because that person is me. Tucking my hair behind my ears, I gather all the papers and duck my head to hide that I'm biting my bottom lip. "So, has Jane texted you at all?"

"Yes," he says with an intentional grin. "She invited me into her circle of friends—her exact words. I must have made a great impression."

I tug my bag over my shoulder and flash him a grin. "Feel honored. The circle is a great place to be. Jane is the best friend anyone could have. Honestly, I don't think you're too heartbroken."

He shakes his head. "I'm not sure we were a great fit, but I think she's awesome and am glad to be included in the circle."

We start walking across the campus to the small café, I like this new tradition. He holds the door open for me, and I know that I'm walking on dangerous ground. My earlier conversation with Axel fades around his brother. I see the problem, but admitting it to myself proves difficult.

"New York this weekend?" he asks once we take our seats near the large window. Jonas glances up from his cobb salad to catch my reply.

"Yes," I breathe out—only peppermint tea for me, my stomach has taken a turn for the worse, and protests every sip. Clearing my throat, I ignore the agitated bile and try my best to smile. "I can't wait. You sound like you're going to have a wild weekend too."

"How did you know?"

"Axel told me," I say. My throat feels gravelly.

144

"About the weekend? Huh, okay that's good then," Jonas shrugs. He's not making a lot of sense. Weird. Jonas meets my eye. "Axel has come down a few times; we always have a good time. This time he's bringing a few friends, and even Logan decided to come up. So, we had to make plans for a big crowd." I grimace, but Jonas notices. "What?"

"Logan is coming."

He smiles. "You really don't like him, do you?"

"It's not that I don't like him—well, I guess I don't—he just loves to get right in the middle of the fighting between our families. I think he likes it. Although, Axel told me Logan was the one who encouraged him to take me out."

Jonas tosses his lettuce on his plate, but doesn't say anything. I sip my tea, feeling sick heat flush my face. Maybe I can't ignore it any longer.

"You okay?" Jonas asks after a quiet pause.

"I'm fine."

"You sure? You don't look very good." Resting my face in my hands a wave of something gross swims around inside. Jonas stands and walks around the table. "Come on, I'll drive you home."

"Don't you have class?"

"Not for a while, and I can survive missing once."

Jonas gathers my things, and pulls my chair out. My stomach tightens even more when he takes my hand to guide me from the café. A tremble ripples down my arms and along the back of my legs as though someone slides ice cubes over my skin. It's not a good feeling, and I'm glad he's

145

guiding me. With my head in fog, my jaw clamps tightly against my angry stomach, I slip into Jonas's car which seems astronomically far from the café. The ride to my apartment is littered with bumps and curves that threaten to spew my entire stomach over Jonas's dashboard, but thankfully I summon the grit to keep it simmering inside.

Taking my house keys, Jonas carries all my books, my tea, my coat since I began to roast in the car, and pushes open my front door with his foot.

There isn't time to thank him. The vomit volcano in my stomach erupts. Running toward the bathroom, I don't even have time to close the door before it all comes out. Tears crust long my cheeks by the time it ends. Keeping my eyes closed, I flush the toilet. At least I feel a little better.

Something about an upset stomach makes me to shake and stagger around as though I live in darkness. I reach up for the towel, but instead feel the damp softness brush my hand. My eyes crack and I think I'm going to throw up again. Jonas holds the wet towel out for me. I groan.

"You don't need to see this," I say, wiping my face and reaching for my mouthwash and toothbrush.

He hands me a glass of water—when did he go into my kitchen? — and stands patiently at the door. "I thought I told you I don't scare easy. How do you feel?"

"Like I want to curl up and die," I swallow hard. My throat is dry and raw, my stomach feels full of knives every time I move. I quickly rinse my mouth and move out of the bathroom toward my bedroom. "I'm going to change."

146

Jonas reaches out his hands in case I stumble, I guess. I must look a sight. When I come out of my bedroom with my extra-large, flowery blanket, he sits on my couch with another cup of minty tea and the glass of water. Without a care, I flop down like a slug, my head comes to rest half on Jonas's knee. Tugging the fleece blanket around my shoulders I close my eyes and try to forget my upset stomach.

"You don't have to stay," I croak.

"No one should be alone when they're sick," he says. "That's what my grandma always said, at least."

"But your class…"

"Brita, I've missed classes before and I'm still pulling good enough grades to get into law school. Don't worry about my class."

I relent and scoot my head, so it rests completely and comfortably on his leg. Jonas doesn't budge, he doesn't tense up either. I offer him the remote and after some time I hear the soft laughter of a studio audience, but I don't know the show. Eventually, when I'm starting to doze, I feel Jonas rest his hand on my shoulder.

Smiling, I whisper, "Jonas, are we friends enough that you'll tell me what scares you?" Random question, but I am a little delirious.

"What?"

"Remember when I told you that I liked Axel, I wanted to know your deepest fear. You said we weren't there yet. Are we there now?"

I hear through the rumbling sick in my gut that Jonas swallows hard. "Yeah," he says softly. "I think we're there."

"So…"

"I'm afraid" – a pause, and another swallow – "It sounds stupid saying it out loud. I'm afraid of disappointing other people. It's why I started school later, so while my grandma was sick I could help out at the shop. Axel went to college a year before me. I think it's why I stay in Minnesota. I don't ever want to disappoint anyone or add to their burdens, you know?"

My heart sort of breaks. Jonas and I really aren't so different; both keeping things from our families, both not giving them a chance to know how we feel. Jonas surprises me though, he always seems so sure about his life. I didn't know he opted to stay home for a year while Axel left. Does Axel recognize the sacrifices his brother made?

"Jonas," I whisper softly, my throat raw and gritty.

"Yeah."

"You could never disappoint me. I'm glad we're friends."

He doesn't say anything for a long time, and I am about to try again when he whispers even softer than me. "I am too."

A dry lump in the back of my throat grows. After the fear of vomiting again passes, I slowly drift to sleep. Right there, with my head on Jonas's lap.

***

I miss two days of classes. It is without a doubt the nastiest stomach flu I've ever experienced. When Thursday evening rolls around and I am still living on broth and 7-Up, my mom starts to worry we'll need to cancel our trip. I make her promise to hang on to the last minute, but I'm worried

148

too. Jonas stops by five times in between his classes and study groups. He brings chicken noodle soup once, but Jane ends up eating it for me. I sleep while they talk with each other. Emma and Natalie bring their collection of romantic comedy DVDs, but I always fall asleep before the first scene is over. I text Axel. He tells me to feel better, but doesn't seem overly concerned.

But then as if I've been reborn, Friday morning brings crisp air and a settled stomach. I step outside to breathe away the sickness. Flannel pajama bottoms, a tattered sweatshirt, and a bun half out of the elastic, I look like I've risen from the dead.

I see Jonas's car pull up. I should probably go clean up, but what's the point. He's seen me with my head in the toilet at least six times now, groaning on the couch, hair sweaty and stringy, yet he keeps showing up. The way I look today is probably glamourous in comparison.

I smile and wave, but then my hand freezes mid-wave. Jonas isn't alone.

Stepping out of the passenger side of the car, Axel smiles his widest, opposite-of-his-twin-smile and takes off a pair of sunglasses. My stomach feel sick again, but an entirely different category of sick. I smell like I haven't showered in two days, my skin is clammy, my hair has enough grease in it that the waves roll into dreadlocks, but there he stands. In all my fluster I can't figure why Axel is walking toward me. He isn't supposed to come until later—or so I thought. I guess I never asked timeframe. We simply assumed we wouldn't see each other. Jonas walks around the front of the car. He doesn't seem all that pleased, but I don't know why. Then, only to add to my shame and sudden desire to melt into the snow, Logan gets out of the back seat.

"Looking good, Brita," Logan calls out.

I quickly brush my hair from my face when Axel stands three paces away. "What...what are you doing here?"

"My buddy's appointment is this morning. We came last night. Two more guys are still at Jonas's with his roommate. It's a full house," Axel says. Oh, no. He scans me.

"I told him you were still sick," Jonas says, coming up behind his brother.

"I'm feeling better. Uh, why don't you guys come inside. I'll just...I'll just be a second."

I rush back into my apartment, leaving them to make themselves at home. Jane is sitting at the counter, sipping her morning coffee.

"Men...coming inside now," I hiss. "Axel is here. And no, I had no idea! Look at me!"

I blurt it all out before she even has time to ask a thing. Rolling my eyes, I turn away when she perks up, and ties her robe tighter. I hope she has clothes on underneath, but there isn't time to ask. I dart back to the bathroom and hurriedly wash away the smell of my embarrassment.

Jane's laughter fills our apartment by the time I pull back my damp hair and battle with a pair of jeans. Axel leans over the counter on his elbows, his flirtatious grin sends Jane into another contagious chuckle while Logan scours our refrigerator. Jonas stands against the wall and is the first to notice me.

"You look like you're feeling better," he says.

Drawing in a deep breath, I nod. "Thanks for helping bring me back from the dead—"

"There she is," Axel says, crossing the small kitchen. His hands find my waist and I forget how to breathe. I like the way his hands feel, but more than before I am keen to the way Jonas watches us. My cheeks blaze when Axel kisses me. Logan scoffs and bites into a cold piece of Jane's pizza.

"Hey," Jane says and lunges for the slice. Rule one of the apartment: don't take Jane's food.

Axel pulls away, his kiss warm on my lips. He's here in his delightful splendor, but my insides are not tumbling, nor fluttering. I instead step back, chest tight with a kind of embarrassed concern that others can see our affection.

"I missed that," Axel says. "So, when are you leaving to the airport?"

I look around his shoulder at the clock over the stove. "In an hour."

At that his impish grin comes to life. "That's plenty of time."

Jane snatches the pizza from Logan's hand, but like the ogre he is he already dives in for a second helping. But if anyone can give Logan a run for his money, it's going to be Jane. Jonas sits on the couch, his back to Axel and me.

I finally offer Axel my best easy smile, and squeeze his waist. "You know, I need to pack still. I didn't get much done while my stomach was turning inside out."

"Keep your hands off," Jane says, flapping a piece of pizza into Logan's face. "If I come back out here and this is gone, you'll wish you never stepped foot in here."

"She means it, Logan," Jonas mutters, without turning his head.

"Fine, I won't touch your pizza," Logan says, then snickers like a gargoyle.

Jane offers a curt nod and brushes past me. "I'll be ready in forty-five Brit. Then we'll go."

I shoot Logan a warning glance when he moves toward the fridge, but he only takes an apple. One of mine. Axel leans against the wall and pulls at the hem of my shirt so I press against him. "Want me to help you pack?" he asks.

I shake my head, and don't miss the way his eyes avert toward my bedroom door. Axel's voice sounds low, sultry, and nearly irresistible. The insinuation can't be missed by anyone in the room. Like I have mentioned, and maybe this makes me the oddest senior on campus, but let me be clear—I've *kissed* guys. Some more passionately than others, but that's the extent of my experience. Clear enough? I'm not going to tell that to Axel, because frankly I've always been okay with that. I'm not sure if Axel expects to take the relationship there, right here, with his brother in the apartment, but I know he would find himself disappointed. I'm not ready. And Logan Snyder is not a face I want nearby when that moment comes. So that's that.

152

Something about the idea feels off, like I've been flipped upside down. Almost…wrong. I shift away from him. Axel is my dream, the desire of my heart, yet this morning I'm not as in sync with the flow of the dream.

"You guys go and have fun," I say. "What are your plans this weekend?"

Axel frees my shirt and shrugs. "Logan heard about a place downtown that should be entertaining. Although, Jonas doesn't seem all that excited."

Jonas glances at his brother. "I never said I wasn't going."

Axel rolls his eyes, but grins. "He's so uptight. Well, if you're about to take off, we'll leave. I'm glad I got to see you before we left. Don't go too crazy in New York."

"Yeah, I don't think I'll be living on the wild side with my mom in tow." I chuckle, back up to the sofa, and pick up two blankets from when I was dying on the couch. I smile at Jonas who hands me a third blanket I didn't see. His eyes cut through my Axel trance and bring a calm to the room, although he says nothing.

With a gesture Axel signals to Logan and Jonas to leave. He pecks me once more, the tingle on my lips gives me hope maybe the dream isn't combusting. Axel is everything I could want. Fun-loving, incredibly attractive, and to be honest, I've never considered much more than that. But as I watch the three guys leave my apartment I wonder if that is enough. Is my dream of loving and being loved by Axel Olsen just that? A dream? Shouldn't I be clinging to man who has my heart, cursing that we'll be separated for the weekend? Shouldn't he have held me and promised he'd call me each night? Shouldn't I *feel* more when my dream-man kisses me? Or is it all a fantasy?

153

I wave. Axel and Logan are talking and don't see. But Jonas does. He waves back and I feel like I can breathe normally again.

Chapter 16

"That was amazing!" Mom sighs when we step onto the curb from the Broadway Theatre. It is a frigid night and the city seems to be coming to life when we leave the show. "Did you like it?"

I nod; my cheeks sore from smiling the entire time during the breathtaking scenes. There is singing, and then there is *singing*. The kind where you can hardly breathe until the echo of the music stops. I tug my black pea coat tighter around my body, the black skirt and knit tights failing to block the bite of the air as we weave through the crowded walk toward the restaurant.

We step into the restaurant lobby moments before my cheeks freeze. Basil and tomatoes with a brilliant scent of oregano warm me from the inside out. When I eat with Mom we eat Italian food. And I don't protest, it reminds me of my great-grandmother who I only met a handful of times.

She immigrated from Sicily. The only trouble with eating from the kitchen of a true Sicilian, my mom and I are extremely picky about our linguini.

It takes another thirty minutes before we're seated, but instantly Mom and I dig into the fresh herb bread the moment it's in front of our faces.

"This is awesome, Mom. Thank you for the trip, it's just what I needed."

Mom smiles and sips lemon water. "I'm glad we did this too. How are you feeling? Still sick at all?"

I shake my head, my long earrings slap my cheeks. I rarely dress up, but my mother bought me a brand-new outfit and accessories for our trip. Who am I to protest getting a little fancy? "Nope, I feel just fine. I'm a little worried I'll have some late nights making up for all my classes I missed though."

"You'll be fine, you always were a good student."

Mom and I chat about school until halfway through my ravioli. She stares at her plate, her eyes distant. Her wine-colored lips don't smile, and I take note how her nails tap along the table.

"Mom, what's up? You zoned out for a second."

She grins, slow at first. Her face is beautiful, and sometimes she looks like she could be my sister rather than my mother. Perhaps I know Mom's expressions too well or maybe it is just that obvious, but I notice a distinct uptick in how many breaths she draws in before she says a word. Something has happened, and it is big.

"Brita, I have a confession. This trip isn't just for your birthday or a Christmas gift. I wanted some time alone with you."

I set down my fork, then pick at my freshly manicured nails. "Okay. I'm always up for girl time, but is there a particular reason you wanted to get me alone to where I can't escape?"

My mom laughs, but she nods. Something is *definitely* up. "You know it killed me when your dad and I split, and I had to say goodbye to you too. I'm not upset at all that you chose to stay, I completely understood, so don't think that, okay? I missed being so close to you, but you've been happy, right? You weren't upset that I took my job?"

I reach for her hand. She meets my soft smile with one of her own. "Mom, I'm fine. I'm all grown up and I have a secret, I don't live with either of my parents most of the year," I say. "Please don't tell me you've thought I've been angry at you all this time."

"No, of course not," she says, dabbing at her mouth. "I just want to make it clear that you're always my number one, no matter how old you get. That's never going to change."

"What's going on?" I ask. My heart quickens.

Mom clears her throat, and crosses her leg. "Brita, I love your dad, I always will. We just…we didn't work after a while. But he gave me you and…"

"Mother," I say with a nervous smile. "You're kind of freaking me out."

She gives a heady look, long enough to set my heart thudding in nerves, then dips into her purse. I hold my breath, too stunned to say anything when she slips a tasteful diamond ring on *the* finger. "Todd asked me to marry him," she says, holding up the ring. "I said yes."

I meet my mom's eyes, she studies me, probably to see if I am going into shock. Maybe I am a little. My parents have been divorced for almost three years. They were married at twenty and had me a year later, they are still young. This day has always been inevitable. It still takes me a moment to form any kind of response in my mind.

"Congratulations," I say softly, taking Mom's finger.

"Really? You can be honest, don't keep anything inside. This is the time to get anything out in the open. No judgment."

I clear my throat and feel my eyes burning with tears. I'm not sad. No, I know the tears didn't come from a sad place. I thought they would, but thankfully I'm drifting between happiness, stun, and maybe a bit of resistance for change. But not sadness.

"I really mean it, Mom," I say. "Todd is a great guy. Does…does Dad know?"

Mom nods. "I spoke with him right when you went back to school. He's okay."

"He loves you still," I blurt out. My cheeks heat at the juvenile response.

"I know," she says. "And I'll always love him too. We're some of the lucky ones to be able to be friends even after a divorce. But I care more about your feelings right now."

"It's difficult to imagine you with anyone but Dad," I admit, picking at the bread instead of my nails. "Are you happy?"

Mom nods, her own tears brim along her dark eyes. "I am, Brit. I love Todd so much. He gets me. You were the first person he worried about when he asked because he knows how much you matter to me. He suggested this trip. That's one reason I love him, because he cares about you. I know you don't know him well, but I hope you'll get to know him."

"Of course, Mom," I say, wiping my cheeks. "I…you deserve the best, and I want to make sure you get the best."

Mom wipes silent tears from her own cheeks, but beams as I expect a woman in love might. She breathes out a sigh of relief and hugs me across the table. "Thank you, sweetie. I've been so nervous to tell you."

"So, when is the big day?" I gush when she finally releases me.

"I wanted to do it this summer, but want you to help me plan it. Will you? Please say you will."

"I wouldn't miss out on this for anything, but you're the designer. Now if you want someone to quote books, I'm your girl. This is kind of embarrassing. My mother is getting married for the second time before I've even had a whisper of a long-term commitment."

Mom laughs. "Now, that is something I do want to talk to you about. You need to tell me what's going on with you and the Olsen boy."

"He stopped by to see me yesterday," I say.

Mom raises her eyebrows. "He came from Wisconsin to see you off? That's…committed."

"No, they came down for the weekend for other reasons," I say. "It was good to see him."

Mom watches me carefully. "Why does it sound like you're trying to convince yourself of that more than me?"

"I'm not," I say, a little defensive. Although getting defensive doesn't seem like the best reaction to make my case. Mom wears a knowing smirk. Rolling my eyes, I finally settle back in my seat and admit something I really hate admitting. "I don't know, I just didn't feel the way I should have felt."

"How should you have felt?"

"If I was head over heels for someone then I thought it would be different, you know?"

Mom smiles. "Like the movies?"

I shake my head. "I don't need it to be like the movies, but I thought it would feel...happy. I was self-conscious about others seeing us the entire time."

"Well, what do you like about him?"

"He's a nice guy," I begin. "He's fun to be around, he's respectful, he's good looking."

"Brita, you've only gone out with him a few times, right?"

"Yeah, what difference does that make?"

"Well, you really don't know much about him to be thinking you're head over heels. You've only started. It will take more time to know if he's your guy. I'm going to tell you something, and I want you to hear me," Mom says, a funny look on her face.

"I'm listening, I've been listening the entire time," I whine.

"You're my favorite daughter, but you tend to take ideas very literal and overthink the smallest of things."

"What? I do not."

"Yes, you do," she says. "It's not a bad thing—not all the time, but right now I can see your cogs hard at work about Axel. You can't force it. That's what I'm trying to say. If he's the one that knows you inside and out, if he's the one who will be by your side through everything, then fantastic. Relax sweetie, you'll never get this time back. Enjoy your last few months at school, enjoy Axel, but don't force love if it isn't there. When you fall in love it will slap you upside the head. It will feel…natural, easy."

"But love isn't easy," I say.

Mom sighs, I know she is thinking of my dad. "No, it isn't always easy and sometimes it fades. Sometimes other things make it so love isn't enough. I don't want you to worry about making a long-distance thing work the entire time you're at school—you've only seen him a handful of times. Don't be afraid to go out and have fun too. You'll know if it turns into something more than just making-out in a car."

I blush, we did have a good time in the front seat of Axel's car. But I start to feel better. She lists all the reasons to stop fretting if Axel is the one who'll plant a ring like hers on my finger. We are new, and he's been sweet. That's enough for now.

"What about his brother, you two are becoming good friends, right?" Mom asks as she takes her credit card from the black payment book.

"Jonas? Talk about different twins," I say, helping Mom with her jacket. "Jonas can be so quiet, he'll say nothing but still, you can't help but enjoy his company. Axel talks with everyone and teases about everything. Well, so does Jonas. Sometimes he spouts off these little jabs that make me laugh for hours."

I'm rambling, but I can't stop. "He's also unsure about certain things, while Axel always seems so confident. Jonas shared a few things that make him uneasy, sort of makes me feel better knowing I'm not the only one who feels vulnerable. But when you need Jonas, he's a brick of confidence and strength."

"Meaning?"

"Like when I was sick, the man stayed in the bathroom the entire time I threw up—then he kept coming back to check on me. Jonas has this way that lets you know he's listening too, you know? It's what Jane first noticed about him; I think it's his eyes. They focus on you and he just listens. He cares what other people have to say. Personally, I feel like that's an awesome quality today, don't you?" I barrel on before she can answer. "He's been a bit of a lifesaver at times, and I wish we'd been friends sooner. I think we both let the feud stop us from getting to know each other."

Mom stares at me with a crinkled expression by the time I stop talking. The corners of her mouth are curled.

"What?" I ask.

"Nothing," she says and steps into the car taking us to our hotel. "Nothing, I just feel like I know one of the twins better than the other."

I don't know what to say. I about blew a gasket spilling all the little things I've learned since Christmas break. I know a lot, she's right, about one twin. This is backward, and I don't think I can bury my head in the sand much longer.

Mom nudges me. "I'm glad you've found such a good friend."

"Yeah," I whisper. *A friend.* "Me too."

That night, long after Mom has gone to sleep, I send two text messages. The same one to each Olsen brother.

My mom told me she's engaged.

My eyes flutter closed before any replies came.

Every inch of my body feels heavy from rich pasta, laughing, and all the excitement of the city. In the morning I have two new messages. Now that the thrill of the night has faded, I ponder more on the reasons why I sent messages to both. Why it had mattered to hear from both. Am I testing them? Betraying them? Am I this person who balances hearts in two palms? I'm ashamed that I don't have an answer just yet.

I reread Axel's text. Short and so very Axel.

Very cool. Awesome news.

He is excited for our family, for me, for Mom. He cares, that's all I need to know, right? But after a moment of skimming back and forth through the messages, I stop trying to figure out why I find more comfort in Jonas's response. I know why. He gets me and the entire purpose of the text.

How are you doing with it? Need me to make a dart board with Todd's name? Or should we help your mom pick out color schemes? You tell me, I'm good either way. Maybe not with the colors, but I could taste test cake. Seriously though, you good?

I respond to Jonas.

Color schemes. It's a good thing, but a little hard too. Thanks for asking.

I wonder if Axel will still be in town tomorrow when I get back. I think I need to take Mom's advice. Give things time. I can still be friendly with his twin, still learn things about his brother. I'll learn things about Axel too, and I'm sure the feelings will come strong again.

Sure of it.

Mom and I part ways in New York, each taking separate flights. Jane looks as though she's just rolled out of bed when she meets me at the terminal entrance Sunday night.

"Fun weekend?" I ask, tossing my duffle bag into the backseat.

Jane sighs. "No. You'll be proud of me for being a studious college student. I had a late study group last night, oh and I need to replenish the stash. Too many Hallmark marathons on TV this morning and the chocolate called to my soul."

"Well, this should give it a good start," I say and dig into the front of my back to hand her an enormous New York chocolate bar. Fancy enough that the chocolate is wrapped in gold foil and cost me fifteen dollars for one candy bar. Call me a true Manhattan Diva now.

"It's like our brains are connected," she says. "So, how was it? Amazing, I bet."

"More than amazing."

"Oh, Jonas stopped by this morning—he left a report he wanted you to look over I guess—anyway he told me about your mom. How are you doing?"

I smile this time. "You know, it was hard the instant she told me. I could only think of my dad, but she's so happy Janey. Todd's a good guy and I can't expect her to stay single forever. Now we need to find my dad a woman just as awesome."

"That's exciting then. I expect to be invited of course, and I get to do your makeup for the wedding."

"Deal. So, Jonas came by, did you see Axel?" I ask.

Jane shakes her head. "Jonas said they were still sleeping, late night, I guess. Sorry, they've already left—at least according to the timeline Jonas gave me." She glances at the clock on the dash. "You're right, though, Axel is a looker. That Logan guy isn't bad either if he could just keep his paws off my food."

"Oh," I say, a little disappointed. "Hopefully they had a fun weekend."

"Hey, I wouldn't worry about Axel being out late," Jane adds. "He was all over you before you left. And Jonas would have said something, I'm sure."

"I'm not worried."

"Brita." Jane tilts her head and smiles. "I know you better than you think."

"I'm really okay," I say, and I'm pretty sure I mean it. "I'm ready to just enjoy Axel and see where it goes."

I add a smile for good measure. Jane lifts a brow. "Well, alright then," she says. "Very mature and secure of you, Brit. You're growing up so fast."

"I would never have made it without your motherly care all these years, Janey."

We laugh as Jane drives too fast back toward campus. I'm grateful when the conversation drifts to Emma and Brody. She really did tell him the truth and it went in Emma's favor.

Jane tells me they've ruined The Lab since Emma hangs around until he finishes his work, or they spend too much time in the corners of the building doing things not related to computers.

I loved New York, it gave me a lot to think about. But when my thousands of pillows mold around my head later that night I settle in with Jonas's report in hand. It also feels good to be back.

Chapter 17

The last few days of January leave me buried in the full burden of classes, and feeling the pressure of my capstone paper. I've gone for the writings of Charlotte Brontë. She fascinates and intimidates me all at once. I find it rather unfair that other classes demand so much of my time— haven't we seniors earned a little down time after years of hard work? Entitled, I know, but I'm not the only one thinking it. And I know the professors don't see it the same way. Because they tell my classes often.

The café becomes a ritual for Jonas and me. Some days all we do is eat quietly and work on various projects. Sometimes we complain. Other days we'll laugh and tease each other, or our families, or he'll joke with me about how much I've kissed his brother. Those jokes make me blush the most.

"Hey, can I ask you something that is a real jab to my ego?" Jonas asks on the first Tuesday in February. We made it through month one of school. Sing praises.

I finish slurping my tomato soup and give him my full attention. "I can't wait to hear it; I love ego jabs."

He laughs ironically and closes his tablet. "I didn't do great on the first test in Nichols's class."

"What? I looked over your reports you did fine on your writing assignments."

"Apparently, I can form a sentence, but it's the basic rules that are killing me. I can't believe I'm saying this, but my freshman English mid-term is causing me the most stress."

Covering my mouth, I try not to laugh. I really do, but the way Jonas hangs his head in shame reminds me too much of a young boy confessing he's stolen a pack of gum from the store.

"Are you asking me for help, Jonas?" I rest my chin on my hands and lean closer.

"Yes, I am," he says with a long sigh. "Would you even have the time? I know we're both busy."

"Well, we find time to come here every Tuesday. How about we work here? I also have Friday nights open. What about you?"

"I could do that; I'll make sure I can. Thanks," he says. His shoulders seem a little lighter.

"Hey, you saw me looking like something that had crawled out of a grave and still tried to make me feel better. It's the least I can do," I say.

"You didn't look bad to me," he adds. Jonas doesn't look at me, instead he eats more of his soup. Is he blushing? My question fades when Jonas snaps his head up and drums the table. "Oh wait, next Friday we're going home right?"

I bite the inside of my cheek and nod. "You're right, I almost forgot. Well, we'll just work longer on Tuesday next week. You don't have class until five, and I'm done for the day after Nichols. By the way, I appreciate you driving me home, I hope it's not putting you out."

"How could I say no when it's your birthday?" He says and points a finger at me. "But you do owe me. My mom's using the weekend as an excuse to take new family pictures. So, thanks for that."

It feels like a sticky web lines my throat. "Axel will be home too?" We text almost every day, and sometimes call, but with busy schedules I've felt cut off from Axel this last week. I want to see him, I need to get that tingling, mysterious feeling back and seeing him is the only way to do it. Following Mom's advice isn't easy, especially around Jonas. I'm not an idiot—stubborn, but no idiot. I recognize the dry throat and tight chest around Jonas lately. But after wanting someone for so many years I ought to fight for it, right?

Jonas looks out the window. "Yes, Axel will be at home."

"Is that not a good thing?" The change in his demeanor comes as a surprise.

169

"No, it's great," he says. "I just think our families will be taking up our time, so I don't want you to be disappointed if you don't see much of each other."

"I wasn't expecting to, just making an observation," I say, stirring my soup into a whirlpool.

Tension tries to build in our silence, but Jonas taps my toe under the table and smiles. "Everything good there? We don't talk about it much, but are you two still going strong and in love?" Jonas doesn't tease other people, but he knows how to make my cheeks boil.

"Did I not tell you that he proposed?"

Jonas chokes on his water, and laughs. "Wow, no I guess he forgot to tell me."

"Well, get caught up, Jonas," I say, then shake my head. "But no, I wouldn't use the words *in love*. It's fine." Is it though? "I guess we haven't talked a lot recently, so I feel a little distant."

"But you're with him? I mean, you like being with him?" Jonas says the words slowly like he's swallowed vinegar. I would like to know what's going on inside his head.

"Yeah. What's not to like?"

He laughs. "Brita, you know I'm not going to stop hanging out with you if you tell me my brother has done something stupid to turn you off. I totally get it."

"Really he hasn't." My cheeks are a hot stove top when Jonas looks at me like he knows different. "You really want to hear all this?"

"Actually, yes. I'd like to know what you're thinking."

Swallowing the tight ball in the back of my throat, I glance at him with a new set of nerves. "Do you think...do you think it's possible to try too hard at something? Something you've wanted for so long, but when you have it—I don't know, it doesn't come natural?"

Jonas isn't smiling anymore and shifts in his seat. "I think everyone has a certain sense about what their heart wants, I guess. If you feel something is off—general you, not you specifically," he clarifies. "I think you should pay attention. Look, Axel is my best friend by default. I want him to be happy, but I also think you should be happy. Do what you think is right, Brita. Especially this weekend."

"I think it deserves a shot," I whisper. "I mean, don't you think?"

"I'm more of the opinion you can't force feelings."

We agree. I stir my soup that is cold now. My voice is soft. "You'll keep all my flip-flopping between us?"

"Not a word," Jonas says.

"So, about my birthday," I say, desperate to change one uncomfortable subject into another uncomfortable topic. "I'm going to tell my family."

Jonas stops lifting his glass to his mouth, his sapphire eyes on me. "About Axel?"

"And you," I say. "I mean if you're okay with that."

"Sure, at least about me. Are you sure you want to talk about Axel right now? Wouldn't you want to wait longer? You know how things can get."

"Maybe you're right," I agree. I'm already on the fence, no sense comes in giving Farfar more fuel to use against Viggo. "You make a compelling argument, Mr. Olsen."

"Thank you." He tips an invisible hat.

"I'm still going to mention you're my chauffer though."

"Fine with me. I'll do the same." Jonas's smile shows off more of his straight teeth. "I think this is so sad and hilarious at the same time. We're adults, both educated, and here we are planning to tell our families the terrible news—we drive to school together."

"It is a little pathetic isn't it? But at the same time, you know there will be a moment where both the Olsen and Jacobson families will think the world is crumbling on top of them. Well, enough with that," I say, clapping my hands together. "Let's get to work."

"What do you mean?"

"Jonas, did you not just ask me for help in Nichols's class? What, did you think you'd get today off? Now start taking notes."

I like the way Jonas smiles and laughs at the same time. It is a quiet laugh, almost like taking a deep breath, but it brightens his eyes in a playful way. By the time Jonas leaves for his evening finance class, he has a strong disdain for adverbs, adjectives, and commas.

***

"Jane don't do anything sneaky when I get back, okay," I warn, and snatch my bag off the counter. Jane sits next to Jonas, who picks out all the gross raisins in the bowl of trail mix. Who eats only the raisins?

She raises her hands in surrender. "I don't know what you're talking about. I hate parties."

"I heard you say the word birthday to him—don't think you're not going to get the same warning," I say, giving Jonas a precarious gaze. "No surprises."

"I'm not planning anything," Jane says. "I told Jonas to make sure he told you happy birthday tomorrow, you know how men are."

"She did," Jonas corroborates. "That's all."

He smiles though, and I glare at the pair of them. "I don't believe either one of you dirty liars."

"Of course you don't." Jane chuckles and gives me a tight hug. "Happy Birthday tomorrow! Have fun, okay? No neighbor drama."

"I never know what to expect from the likes of him," I reply, my whisper husky and intentionally loud.

"We are not the problem. It's you people," he says as he stands. I almost hear Viggo in his voice, but he makes it funny. "Ready to go?"

I nod, grab a grocery sack filled with snacks, and follow Jonas into the snow. The night is growing darker and colder, but the inside of his car smells like hot chocolate and sugar. This week we've spent more time together working on Nichols's study guides. I have now learned that Jonas taps his pencil as he studies, sometimes it has a rhythm, other times it is an incessant thwack that echoes in my head. But he told me I bite my tongue when I concentrate. And much to my regard it is now sealed in my brain that Jonas has the same obsession with cocoa and sweets as me— bakery kids, it must be our lot in life.

We've survived on Swedish cookies I made last Friday night. So of course, on Tuesday Jonas had to squash my love for spritz with hot Æbleskivers from a local bakery. The feud continues, in a much sweeter sort of way.

A few miles outside of Lindström a new war builds full throttle inside Jonas's car.

"You're telling me you'd rather spend a weekend in snowy mountains than spend an entire *week* in Hawaii?" I gape as Jonas pulls off the highway. This drive went even faster than the last one. We haven't even jammed to eighties—the radio isn't on—just our voices and candy entertaining us the entire way.

"There's nothing wrong with a mountain cabin. Fire, snow, pine trees. Yes, I'd take that over sharks and eels and sunburns."

"Sharks? Do you think they're just waiting in the tides?"

"I don't know, maybe. I don't want to find out."

"Ugh, we can't be friends," I say and slump back in my seat.

"That isn't fair," Jonas says. "I forgave you when you picked the Hulk over Batman. Who picks The Hulk?"

"That question doesn't even compare to mine. I asked a real adult question, not a fourteen-year-old boy's fantasy."

"There is nothing fantasy about Batman," Jonas says, his tone quite serious. "It could happen, and I plan to appeal to all the multi-billionaires of the world to create a vigilante."

174

"You're impossible. Well, I'll enjoy my trip in paradise, and you can go cuddle in the frigid winter with your fire, as if we don't get enough snow in Minnesota to last us a lifetime."

"Oh, no you have to come," he says, laughing deep and real. "I will prove how awesome it is. Think of it—all the hot chocolate you can drink."

"Fine, I'll go freeze if you come snorkeling in the ocean." I jab him in his ribs.

Jonas keeps his smile, but he goes quiet. The pause brings my attention to the pulse in my neck. He looks at me, then nods. "It's a deal."

"Alright then," I say.

My bottom lip rolls over my teeth and I turn forward again. We are teasing, that's all. Yet, I can't hide that I sort of like the idea. Okay, I'll say it—only to myself—bits and pieces of my heart are drawn to Jonas. I like that he is a little scruffier right now, sporting his facial hair before Sigrid forces him to shave for the picture. His hair is a little longer over his ears, and I like that it isn't the clear-cut blond like his brothers. His color is darker, with more red. A different color. But Jonas is my friend, I'm dating his brother. Thoughts like this aren't fair to anyone. Maybe closer to being on the wrong, since I've told Axel that I care about him. How would he feel if he knew I'm planning romantic fantasy vacations with his brother? And that I like it.

"I'm pulling right up to your house," Jonas says, his voice breaks me from my private thoughts.

"You like to live on the edge, Jonas Olsen." I wink as I gather my bag and gummy bears.

He parks unafraid outside the bakery. Warm lights flood the back windows of my house, and I can see some movement across the street inside *Clara's*. Probably Viggo or Sigrid getting ready for the next morning.

"Hey, I uh…I got you something for your birthday," he says.

"Jonas," I breathe out when he hands me a large box that is wrapped like Agnes had a part in it. He flushes.

"I'm not a professional gift-wrapper, but I did my best."

"I think it's great. I'm lazy and would have used a bag, so you're a level up from me. Thank you so much," I say eyeing the box. "Want me to open it now?"

"No." He rakes his fingers through his hair. "No, you've found my shy spot. Just open it whenever, but after I leave."

"You're a weirdo," I say and wrap an arm around his neck. Jonas hugs me back. We pause, stuck to each other as though we've forgotten how to let go. His strong hand rests respectably on the small of my back. I feel like I will be wholly content if it never left. My face turns into his neck, subtle. I don't even realize it myself until I draw in a long scent of his sweet cologne. His hand travels my spine softer than a whisper.

Clearing my throat, I finally release him and hold up the box. "Thanks again."

Jonas looks at me like he's seeing me for the first time. "Have a happy birthday."

I jump out of his car, my heart still thumps in my neck as he pulls away only to wrap around to the back lot of his apartment building. I clutch the gift to my chest. Unable to wait a moment longer I rip off the wrapping and lift the lid on the cardboard box. Smiling and looking across the street I say the words my mom used for Todd. Jonas gets me.

In the box are four containers of hot chocolate, all different flavors, but my favorite part is the teacup. Jonas put some thought into the gift which makes it better, because the teacup is certainly ordered from some online shop. On the front there is an image of William Shakespeare with all his written works in different fonts bouncing around his head.

Caressing the delicate cup, I fight the urge to knock on *Clara's* door and hug Jonas again. Tucking my cocoa under my arm I smile across enemy lines at the Olsen's property. Things are changing, maybe Farmor was right. Change might happen. One car ride at a time.

Chapter 18

Delicious scents of cinnamon fill my room the next morning. Rubbing the sleep from my eyes I hurry downstairs. I hardly step into the kitchen before Agnes wraps her tiny but strong arms around my waist.

"You're home," she squeals. "Happy Birthday!"

I kiss the top of her head then pick her up. Her pale eyes look tired and a little red, her cheeks flushed, but still she beams. "I missed you. How early did you wake up to help make cinnamon rolls?"

"Before the sun woke up," Agnes says.

"I bet they will be delicious."

Setting Agnes down, Inez wraps me in a tight hug. "Brita, happy birthday, beautiful girl."

"Thank you," I say, and dip my finger in the icing bowl. "Hey, is Agnes okay?"

Inez frowns. Agnes struggles to tie her apron, and doesn't hear us. "She's had a bit of a cough, and you know for her it's harder to fight off. She'll be okay, the doctor gave her an antibiotic. We just have to keep watch on her oxygen sometimes at night and make sure it doesn't turn into something else."

I squeeze Inez's shoulders. "You'll keep me updated, right? I miss that girl when I'm away and I'll just worry if you don't tell me things."

"Of course," she says. "Now go sit down. It's time to eat."

"Lilla älskling! Happy Birthday."

"Farfar," I almost squeal like Agnes when I hug his thin body. "I missed you."

Farfar kisses my forehead and pulls out one of the chairs at the table for me. I know Dad has headed into work early so he can be home at lunch and stay home the rest of the day. I want to see him, but I'm not looking forward to talking about Mom's engagement. Oscar scrambles through the front door of the bakery, still in his pajama bottoms and his hair standing on end, Karl right behind.

"Glad you could make it," Inez says with a scowl at her son.

"Mom, I was out late after the game," Oscar whines and pours a glass of orange juice.

"Yes, I know," Inez says. "I waited up if you remember."

"Yes, I do." Oscar kisses his mother's cheek. "Because you love me so much. Ugh, what are you doing here?" Oscar looks at me, a dramatic look of disgust pulling at his face.

"You stink, maybe you should shower before you step out into public," I retort.

He laughs through a bite into his cinnamon roll. "Happy birthday, dork."

"Thanks, dweeb."

It feels good to be home.

Every birthday in the Jacobson household one can expect to hear at least three renditions of the *Happy Birthday* tune. Never sung in English, that would be silly. My family sings to me over breakfast, then when Dad comes home for a big lunch of my favorite open-faced sandwiches on Farmor's famous rolls, and now I blush for a third time as they sing over a stunning chocolate cheesecake Inez made. Oscar even admits that he helped with the crust. Chocolate and cheesecake mixed, there really isn't anything better.

Yes, Jacobson birthdays supply plenty of singing, plenty of food, and plenty of laughter.

"This is delicious," I say, gnawing on a clump of cake.

Inez smiles, rather pleased, and reaches for a small gift bag. "Here, open our gift before Agnes bursts out of her skin."

I tap Agnes on the nose, who was in fact bouncing in her seat. She drops her fork and spills some of her whipped cream down her front. No one minds, and Karl quickly helps wipe her dress as though nothing happened.

"You guys," I say, breath lost. A small pair of diamond stud earrings sparkle in my palm.

"They're real," Oscar says. "Real diamonds. You're welcome."

I feel tears swell. Oscar snickers when Karl shoves him in the shoulder.

I look at Inez, then to Karl. "You can't be serious."

"We want you to have something special. You're graduating, Brita. You've accomplished so much, we just wanted to show you how proud we are of you."

Quickly I stand from the table and wrap my arms around both my aunt and my uncle, then to Agnes, a full bear-hug, as she calls it. Oscar even lets me give him a side-hug. I wipe away a single tear when I return to my seat and put the earrings in my empty lobes.

"Well, now that my sister has shown me up, here's this," Dad says.

I take the envelope and grin. "It's going to be great."

"It's from both Farfar and me," Dad adds. Farfar points at the envelope as though to urge me to go faster.

My stomach flips when I study the check in my hands. "What is happening?"

Farfar claps, apparently overly pleased with my reaction. Dad squeezes my hand. I'm still reading the amount. "Now you can have a little something to get started with real life after graduation. Maybe even get a car."

"Farfar, Dad…this is too much, really," I say.

"Brita, no it's not," Dad interjects. "You deserve it. Just don't spend it on something like chocolate."

"That's exactly what I'm buying. You've made mine and Jane's life," I say, hugging my dad long and with meaning. I kiss Farfar's cheek and let him pat my face.

"So how has the semester been?" Inez asks once we all settle back into our cheesecake. "Anything fun happening?"

"It's been good, challenging, but good," I say.

"Hey, how are you dealing with Aunt Judy getting engaged?" Oscar asks. I am glad Oscar and Agnes still call my mom *aunt*. It makes her still feel part of the family. I steal a look at Dad. He doesn't look too terribly upset, but he doesn't smile either.

"Um, it was a little bit of a shock at first, but I guess if she's happy—
"

"That's right," Inez says. "We'll always be family. I offered to do the cake, that's how important it is to keep our relationships."

"Dad, how are you?" I dare ask.

Dad smiles and pushes around the final piece of cheesecake on his plate. "I'm happy for your mom, really. We had a good talk right after Todd asked. She said if I didn't agree with it, she wouldn't do it. I, of course, appreciated that, but I would never stand in the way of her moving on with her life." Oscar snorts a little bit and I slap his back, thinking he choked on his water. Dad laughs. "Can't say I wasn't tempted to say no in the most animated way."

I'm relieved that Dad smiles. He is a good man. I will always be sad my parents divorced, but I can now say that I do only want them both to be happy. I'm confident they both will be.

"So how long do we get you tomorrow?" Farfar asks. "When does the last bus leave?"

My fearless Viking moment arrives. The way my stomach drops like a lead weight into my feet tells me so. I haven't mentioned anything about the Olsens like I promised. I watched them leave earlier that day, probably for pictures. Axel texted me happy birthday, so had Jonas, but the only evidence that I consort with the enemy remains in Jonas's gift upstairs on my bed. Dad's knee bounces under the table, but then he already knows and sits back, letting me face my own fate.

Taking a deep breath, I glance at my grandfather. "I'm not taking the bus, Farfar."

"Oh, Nils are you taking her back?"

Dad looks at me out of the corner of his eye and shakes his head. "Nope, I'm not."

"Well, then how are you getting to school?" Inez asks. "Unless you really are going to buy a car."

I splay my fingers out on the lace tablecloth, close my eyes for a long breath, then somehow find the strength to speak. "Okay, you guys. I need to be honest with you. I've been getting rides to and from school."

"Good," Farfar says. "Why the secrecy?"

"Because Farfar," I begin. My throat feels like a desert. *Be a Viking*, I tell myself. But that is just the problem, my confession will fall to a table filled with Vikings. "I've been driving with...Jonas."

Nothing. Only blank stares, except for Oscar—he looks at me like I've lit the table on fire. Dad drinks his water like a man with an unquenchable thirst.

"Do you really not know their names?" My stomach backflips. All I need to do is say the last name. Say it, that's all. Say it, *say it*. Clearing my throat, my voice breaks as I whisper, "*Jonas Olsen*."

Then it begins.

Farfar shouts in Swedish, and my limited vocabulary is enough to know the words aren't polite. Inez stares at me, her grip wraps tightly around her fork, and Karl takes the initiative to shuffle Agnes from the table, using a bath as the excuse.

"How could you do this, Brita?" Farfar bemoans during a moment of clarity.

"Pops, think about why you're angry. Is it really such a big deal that she is riding to school with Jonas?" Dad referees.

"You knew about this, Nils?" Inez asks.

"Mom..."

"I don't need your input," Inez snaps at Oscar, who abruptly closes his mouth.

184

"She's my kid, Inez," Dad says, brisk and rough.

"Listen!" I hold up my hands. "Jonas is nice. He's a friend."

"How long, how long have you been…betraying us for them?" Farfar asks.

"Betraying you? Farfar, can't you hear how ridiculous that sounds? He goes to school with me, he's nice. You'd like him—"

"No, stop. Enough. I refuse to hear any more of this. You, Brita, do not understand how…*despicable* that family is. You don't know what they've done to us. You won't ride with that boy anymore."

For a moment I'm worried Farfar is having a health spell by the way he gasps, but I realize his temper is behind the jagged breaths. And I'm burning. I'm furiously angry. My fists curl and I stand, in defense of Jonas.

"No, he is not," I say firmly.

"What?" Farfar says.

"He is not despicable. I don't know why you hate Viggo, you're right. But that is who you hate, not his grandchildren. You didn't even know Jonas's first name. You don't know him at all." My fingertips are numb, but I won't stop. "He is *wonderful*. He's kind and smart. When I was sick, he took care of me. He is a true friend, and no one at this table has the right to tell me who I will be friends with. Not anymore."

I can hear the winds of change and I feel empowered.

"Brita," Inez says. "The Olsens are not kind. I don't know what sort of game this boy is playing but—"

"Is it so hard to think he might just like me too?"

"That's not what I meant."

"What have they done to you? Tell me, what has Elias, or Sigrid, or Viggo done to you personally Inez? Has Bastien been unkind to you, Oscar?" My cousin glances up, warily checks his mother's set scowl, but he finds the good-old Viking courage and shakes his head no. "Why does having the name Olsen suddenly mean Jonas must be using me, or plotting something sinister?"

Inez angrily gathers the plates. "I would never expect this blatant disrespect from you, Brita. Not you."

"Inez, stop," Dad warns. "You don't get to talk to her like that."

"I do, Nils," Inez spits back. "Brita is like a daughter to me, always has been." Great, I've caused a fight between my entire family too.

"It doesn't matter," Farfar says. "Brita, you don't need to know the history of our families. All you need to have is respect for this family and the pain caused at the hands of those...*people*."

My pulse is violent in my ears as I stare at my family. My dad's jaw tightens, Farfar has red cheeks, and Inez avoids me. For the first time in my life, I've brought utter disappointment and yet, they disappoint me in this moment too. I can't stay here any longer. Snagging my coat and purse from the rack by the door, I burst outside, rush down the sidewalk; wretched, ugly tears fall. And my heart shatters.

Chapter 19

The icy air doesn't bother me. I find refuge on a bench bolted to the cement at the end of the walk. A measly hundred feet from the bakery, and feels much too close. Thankfully no one follows me. In fact, I won't be surprised if the doors are locked tight when I return. Chiding myself for thinking so little of my family, I watch the streetlamp flicker to life. I'm cast in blue, frosty light, cheerful and out of place.

My fingers hover over my phone—I'm half tempted to text Jonas, I suppose I should want to text Axel, but the argument didn't bring up his name now did it. I tuck my cell back in my pocket. No. I can do this on my own. I've already confessed a bit of my feelings toward the Olsens, I can face troubles. Time to stop running to others when I'm in distress. My feet need to find their own ground. A watery smile spreads over my face, maybe this is the start of that strength Farmor mentioned in the letter.

This still aches and absolutely, unequivocally sucks. My heart feels shredded, like a cheese grater had its way with my chest. Wiping my eyes, I think of my grandmother. Soft-spoken, sarcastic Farmor. I've no doubt she'd have my back tonight. Then we would have gone to get manicures and sodas.

Headlights approach and I curl away, embarrassed if anyone sees my red face. *Oh, you are kidding me.* I bite my tongue, taste blood, and cover my face with my hands. Jonas's car is inching down the road.

If I get up now, he'll notice me for sure. Cursing the streetlamp above, I duck away. He won't stop, maybe it's not even Jonas. Oh, please don't be Axel. I have a feeling Axel is not the kind who will want to deal with tears on a Saturday night.

The car slows while passing my bench but doesn't stop, and after it's gone, I dare peel my eyes after the red glow of the brake lights. Two people step out, Jonas instantly recognizable. The other is Bastien. His face is glued to the screen of a cell phone, and he has hair that falls long over his ears. I turn my back on the brothers, confident Jonas hasn't seen me. Knowing him as I do, he'll feel guilty if he finds out that a bomb has exploded in the Jacobson house.

I hear the jingling bells of *Clara's* door open and close. Releasing my breath, I straighten once again on my solitary bench and glance across the street.

Groaning, my head hangs; I stare at my boots, acutely aware of the sticky mess of tears on my cheeks. I probably look like a pufferfish with my swollen eyes. Jonas jogs across the street; his hands tucked deep in his coat pockets. A part of me yearns for those dark blue eyes, and calm, confidence unique to him. I don't even care that the thought passes my mind, it's the truth and I am owning the truth tonight.

"Brita, what are you doing out here?" Jonas asks, sitting next to me without waiting for an invitation. I scoot closer to him. "Are you crying?" Jonas's arm is already around my shoulders before I can stop it and my senseless chin quivers again.

"I'm sorry, I hoped you wouldn't seen me, I don't want to bring you into things you don't need to worry about," I say, but then scoff bitterly. "Well, I guess in a way this is your fault."

"My fault? What happened?"

"I told them." My voice is nothing more than a wet sob. I suck in sharp air, look away, and bite my lip to keep my emotions in check. A rattle is in my breath when I look at Jonas. He is doing his thing—how he stares, eyes intense and focused, listening. "I told my family that we're friends."

Jonas leans back against the bench, his arm falls from around my shoulders, and I feel rather empty. Leaning forward on his knees Jonas keeps his voice low, and I take note how he softly cracks his knuckles. "I don't know if I'm the one you need right now, but you shouldn't be out here all alone."

"You're wrong," I whisper, wiping my cheeks. "You're just the person I need tonight." It wasn't a lie. Jonas doesn't wallow, but he listens. He validates hurt. I want him tonight.

He smiles, shoulders relax, and he stops cracking his knuckles. "Here," he says and reaches into his pocket. Revealing an unopened pack of gummy worms, I grin.

"See," I say. "Just who I need."

"Thank Bass for being a procrastinator. He needed a few things for a project at school on Monday, so I took the opportunity to stock up for the drive back tomorrow. I'm good digging into them early though."

"I'll be sure to thank him."

Jonas eats a red worm and looks up at the sky, though with the brightness of the bulb shining over us, stars are rather difficult to see. "Want to tell me what happened?"

After gnawing off the head of a blue worm I carefully recount the explosion over the cheesecake. I don't embellish, there isn't any need. The story is almost as uncomfortable recounting it as it has been living through all the angry words and hurt feelings. My shoulders cave forward, the spaces between my ribs pit a bit as I fight new bitterness. Fists curl, and my nails dig into the meat of my palms.

Jonas runs a hand through his hair. There is a twitch to his jaw, as if he fights against what he really wants to say.

"I'm sorry," he says softly. "I wish I had some great words of wisdom I could give you, but honestly—I'm just mad."

"No, I'm sorry. I dragged you into my family's bitterness, and you don't deserve that," I say, dabbing my coat sleeve against my eye.

"I did the same thing to you," he says. "I told my parents. My dad didn't seem that upset—"

"Really?" I ask, brows lifting. "I thought your dad hated us as much as your grandpa."

190

"Yeah, shocking huh?"

I'm afraid to ask, but want to know. "Um, did Axel, did he say anything?"

"No," he says, firmly. "Axel isn't around tonight."

I nod, and don't ask where he is. I'm not sure it matters. "So, your dad was okay?"

"I mean, he didn't seem thrilled, but he basically said I'm twenty-three, so what can they say?"

I laugh, not because it was funny, but ridiculous. "Yeah, turns out I'll always be twelve to my family. At least Dad tried to stop it. I kind of left him to the wolves back there."

"He's an attorney, he can get out of a heated discussion," Jonas says.

"So, what else did your dad say?"

"He asked to be the one to explain it to Grandpa. I didn't argue about that. Hopefully they'll talk when I'm tucked safe and sound back at school. See, you're braver than me." He nudges my shoulder with his. "Really though, I feel bad. Part of me wonders if it would be easier if I just…you know, kept my distance."

"Don't say that again, or I'll coat my next batch of cookies in soap," I snap. "Jonas, I never want to go back to the way things were. You've become one of my greatest friends—your gift by the way—that just proves you know me more than almost anyone. You're up there with Jane and my parents. Even if I wanted to, I can't go back now. You're just hitched to the Brita bumpy ride and will have to deal with it."

"Good," he says with intention. "I don't want things to go back either."

"So, tomorrow we still drive to school together like heathens?"

"Yes."

"Perfect. At least Agnes will speak with me still. She loves me no matter who I hang out with."

"That's Oscar's sister?" I nod and lean my head against his shoulder. Yes, I did, and I am not ashamed of it. He tugs me close. "You're close with her? Isn't she like four?"

I laugh. "She's six, and yes, we're very close. I'm close with Oscar too, they're basically the siblings I never had. Agnes, though, that little girl is just a bright spot in the world. I could listen to her little laugh all day long. I'll let you in on a secret, I saw her wave at your mom once— your mom waved back. No one can resist Agnes."

He peers down when I look up from his shoulder. "Can I ask, why does she have to wear those things on her legs?"

I stare at a dying bulb in the lamp across the street. "Inez and Karl thought they'd only be able to have Oscar. Agnes is a pleasant surprise. But her birth was really tough, and she had some injuries. She has cerebral palsy. One hand doesn't work well, but walking has been the biggest challenge. She used to use a walker, but the braces help her stand on her own. She's done so well though. Don't tell anyone, but I miss Agnes the most when I go to school."

"Well if no one talks to you tomorrow, I'm glad you have Agnes. Who knows, maybe she'll even be friends with me. Two Jacobsons, friends with an Olsen—that would be something to talk about."

192

"Three, actually," I say slowly. My heart pounds. I think of the letter.

"What?"

"I want to show you something, okay?" Digging through my purse, I gently hand Jonas the letter my grandmother had left me. "Read this."

Jonas obeys and unfolds the worn paper. I watch him skim through Farmor's neat writing. He smiles a bit and nods—he must agree with something, but then—there it is, I know he is at the end.

"What? What does she mean?" he asks, looking up at me, his eyes wide and searching.

"I think she means exactly what she wrote."

"Our grandmothers were…friends? Why wouldn't they tell anyone?"

"I don't know. Do you have any idea what happened between Farfar and your grandpa?"

Jonas isn't looking at me. "All I've been told is grandpa felt deeply cheated by something and he blames your grandpa. That's all I know. Have you ever shown this letter to your family?"

I shake my head. "Nope, you're the only one. She wanted me to change what happened, you read yourself, it's her biggest regret. That's why tonight makes me so angry. I specifically asked what happened between the families. My grandpa told me I didn't need to know our history."

Jonas has a mischievous look on his face that reminds me of Axel. "I'll admit all this talk is making me want to have you over for dinner or walk inside *Hanna's* and buy my own cookies—just to defy all the insane grudges. What do you think? Would I be offered service if I went inside?"

I laugh, but truly I'm not sure. "You'd probably be accused of coming in to steal all our recipes."

"I know this isn't easy, but I say we let all this go. I like hanging out with you, and I need to use you for your English skills. My future is at stake if I stop seeing you."

I flush at the words *seeing you*—but in a way it is true. I see Jonas ten times more than I see Axel. Something burns in my chest, breaking through the agonizing wall of bitterness. For the first time, I don't mind that I see Jonas more, and I don't need to worry about what that means. I can just enjoy some gummies and enjoy his company.

We quickly move away from the pain of the night and are already talking about who will be in charge of bringing the food to our Tuesday study session when the ice crunches along the sidewalk. I whip around and jump up from the bench.

"Oscar, you're still here?" I say. Jonas goes silent. He looks between me and my cousin.

Oscar shivers in the cold, and he glances with caution at Jonas. "Agnes fell asleep, so Mom and Dad opted to stay over. I came out to look for you and make sure you're okay. Hi, Jonas," he says.

"Hey, Oscar."

"How is it in there? Is Farfar going to survive, or am I burned from the family tree?" I ask.

Oscar rolls his eyes. "Not you anymore, but Uncle Nils might be. He changed the topic from you and admitted how he hired Jonas over Christmas break."

"He didn't," Jonas says, looking concerned. "The partners hired me."

Oscar smirks, his smile less awkward the longer he talks. "I know. Uncle Nils tried to say that, but in our grandpa's mind he might as well have sought you out to hire you. I thought you'd want to know I think he's softening grandpa a bit." Oscar steps next to me. "Brita, I don't care who you're friends with. In fact, I like Bastien." He looks at Jonas. "There, that's my secret, I guess. I've gotten to know him during the bus rides and games this season and I like him. He's a cool kid who hasn't mentioned my last name or his once. We just get to be teammates."

Jonas seems pleased. "I'm sorry, for everything this has caused."

"Don't be," I say. "Tomorrow, just pull up in front of the house. No gas station. Heathens, remember?"

Jonas laughs. "Fine." He faces my cousin. "I appreciate you looking after Bass."

Oscar offers and embarrassed smile and nods. Jonas stands still for a long moment and I want to hug him again, like in his car. I think maybe that is what he's waiting for, but then he leaves with a wave back to *Clara's*.

"Come on," Oscar says through chattering teeth. "It's freezing out here."

Inside the house is dark. The table has been cleaned and is tidy, no evidence of the confrontation visible at all. On the sofa bed, Aunt Inez and

195

Uncle Karl are already asleep. Oscar takes an air mattress in the bakery, probably to sneak all the treats all night.

By the time I slither beneath my covers my body quickly succumbs and my mind fades to syrupy black.

***

Farfar sits at the table in the morning when I tromp down the stairs. I hear pleasant talk in the bakery as a few customers come in for Sunday brunch. Dad sits on the couch reading the paper, and a notable tension builds from the floorboards to the eaves; thick enough to taste. My bag weighs on my shoulders, and I strategically give myself only a few minutes to say goodbye so we won't have time to rehash the bitterness of the night before.

Agnes sits in the middle of the floor coloring a pony in her unicorn book. Her cough draws my attention away from Farfar's downturned lips as he studies his crossword puzzle.

"Agnes," I whisper. "I'm leaving kiddo. Give me a hug."

Dad peeks over the newspaper as Agnes covers her mouth and coughs again, but her brilliant smile sets in place when she squeezes my neck. "Bye, Brita. You'll be back for the big party?"

"What big party?" I ask, looking at Dad.

He folds the paper and takes off his glasses. "We never got to it last night. The Chamber of Commerce is hosting an award dinner for influential businesses. Our family was invited. There are all sorts of prizes, a dance and all that. Should be nice. It's in two weeks."

"Sounds nice," I say.

Dad is too keen. "You'll be there of course." He stands and opens his arms. "Come here." I hug him, letting him squash me against his chest. Dad lowers his voice, whispering close to my ear. "Don't let last night upset you for a second more. Be happy, Brit. That's truly all anyone in this house wants for you—even if they are a little hot-headed sometimes."

"Love you, Dad. Thanks for everything," I say when we pull away. Oscar isn't around, but I'll send him and Uncle Karl a goodbye text in the car. When Farfar and Aunt Inez stand near the door, I gulp, a loud one too.

"Brita," Inez begins. "Last night should not have happened—especially on your birthday."

"You should not have lied," Farfar insists. He still sounds so angry. I can't remember a time when my grandfather spewed his anger at me.

"Pops, we talked about this," Inez says. "Brita, if riding with the Olsen boy—"

"Jonas," I correct.

Inez sighs. "Jonas. If riding with him gets you to school safely, then we're fine with it. He seems respectable enough."

Farfar huffs, his brow knits together in an angry furrow.

Inez ignores him. "Just understand the Olsens have been fed untruths about us as well. I'm a neighborly person, but I've never had much trust for that family—so just be cautious."

"Are you really giving me permission to ride with someone?" I ask, my jaw clenching.

"Yes," Farfar says. He must have misinterpreted my tone, because he looks at me like he has bestowed a gracious gift.

"If that makes you both feel better then fine, give me your permission." I point to the window; Jonas has pulled alongside the curb. He even steps out of the car as though he is considering coming to the door. I won't put him through that. "But I already gave myself permission. I love you both, but you can't tell me who I can care about. And I care about Jonas and his family. Farfar, don't let this cause more anger between you and Viggo, please. We're big kids now, and can make our own choices. Love you."

I kiss his cheek quickly. He grunts in response. Inez gives me a stiff hug, but her attention turns to the window. Jonas takes a step toward a front porch.

I open the door and slam it before he's forced into the tension. Jonas grins when I look at him.

"Hi," I say. "Ready?"

"Yeah." He hesitates and glances at the house. "Everything good?"

I shake my head as he opens the door for me. "Not really, but it will be. Remember what I told you last night, you're stuck with me as your friend. They will need to get used to it."

Jonas smiles and seems relieved. Inez catches his eye through the bay window, but hurries and hides behind the curtains. Jonas slips into the driver's seat, and I glance across the street at *Clara's*. Sigrid and Elias stand on the front stoop. They aren't smiling, but they do offer Jonas a final wave. It will take time, I keep reminding myself. It will just take time.

198

Chapter 20

By the time we arrive at my apartment building, my stomach gurgles in that awkward feeling between stuffed and hungry again. Jonas and I haven't been as talkative on the drive home, but when he parks in one of the stalls at my building we both seem at ease now that Lindström, the bakeries, and our families are at our backs. Axel texted me during the drive. He apologized for not seeing me on my birthday, or getting me a gift. I don't respond.

"Want to come inside and eat something besides sugar?" I ask when Jonas shuts off the ignition.

"Oh, I planned on it," he says through a smile. "I know you and Jane have real food, I'm going to go home to dry cereal. I don't even have milk. So, yes I'm coming inside."

"Good." I grab my bag and the boxes of hot chocolate Jonas gave me. "By the way, are you going to the Chamber of Commerce dinner?"

"It was the talk of the entire weekend. Wait, is your grandpa invited too?" I nod, linking my arm with his as we trek through the snow. The transition from not touching to touching is as smooth as silk. We both don't even notice I've done it.

"That's going to be an interesting night," Jonas says. "My dad said there will be awards. I can see that posing a problem with their level of competition with each other."

"I'm going, and you still haven't answered if you are going?" I press again, fumbling for my keys.

"There's no way my mom would let me miss it. You know it's like a suit and tie affair. Anything to get her sons dressed up, my mom will take it."

I laugh, but can't say I disagree with Sigrid. The Olsen boys in dashing suits and black ties, I can handle a night like that. Plus, Jane will die to help me buy a new, fancy dress. I vow to ignore the inevitable tension between the two bakers of Lindström.

We step inside, the apartment is dark and eerie. Setting down my bag, I look around the corner for any sign of Jane.

"Janey," I call, looking back at Jonas. He slings his coat over the back of the couch. "Hmm, I guess she's not home. Usually Sunday is relax day."

I flick on the kitchen light and a swarm of loud, vivacious, overly excited college students leap out from behind any piece of furniture they can find.

"SURPRISE!" They scream as one. Jane bounces forward and sprays my head with blue silly string.

"Happy Birthday!" she squeals. She wraps me up in her arms and jumps up and down, so I am forced to do the same.

"Jane!" I smile as she crowns my stringy head with a toddler's plastic princess tiara. "I told you no surprises."

"Like she would ever listen," Emma says, her hand clasped tightly in Brody's thick fingers. "Happy Birthday!"

"Joe, you did such a good job getting here at just the right moment." Jane squeezes his arm.

My jaw drops and I stomp right up to his arrogant, smirking face. "You were a part of this? I feel betrayed."

"Oh, it was his idea," Jane shouts across the room. She's already holding a large punch bowl, and revealing stacks of hidden pizza boxes. "He called me up, and I put all this together in like three hours. It's going to be *epic*!"

Jonas peels away some of the string from my hair. "You deserve a birthday redo," he says softly, and I feel my throat tighten. "The original was ruined because of me, so I plan to make up for it."

"It wasn't ruined because of you," I argue. "You, in fact, saved it in the end."

My head sort of feels like it has been dunked in a bucket of water when Jonas takes my hand and pulls me into the middle of the room. That drive to make things work with Axel, yeah, I need to admit the drive has faded. Soon I huddle in the center of the overstuffed room, laughing and loving every moment. Some people I don't know well—but the ones who mattered are all there. Jane isn't kidding. She has planned everything. Brody and Matt handle a video game station and I wallop Matt in Mario Kart, thank you very much. Jonas decimates me in one of those Minute-to-Win-it games where stacking cups is involved. But I destroy his roommate, Brett, in ripping tissues out of the box as fast as possible. It is the first time I've met Brett, but I feel like games, music and pizza are the best sort of icebreakers. I do hate surprises, I really do. But the effort and thought everyone in my college life has gone through to put it all together keeps the smile on my face well into the night.

At the end, streamers, empty pizza boxes, plastic cups, and a few sleeping people scatter across the apartment. I yawn and reach for my coat to walk with Jonas back to his car.

"Did you have fun?" he asks.

"I did, thank you. I never thought you could be so cunning," I say and wrap my coat tighter around my body when the wind picks up.

"You don't know the half of it," he says. "I was being serious though, Brita. You deserve to be happy. I really didn't like seeing you so upset last night, especially when it had something to do with me."

My fingernails dig into the layers of my coat when he steps closer. He pulls me against his chest, naturally my arms find a place around his waist. I wonder if he can feel the way my pulse thuds like a jackhammer in all my major arteries. We've hugged before, but this time is different—I want Jonas to hold me longer than normal. Maybe, even a little more than a hug. Ashamed of myself, I push those thoughts out of my head. I haven't even cut things off with Axel and already I think this way about his brother. Jonas pulls away slowly, our faces brush as we part. Jonas always calls me his friend, so the way he looks at me in that moment is only that—a friend to a friend. I think.

"Don't worry about what happened back home, okay? I'd do it again," I tell him, trying to keep my eyes locked with his instead of inching down to his lips. "Thank you, Jonas. You've made this birthday the very best."

"I'm glad. I'll see you Tuesday?"

"Yes, you will. Goodnight, drive safe." I say drive safe, but really Jonas lives less than a mile from my apartment. All these years and I've never known.

I quickly rush back to the warmth of the apartment when he's gone. Jane stands right behind the door, and when I jump back in surprise I slip and bang against the wall. We stifle laughs at our clumsiness, and so we don't wake up Natalie and a girl from my literature classes sprawled out on our sofas.

"You scared me," I whisper.

"Obviously." Jane smiles, her pink painted lips wide. This smile isn't her regular full-of-joy grin, this one has a purpose. "So, when are you going to tell him?"

I scoot past and slowly drift toward my bedroom. "Tell who, what?"

"Jonas," Jane says. She tries to keep up with me in the hallway.

"What are you talking about?" My face heats like a fever, and I turn my back on her, so she won't notice.

"When are you going to tell Jonas you're in love with him?"

"Jane! W-what are you...I am not," I stammer. "I don't like Jonas like that, okay?"

"Because you're in love with Axel?"

"I didn't say I was in love, but he's the one I've been seeing, yes."

Jane laughs loud enough Natalie grumbles something about silence, but it doesn't stop Jane from pressing the issue. "Seeing him? Brita, most of your free time is spent with Jonas. You've seen Axel once since coming back to school. Oh, and it isn't one way. Jonas blesses the very ground you walk on. He wouldn't have called me about this party if he didn't."

"We're friends, our families sort of flipped out when we told them we'd been hanging out, so he—"

"I know, he told me what happened. It still doesn't change anything. Don't worry, if you're not ready to admit that you're smitten, star-crossed, and passionately in love with Jonas yet, I'll be there to say I told you so when you come to your senses. You can count on it, but you also don't hide it well."

Jane flips around, done talking, I guess until I start to rub the sides of my head. She pauses. "Are you okay?"

My throat feels scratchy, like sand. "I think—" I can't believe I'm going to say this. "I think I need to end things with Axel."

Jane grins. "Now we're talking. Hey, don't hyperventilate on me. Talk me through what's going on in your head."

I look my friend. "I don't know. I've never…felt this before."

"With…who? Which one, because I'm getting confused with the twin brother thing."

I laugh and slump against my doorframe. "When he touched me tonight, I felt like I was going to burst. Even before the semester started, I don't think I ever felt that with Axel."

Jane smiles wider. "Now, we're really talking. You've got to tell Jo, Brit."

"What if I'm wrong, and Jonas only wants to be friends?"

Jane rubs my shoulders. "But what if you're not wrong. Think about that. And don't worry, I'll help you wrap up the make-out relationship with the brother. I'm a pro at dumping guys."

My hands tingle, they're going numb. All of me is tingling. Did I just admit I have feelings for Jonas—out loud? I touch my lips, and feel giddy and terrified all at once.

Burying myself in my sea of pillows, I beam in the fluff privately. Jane is right about one thing, I need to tell him.

On Monday afternoon my thumb hovers over Axel's name on my screen. Maybe I should text him—no, that is immature and I refuse to be cowardly. With Jane sitting on the edge of my bed, I tap his name and wait.

"Hey," he says after three rings. "How's it going?"

"It's okay," I say.

"Yeah, that's good. I'm just on my way to study group so—"

"This won't take long, I just...uh, I just have to talk to you about something."

"Oh, okay," Axel says, his voice chipper and pleasant like always.

"Okay," I take a deep breath, and Jane squeezes my hand. "I've just been thinking a lot. I think..." My stomach coils in tight, painful knots. "I think it might be good if we don't see each other anymore."

Axel pauses—although not as long as think someone might. "That's cool," he says almost as chipper as before. "You get a guy?"

I stare at Jane, my eyes wide. She shrugs her shoulders and mouths *what*. "Um, not exactly," I say slowly.

"Okay," Axel says. "It's fine."

"You're okay?" I question, sort of wishing he might have some semblance of sadness.

"I'm fine, Brita. It's nothing serious and things change. It's all good."

He speaks so easily, like it has never been anything to begin with. I don't know how to react. Is this how every breakup is supposed to go? I cover the phone and whisper, "He's fine, should I tell him?"

"About Jonas? No, don't," she says. "Just leave it between brothers."

I nod and return the phone back to my ear. "Okay then. Thanks for understanding."

"Sure, don't have too much fun. I gotta go, okay?"

"Yep, see you later." Stun coats my tone. Not so heartbreaking as I thought. Then I get a little frustrated. Clearly, Axel has been invested in our relationship about as deeply as a drop of water in a glass.

"So, how did he take it?" Jane asks.

"Perfect," I mutter. "He acted like I'd just found another guy, and that was totally fine with him."

Jane chuckles. "Well, you kind of did. You're lucky, it can't get better than that when you're breaking up. I mean, if he really is that cool with it. Maybe he's crying right now."

"He didn't sound like he was about to cry," I admit. "He almost seemed like he didn't understand why I even called him to call it off."

"Well," Jane says, clapping her hands. "Now all that is left is talking to the man of the hour. Tomorrow?"

I nod. "Tomorrow."

Tuesday night study session is about to get a whole lot more interesting.

Later that night, I try to compose a few pages in my capstone paper, but I can hardly think clearly when Tuesday is only a few hours away. I haven't spoken with Jonas since the party, by intention. I needed to analyze my thoughts. Jane declares Jonas feels something more for me, but what if she ends up being wrong? Straightening my shoulders, I push the fear aside; it is a risk I am just going to have to take. Ironic, Axel urged me to do something crazy this semester. Confessing feelings for Jonas Olsen feels pretty certifiable and epically awesome all at once. I like Viking Brita.

Then all my Northman power evaporates when my phone buzzes next to my laptop. Jonas is calling. Puffing no less than five sharp breaths, I answer.

"Hey," he says. "I'm not interrupting you at all, am I?"

"No, no I needed a break. What's up?" I feel as though I've forgotten how to talk to the man.

"Good. So, I wanted to call you about tomorrow."

"Yeah, what about it?"

"Well, would you hate me if I canceled the after-class study session."

I choke on my own spit, feeling my nerves sink back into the pit they slithered from. "Uh, sure. No problem, do you have plans or something?"

"I didn't, until like ten minutes ago. Brett, he's embarrassing himself and going after a girl in one of his classes. She agreed to go out with him, but didn't want to leave her cousin, who is also her roommate, at home. So Brett volunteered me to go on the date too."

"You're going on a date?" I didn't intend to ask the question out loud, especially not in the disappointed whisper that is my voice.

"If being volunteered without my knowledge means going—I'd say more like forced," he laughs, but I don't. "You okay? I can cancel if you want, I mean we did have our thing set up first."

Our thing? My heart sinks even more as my brave Viking bubble pops. I'm foolish, and Jane is wrong too. I've allowed myself to get caught up in Jonas's attention, his caring nature. Jonas only sees me as a friend.

"No, of course not," I sigh. "Have fun. I'll just see you in class tomorrow."

"We're still on for Friday, right?"

"Of course. Since you're bailing, you need to supply the food," I tease. There, I can still banter. I can forget my lack of judgment about our relationship as well.

"Deal. Sorry about bailing, really."

"Don't be. Who knows, she might be your true love."

Jonas laughs, but it isn't sincere. "Doubt that. See you tomorrow?"

"Yep, see you later."

Sitting at the table I close my laptop. I almost made a complete fool of myself. I might have ruined everything great Jonas and I have built. Pulling out one of the chocolate bars from the stash, I shut away Brontë for the night and turn to late night reruns instead.

On Tuesday, I have reservations around Jonas. He talks to me for a few minutes after Nichols's class. I try not to notice how nice he looks in his jeans and blue collared shirt that makes his eyes impossible not to admire. Then Brett calls him and ruins it all over again.

"I better get going," he says after he hangs up. "Get ready for Friday, my treat is going to blow your mind." He animates an explosion at the sides of his head for effect. I laugh the way I always do, but inside a sheet of ice spills over my insides as I watch him walk away. A few days, that's all, then things will be back to normal, everyday friendship.

Jane has to pry the truth out of me, but once I tell her, she gives up studying and crosses her legs on the floor in front of me. "What do you mean he's on a date?"

"How else can I say it? His roommate set him up on a blind date."

"Oh, that doesn't mean anything then. He didn't even do the asking."

"Yes, but he canceled our long-standing study session for a blind date. We're friends, Jane. Like I said. I got caught up in the idea of it."

Jane shrugs. "I think you should talk with him still. Or don't. Whatever makes you happy, girl." With that she returns her earbuds in place and goes back to her studying. I leave to shower and sleep. My mind needs to shut off. As I step into the shower, I don't notice the text from Jonas lighting up my phone.

Well, definitely shouldn't have canceled tonight. Don't worry though, I'll make it up to you.

Chapter 21

Jane wraps a cashmere scarf around her neck and practically skips to the front door when six o'clock comes on Friday night.

"You don't need to leave," I say, straightening the grammar books on the table and pulling my hair into a high ponytail.

"Despite contrary belief that I spend my life glued to a computer screen, I actually have a social life too. That guy I told you about, Ben, he asked me out to this little dive across town. I guess there's live music. So, yeah I'm out of here."

I smirk when she checks her reflection once before opening the door. "Have fun, be safe."

"Always," she calls back. My throat goes dry when I hear her snicker and say, "Oh, sorry Jo, almost ran you over there. Have fun, be a gentleman."

I pinch my cheeks, not really knowing why, but they do it in the movies so it seems right. Jonas comes around the corner carrying a pink box filled with something Danish and delicious. I lean against the back of the chair, trying to convince myself I've never felt anything near stomach flutters, or desire, or sensations of the kind for Jonas. But when he grins over the box I am brought back to those forbidden feelings.

"What have you brought tonight?" I say, trying to lift one side of the desert box.

"I told you it's going to blow your mind," he says. Placing the box down he removes the lid. Inside is a square cake. It has a crumb topping and smells divine. "I would like to introduce to you, drømmekage, otherwise known as dream cake. It's amazing. My grandma would make it for me and Axel on our birthday. Except Axel preferred store-bought cake—can you believe it? Just a grocery store bakery."

"Anarchy," I tease, dipping my fork right into the cake. "Oh, you'll need to deal with me eating this right out of the box."

"It's the only way to eat a cake," Jonas say, and plops into a chair next to mine. Our knees touch. My hand could rest on his leg if I moved half an inch. I lift my forkful of cake and pretend like my stomach didn't backflip. He watches me take the first bite. The second the sweetness melts on my tongue I'm ruined, but I can't let Jonas win so easy. I make a few faces, let him sweat a little.

"I concede, Jonas," I say. "This is amazing, and has officially blown my mind."

Chuckling, he joins me in cutting out the middle pieces with his fork. Two hours later, the cake is gone and Jonas has a grasp on grammatical rules. He pats his stomach, and closes his book.

"My brain needs a break, so does my stomach."

I agree, stretch my sore muscles that have been stuffed in one position for too long, and drift over to the couch. Jonas follows, of course, and settles about a foot from me. He sits close enough I catch the clean scent of him that whirls my brain and adds longing. He is a new weakness, and truth be told, I think I'm setting myself up to be hurt. Somehow, I find the strength to turn away and glance out the small window toward Emma and Natalie's apartment.

"So, you never told me what went so wrong on your blind date," I say. Jonas and I usually text every day, about nothing really, and in all my pride I never asked about Tuesday night. A real friend would so here I am, asking about Tuesday.

He laughs, a real throaty chuckle, and rubs his hands over his face. "Oh, it was so awkward. The girl Brett likes, she's alright, a little demanding, but her cousin—the woman looked like she had just stepped out of high school, she spoke like a mouse—when she did speak. Brita, I'm not exaggerating. I thought I was quiet, she made me look like the most outgoing person on the planet. I started counting how many times I asked a question and she didn't answer. Flat out, looked at me in the face, and turned away with no answer."

"How many times?" I ask, my smile grows the longer he speaks. Shameful—being pleased his date went terrible and all.

"Twelve! Twelve times. She told me where she was from, her major, and her favorite food. That was it. I asked her about her hobbies, blank stare, no answer. I asked about classes—I could really go on. And to make it worse, if she wasn't obviously ignoring me already, she played on her phone all night."

"She must have been too smitten by all your charm; you left her breathless."

"Or terrified. Even Brett noticed and laughed about it all night."

"Well, serves you right," I say and shove his arm. "I spent the night eating chocolate and watching *Fresh Prince of Bel Air* reruns. It was perfect."

Jonas groans. His head falls against the couch. "You know how to make a guy feel worse. You didn't even invite me to come over. That was my favorite show as a kid."

"Jonas, I'm not going to be your rebound girl after you've spent the night schmoozing some other girl. Just who do you think I am?" I say in my most pompous voice.

He shifts, so his shoulders are square to me. "Trust me, you would never be a rebound girl."

Something about the way he says it sends me tumbling down a hill when certain destruction lies ahead. Kind of like the feeling of falling except you are so relaxed you don't even brace for impact. Like in a dream. My smile fades and I study Jonas, with real intent. I love the way his eyes burst like crystals shattering on the ground when he looks at me. Maybe I'm wrong and I'm not the only one lost in the whirlwind. A dangerous

217

connection has shaped with Jonas, one I am hesitant to keep, yet so reluctant to break.

"Hey, come here," his voice is soft. He reaches for my face. Blood pumps like a raging river through my veins.

"What is it?" I ask, unsure if I should pull back or lean my face into his palm. I opt to lean in, how can I not?

Our faces drift closer, Jonas scoots right next to me on the couch, one leg tucks beneath him, the other still hangs over the edge. Drawing in one lasting breath I tremble when Jonas's thumb skims across my cheek. My head spins, still like falling, but underwater. I can hardly think straight except for the heat in my skin.

"You had a little cake right there," he says, and my heart sinks into my gut.

I am about to curse myself for thinking Jonas thought of me as anything else but a study buddy when I realize his hand still cups my cheek. His skin feels warm. Jonas remains close; our shoulders brush, and his nose is inches from mine.

His thumb gently strokes my cheek, and my shoulders lift in heavy puffs. I keep swallowing away the sand in the back of my throat. His perfect eyes align with my gaze. His face draws serious. In the moment the way Jonas looks at me isn't how a friend looks at a friend.

One might think closing the gap between a few inches might take a matter of seconds, but for me it is a breathless eternity. Time slows enough to leave me aware of what is about to happen; enough time for my heart to nose dive into my stomach; enough time for me to question whether I should stop it; and enough time to realize I don't want to stop it.

Jonas kisses me. Our lips brush gently at first, then deeper, with more fervor. I shudder when his fingers trace the lines of my neck, across my shoulder. My fingers dig into his hair. I lean back against the arm of my couch and draw him closer. His body presses to mine. I'm not swimming anymore, but floating and grounded all at once. I'm kind of in control, and out of control. All I really know is this is the way a woman should be— no, *deserved* to be kissed.

His hand rests on my waist, and he pulls back just enough to say, "Brit, I don't know if Ax—"

"Took care of it," I say, and urge his mouth back to mine.

Jonas doesn't question again, his arm holds me steady. He kisses me, and kisses me, and kisses me. One slides into the next. I fit against him, like he's molded for me. For the first time, in forever, I think of nothing but the moment. No need to analyze, no need to be afraid.

When Jonas kisses me, I finally know what it feels like to be free of thought and simply, *feel.*

Chapter 22

There are some people in the world who are so sincere that you know every emotion they feel at any given time. Jane is one of those people. She asks for every detail, then makes me repeat, then squeals most of the next day.

"What we need to worry about now is this dress for next weekend. Shopping for sure," she says.

I grin and nod. The commerce dinner is coming up, and I plan to fancify, and stay close to a certain Olsen all night. He must have known I was thinking about him because a minute later, a knock comes to the door and Jonas is accosted by Jane.

"Joe, you dog."

He chuckles shyly and slithers into the apartment, his eyes locking on mine. I can't breathe in the best way.

"We were just talking about this fancy dance thing," Jane says nestling on the loveseat. "I'm coming, of course."

"Yes, you are," I say. I have more than a few plans for that night, Jane is in on them and she needs to be my sounding board.

Jonas sits next to me, and I close my eyes to keep from sniffing him, because he smells that good. I do lace our fingers though. He grins and squeezes my hand.

"But Joe that means I'm driving with Brita, you're on your own," Jane says.

"Just come with us," he says.

Okay, the word *us* is my new favorite word.

"Uh, no," says Jane. "Girls need to get ready with just girls sometimes. Let me live out my romance fantasy through you two."

"Aren't you getting pretty sassy with Ben?" I ask.

"Yes," Jane says, looking at her phone. "That reminds me, I better get going. We're meeting for coffee." She stands and starts down the hallway before turning and snapping her fingers. "Hey, keep your distance until I'm gone. New rules."

We laugh, but listen. No worries, distance is closed once the deadbolt clicks.

***

Jonas hasn't spoken to Axel about what's happening between us. I'm not sure why, but we sort of avoid talking about the situation. He knows I

221

called Axel, and we leave things at that. I don't know what will happen at this dinner. I'm nervous Axel will be angry, maybe at me, maybe at his brother. But more, I'm worried any drama will stoke the flame between our families.

I refuse to go backward.

"Why can't we talk now?" Jonas asks on my doorstep. "At least tell me what it's about."

I've been trying to get rid of him for the last half hour. Someone like him is not easy to part with.

Sighing I cock my head. "Can you let a girl stick to her plan? I have reasons why I don't want to deep talk right now. I am more romantic than that."

Jonas smiles now and my head feels heady, like a rush of adrenaline. "I like romantic moments too. We can make this one right now." He cages me against the wall, palm against my face. I peck his lips, wanting more.

No, I am not getting caught in his spell. With a nudge I urge him back. I will save spells and swooning for tomorrow night.

"You are tricky," I say. "And addicting, but if you don't leave, then I will never get anything done, and I won't make it to the dinner, and my plans will be ruined."

"Tell me to leave then," he says.

"Not nice." I trace the line of his lips with my thumb.

He groans and peels back. "Fine, you win."

"That's more like it."

He grins. "I'm dancing with you tomorrow, Jacobson. In front of *everyone*."

"I will never speak to you again if you don't."

"Tomorrow then."

"If you're lucky I will call you tonight."

He chuckles and fiddles with his keys. "Then I have something to look forward to."

I'm in enormous trouble. When Jonas finally drives away, I clutch my chest before my heart beats a hole through the center.

Tomorrow everything could change. I hope, in the best kind of ways.

***

"That's the one," Jane says when I step out of the dressing room. She stands from the plush cushion, sets down the fashion magazine she's been reading, and circles me. The surrounding mirrors show off every bit of the form-fitting black dress. The cap sleeves top just over my shoulders, and the swooping neckline is a little lower than I've worn before, but still acceptable for my father to be in my company. Biting my lower lip, I enjoy the thrill passing through my stomach and admire the way the dress gathers along one hip, giving the illusion I actually have curves.

"Add some red stilettos and you're set, my friend," Jane says. "Jonas won't be able to take his eyes off you."

"I can't believe I'm going to do this."

223

"Oh, I can," she says. "I've been waiting for this for weeks."

I laugh. "Maybe this is all too fast."

"Maybe so, but maybe not."

"Have I ever told you how frustrating your vague bits of advice can be?" I laugh and spin once more.

Jane sits again. "Okay, let me be honest."

I stop spinning, a little nervous. "About what?"

"Calm down," she says. "I'm not going to say anything bad. I've seen you date a few guys these last four years. Remember peanut butter Tony?"

I scoff. "How can I forget." My only semi-serious relationship had an unhealthy love of peanut butter. Now, I have a strange distaste for the flavor.

"I thought maybe you were sort of smitten with him, but Brit—Jonas is a new level of smitten. Like, the first second I saw you together I thought you'd been holding out some secret love back home. Remember? The first second."

I think back our first road trip to school. It seemed so long ago, but only weeks stood between that moment and now. "I'm still terrified."

"No, not terrified," Jane says. "Words are important. Excited. You can be nervous, sure. But this is what you want, right?"

"For once, yes. I know this is what I want."

She grins. "Alright then. Let's buy this thing and hit the road. I want to see that goofy cousin of yours again."

"He's like three feet taller now."

She helps me gather my things, and her new red dress. We pay, grab some cocoas at a café next door, and pile into Jane's car.

I try not to think of tomorrow too much. I even try to study for midterms once we get to my house, Jane tries too, but Oscar is distracting. I sneak away and steal a few minutes on the phone with Jonas. I can't sleep. My thoughts whirl uncontrolled about the moment when I will finally tell Jonas Olsen I am falling headfirst, unashamed in love with him.

Chapter 23

Oscar shamelessly flirts with Jane at the breakfast table Saturday morning. Farfar finds my roommate interesting, retorting in Swedish when Jane says something in French. They aren't having a real conversation and are the only ones who find it side-splitting. The Chamber of Commerce delivers a large bouquet of flowers that stand proud in the center of the table. A silk ribbon runs through the center of the plants with the entire name of *Hanna's* written in gold lettering. The Chamber plans to have the history of the bakery on display for guests to read, so last night a member of the council came and did an entire interview with Farfar. I loved hearing his story again and again.

Farfar and Farmor immigrated with a cluster of Scandinavians a few years after World War II. Farfar was only nineteen when he left Sweden. I know he met my grandmother on the ship bound for Ellis Island, but hearing how he was smitten with her from his first glance like she was him, is my favorite part. One thing I always loved about my grandparents before Farmor passed away, no one would ever doubt their love for each other. Always dancing after hours; Farfar always washing dishes at her side. To me, their story held magic and a sense of pride came in knowing others would know the same inspiring tale of *Hanna's Swedish Pastries* tonight.

Jane and I sit outside on the front stoop so I can show her the Olsen's side of the street. There isn't a lot of movement on their territory, but they are there. I smile at the thought.

I fall back slightly when the door swings open and Dad steps outside. "Girls, the dinner is in a little over an hour, you might want to get ready."

"We're coming," I say. Jane smiles like she is ready to cause mischief and drags me upstairs to my bedroom.

I help Jane pick the perfect pair of earrings and do the makeup on her eyes. She is bold with a pair of black and white heels that make her legs go on for miles.

Then we set to work on me, arranging my hair in loose curls around my shoulders. Jane lets me borrow a gold teardrop necklace and thin bracelets to match. I know by the end of the night I will either forgo the red stilettos or I will come home with blisters. I like the way Jane paints my lips in a nude pink and adds a little more color to my cheeks. Tonight I look more like the Italian in me, but it suits.

"You're going to kill him, Brit."

Fanning myself with a crumbled piece of paper on my desk, I shake my head. "My heart is going a million miles an hour."

Jane laughs and pulls me out of my room where Oscar waits to drive with us, all tidy in his gray suit. "That's a good thing, Brit. That's a really good thing."

It might not sound like a classy award dinner since the setup is in the high school gymnasium, but I hardly recognize the place. A white canopy covers the bleachers, and twinkling lights along the fabric add that little romantic nudge this night needs. Tables with white linen cloths are set on one side of the room, and soft music plays while people gather. Two young men take our coats at the door and usher us inside.

A photographer is snapping a picture of the butcher, whose shop is next to ours. Jane enjoys seeing the owners of the hardware store that has been in Lindström since the early twenties respectfully set up a large picture of the original owner, Mister Daniels. They purchased the store when he passed away. Mister Daniels's picture wasn't the only one placed on stands and tables. All kinds of black and white photos are lined along the flowing edges of the canopy. I want to look at them all, until Oscar points across the room to the tables where Farfar and the others are seated.

"Oh, you all look wonderful," Inez says, cupping Oscar's face. He tries to get away. Agnes giggles, then coughs.

"Still coughing, kiddo?" I ask.

She nods, her voice raspy. "A little."

"They're going to start dinner orders soon," Dad says, glancing over a thin cardstock menu of the catered options.

228

"This is awesome," I say. "Congratulations Farfar." I wrap my arms tight around my grandfather while Jane takes the seat next to Oscar, much to my cousin's pleasure.

"Thank you," Farfar whispers. "You look very much like your beautiful mother tonight."

I smile, grateful he's no longer upset after the birthday fiasco. Farfar always seems to know what to say to make me feel like I am his number one—although Oscar says the same thing about our grandfather often, and I'm certain Agnes will say that too.

I round the table to sit next to Jane just as high-school aged servers go about taking orders. That's when I freeze.

My wandering gaze locks across the dining area. Jonas is there. I don't see Axel yet, but ugh, Logan stands next to Jonas while he holds out Sigrid's chair as she sits. As if our eyes are magnets, Jonas glances up. The muscles required for breathing close shop for a moment when his piercing stare studies me. He looks perfect; his tailored black suit brings that head-fog back I love so much. I don't even mind when Logan waves at me.

I snap out of my trance only when Jane tugs on my arm and snickers, I take my place at the Jacobson table. She glances over her shoulder with a touch of arrogance.

"Oh, Brita," Jane whispers. "He's ruined. Did you see the way he looked at you?"

"Did you see the way I looked at him?" I rest a palm on my chest, trying to slow my heartrate.

"Yes, yes I did."

The back of my neck tingles, I hope it means Jonas has me in his sights, but I don't dare turn around. Giving my order to the server, I sip my water, and fall into easy conversation with my family and Jane until our plates are cleaned.

Dancing will follow the dinner while people mingle, and a raffle for a basket filled with an item from every honored business will wrap up the evening. Dad and Inez are looking forward to that part the most. People take to the dance floor, or wander about the pictures and awards. The younger crowd seems more interested in trying their hand at snagging the grand prize. Oscar goes with my dad to enter their names into the raffle drawing and Jane asks me to show her toward the bathroom when she pushes her plate away.

"I can go alone," she insists when I try to follow. "You know I'm not a group bathroom girl. Let me go in peace, I say."

Laughing I show her the way then fall into the crowd surrounding the display tables. I look at the framed black and white moments of early building construction, or smiling faces with new open signs on shiny new businesses. Then the brush of a hand goes to my arm. Fireworks spread along my skin where he touches me. I bite the inside of my cheek and meet his eye. Even with my heels he stands several inches taller than me, and I like the way he looks at my face and eyes as if he is meeting me for the first time. Did I mention he looks perfect?

"Hi," I say breathlessly. Jonas steps closer so our bodies touch.

"You look beautiful," he says.

"Thank you," I whisper. "You are delicious."

He cocks a brow. "Delicious, huh? I like that, but don't give me the credit. I tend to pull it off when my mom dresses me."

"She did well." I purposely scan him top to bottom.

"Would you want to make a few waves," Jonas says, leaning his lips next to my ear, "and dance with me?"

He holds out his hand, the smile I'm in love with spreads over his face. Nodding, I clasp his hand and allow him to lead me to the center of the wooden floor. Most couples are old enough to be our grandparents, but I don't care. My hand is laced with his, my arm around his neck where I start caressing his skin. The warmth of Jonas's hand on my back sends a shiver up my spine.

Neither of us look around, though I know it won't be long before both the Olsen table and the Jacobson table are fully aware of what is happening on the dance floor. We watch each other, as though every other breathing thing in the room disappears.

"What did you want to talk to me about?" Jonas asks after a few moments.

Swallowing hard, my lips lift in a nervous smile. "About how I'm really glad we started studying together."

Jonas tugs me closer against him so I catch a long breath of his aftershave. Our cheeks align, and I imagine staying in this position forever.

His voice comes rough next to my ear. "I don't study that much anymore, and I'm pretty sure I'm going to fail my midterm."

We sway a few more beats, my cheek rests against his. The way my heart soars, everything feels so right. I promised myself I would do this. Reluctantly, I pull back so I can meet his eyes. My hand around his neck inches forward, and I brush my fingers along the collar of his shirt while my thumb caresses his cheek. Now Jonas looks as though he can't breathe.

"Jonas there's…more I want to talk about, but I don't want to do it here. Do you think we can go somewhere?"

He nods quickly and stops dancing. I suppose he takes my request as go somewhere right now, before the song even stops. "Do you have a coat ticket? I'll go grab it."

I bite my lip, hardly able to contain my happiness when he rushes away. Dad stares at me while Inez whispers something to Karl. I don't know if she is pleased or not. I don't care. Farfar is buried in a piece of cake, not looking at anyone.

"Brita, oh my," Jane says, suddenly at my side out of nowhere. She drags me toward the photo tables. "Are you dying? Where did Jonas go? What happened?"

I chuckle and scan a few pictures in various frame sizes. "He's getting our coats. We're going to go talk."

Jane squeals and shakes my shoulders as though she can't quite contain her excitement. But I stop. My eyes widen as I reach for a picture, studying with new intent the four smiling faces. I know what my grandparents look like in younger years. I've seen many pictures. There stands Farmor, snuggled against Farfar. She has tight, light curls that tuck under her jaw, and he has darker hair. But two more people stand in the photo, smiling with the same excitement as my young grandparents.

232

The woman has dark hair, styled much like Farmor's, and the man who has his arm slung over Farfar's shoulder has striking eyes I recognize even in black and white. They are nearly identical to Jonas's. Together they hold a large copy of a business license that reads *Scandinavian Market*.

Jane steps next to me, examining the picture over my shoulder. "What is it?"

"These are my grandparents," I say. "And these two…I think these are Jonas's grandparents. Look at the business name. Janey, there is no *Scandinavian Market*, just the two bakeries. I think they were once business partners."

"You guys really don't know the story at all?"

I shake my head. "My grandpa won't talk about it. I knew they were friends, but not business partners. They seem so happy."

I feel sad looking at the picture. Young Viggo and young Farfar did look happy, like they might've been brothers. Flash forward to today and their voracious hatred for each other, I can only imagine what might have happened to drive them apart.

"Brita," a deep voice booms. "And Pizza Girl."

I roll my eyes and face him. "Hi, Logan. How are you doing?"

He smiles, his tanned skin a stark contrast to his white teeth. "I'm doing great. Thanks for asking. How are you ladies?"

"We're amazing," Jane says sweetly, though I hear the sarcasm. "By the way, I'm still waiting for you to buy me a new pizza."

"Name the time and place," Logan flirts.

Don't fall for it, Jane, I think. But she can hold her own. I glance around Logan and catch sight of Axel. He's not alone. A young woman with long auburn hair and a skimpy, pale dress links her arm with his. Axel dips low, whispers something into her ear, and she giggles.

"Jane, look," I say, nodding toward Axel.

"Well that was quick," Jane mutters. Logan follows her eyes.

"Quick with what?" Logan asks.

"The girl," says Jane. "Moved on quick."

To be fair, I ended things because I moved on too. I'm still a little surprised to see Axel with his mouth on a girl's neck. I mean, his mother is five feet away.

One of Logan's brows climbs. "Axel and Shay have gone out loads of times this semester. She lives here too, but was a few years behind us in school."

I don't recognize her, but then I don't recognize people from my own graduating class sometimes. I peer at Logan. "What do you mean loads of times? They've been dating?"

Logan chuckles, and looks at me funny. "Well, she's *one* of the girls he dates. Things picked up with her back in February—I guess the Olsens had family pictures or something. They went out a couple times. But there's a girl in his therapy classes named Lily, I think, and then..." Logan trails off. He has a kind of wicked smile. "Wait, Brita, did you think Axel was only dating you?"

I hardly know how to respond. I'm glad Jane does for me. "Well," she says. "Typically that is what most girls think."

Logan laughs and I would like to punch him. "Oh, Brit. Ax dates a lot of people. I know he viewed you two as just having a good time together."

"Sure, just a good time," I say, feeling sick. All those times we spent together I actually thought…and on my *birthday weekend* he was out with another girl. I remember that night, sitting on the bench with Jonas. My stomach flops over and over like a storm. Jonas told me Axel wasn't home. "Logan, did Jonas know about all this?"

Please say no.

"Brita, Brita. They're twins."

I guess I'm supposed to get something from that.

"They have the same type, and Ax usually sets Jonas up with girls he dates too. By the way you were all over Jonas out there, looks like you're the flavor of the month." Logan starts to laugh, but the sound fades when I clutch my stomach to keep from heaving. "Brita are you upset? Come on, you had to know with the history of your families. It wasn't real, not like *real*, real. Don't tell me you fell for that."

"Hey you," Jane snaps. "Shut up." She turns to me, arms on my shoulders. "What's going on in your mind?"

I'm already walking toward the exit. "You heard him," I say, a wash of dizziness comes. I hold onto the wall until it passes. "Logan's right, I did fall for him."

"Whoa, maybe you ought to talk to him."

235

I think I will throw up if I talk to him right now. I shake my head. "No, it makes sense, Janey. He's never talked to Axel, because he probably already knows." I grip my hair. "I'm an idiot. It's what twins do, I'm their *flavor*."

So that's what this is. That's why Axel doesn't care, that's why Jonas never talks about the fact that I've dated his brother. It doesn't matter to them. I'm a girl passed between brothers.

My heart breaks into a thousand pieces when I see Jonas. He smiles, holding my coat.

"Ready to go?" he asks.

"Is this a game to you?" I snatch my coat from his hands.

"What?"

"Is it a game? You and Axel, both seeing if you can get the Jacobson girl?"

"Brita I have—" Jonas starts.

"I'm not just something you can share between the two of you," I say, my voice breaking.

I storm past him, Jane fumbles a bit as she bounces between Jonas and me, but in the end she follows me.

"Brita," Jonas calls out, tugging on my elbow and following me out into the night. A soft rain begins to fall, the drops frigid like snow, but I don't feel the cold. "What are you talking about?"

I wheel on him, while Jane slinks off, hopefully going to get her car. "All this time you knew Axel was seeing tons of girls, yet you let me believe I was the only one. You lied for him. What was your part of the deal? That you get some of me too?"

Jonas tightens his mouth and looks at the sky. "How could you think that?" His voice is strained and dark.

"Did you know? Tell me, Jonas."

"Alright, yes. I knew Axel wasn't exclusive with anyone. But how could I tell you? I didn't want to hurt you. After Christmas, you acted like he was your boyfriend. I told him that you saw the relationship that way, but he didn't believe me. I should have told you, but I thought it would just fizzle naturally if I stepped back. I'm sorry."

"So instead you thought you'd keep me company in the meantime and move things along? You brothers know how to share, huh?"

Jonas presses closer, his voice filled with barely contained fury. "What do you mean by that?"

"Logan told me everything," I cry. My tears are hot and painful. "He told me how Axel sets you up with girls he dates. That I'm the flavor of the month. How fun it must have been to conquer the enemy. To get me to fall for the both of you."

Jonas reaches for my hand, but I rip it back. "I don't know what Logan said, but you're wrong. Brita, you think I would do and say everything just to mess with you?"

Headlights pull up behind us. Jane is brilliant and *did* go to get her car. She knows the night is over. Glancing back at Jonas, I shake my head.

237

"You know, I planned to tell you that I love you tonight. Not like you; I fell in love with you, Jonas."

"Brita…"

"No," I hold up my hand. "I fell for it all. You and Axel won." Speaking of Axel, I see him, and Logan rush out into the parking lot. They look around until they catch sight of me marching right up to Jonas's face.

Jonas doesn't back down and takes my hand. I love his touch; that hurts even more. Standing in the rain, I tremble in rage, or a broken heart, or both. "I would never do that to you," he says. "Because I love you too."

I gently take my hand from his. "You lied to me Jonas, for so long. I really can't believe you right now."

"Can't, or won't?"

I hold my breath and back away. "This has been one pitfall after the other. My life was fine before…before you. I think I've had my fill of Olsen brothers for now. I'm going to go. I'll see you in class."

"Brita, don't leave," he pleads.

I slip quickly into the passenger side of Jane's car and slam the door. Jonas calls my name when Axel and Logan join him. He slaps his hand on the roof of the car, but I only turn toward Jane.

"Please go," I whisper. "Let's get out of here."

She nods sadly, but she doesn't say anything. Jane drives me away from Jonas and lets me crumble on her front seat.

***

I leave a note for my family stating Jane and I went home. I know they will need an explanation about my quick departure eventually, but it can wait until tomorrow, or next week. Jane and I say little on the way home. The second I walk into our apartment I sluff my bag off my shoulder, strip out of my new dress, and shower, wiping away all memories of the night. But some things don't wash away with soap and water.

I step into the kitchen after I am scrubbed and in my pajamas. Jane is on the phone, her back turned away, but I know exactly who is on the other end.

"Joe, just give her a little time, okay? Yeah. Yeah. I will. Okay, bye," she whispers. My eyes burn again thinking of Jonas, but then I feel angry all in one painful emotion.

"Hey," Jane says when I take a curled position on the couch. "That was Jonas. He, uh, says he really wants to talk when you're ready. He says he loves you, Brit."

"Of course, he does, he's been caught in a lie," I mutter, but inside what I want is to go back in time to the moment we danced and held each other.

Jane holds the basket of chocolate bars and smiles at me cautiously.

I wrap a blanket around my shoulders. "Sorry, Janey. I don't think chocolate is going to fix this." Jane finds a place next to me, her eyes soft and patient as she waits for me to say anything. "Do you believe Jonas?" I ask after a few new tears well in my eyes.

"All I'm going to say is, think of the source."

I bite my bottom lip. Logan. His stupid love of our families feuding has been a thorn in my side since high school. I've never liked Logan, but I love Jonas. My stomach turns, coiling like barbed wire as I bury my face in my hands. "What did I just do, Janey?"

Jane sighs and leans forward on her knees. "Brit, I've seen you at crazy ends of the emotion spectrum this semester. Euphorically happy and now . . . this. What made you turn on him so quickly? I gotta say, it's sort of like you wanted a reason to prove this wasn't going to work."

"No," I insist. "That's not it. I just—" But what? Maybe she's right. First, Axel was a fantasy I never believed I could ever have. A secret that, when I truly think about it, I never plotted out when I'd tell my family about him because I'm not sure I ever planned to. Then knowing Jonas, loving his shyness, his gentle hands, the way he understood my worries, maybe I allowed my own prejudice that we would never be accepted interfere.

I hold a hand over my chest when it feels as though my heart will break through my ribs. Did I give in to the broken families at the first bump in the road?

"I think you're following me," Jane says softly.

My phone rings before I can answer. I lick my lips and look at Jane. "It's Axel."

"Your choice if you answer or not."

She leaves me, and like a coward I wish she'd come do this part for me. My hand trembles as I answer the call.

"Brita?" Axel says when the pause extends to an uncomfortable silence.

"Is he there?" I croak out.

"No," he says; I've never heard Axel Olsen sound so somber. I doubt he's smiling like he always does. "But maybe you'll tell me what's going on and why Jonas just about broke Logan's jaw."

"Can't say I'm sorry to hear that."

Axel laughs softly. "Logan admitted what he said. I guess, I ought to apologize first. I sincerely had no idea I'd given the impression we were exclusive. Brit, I like you, and wouldn't ever want to hurt your feelings."

I rub the bridge of my nose, forcing the burn behind my eyes to simmer to an ache.

"Now," Axel goes on, "I'm switching to brother mode. What are you thinking? You really believe Jonas and me would be jerks like that? That we'd use you?"

I feel like an idiot. There isn't another way to put it. I'm wholly embarrassed when my voice cracks. "I was angry, and I think part of me believed maybe it was only a matter of time before it ended because of the family history."

"Well, that's stupid," Axel says. He definitely isn't smiling.

"You're not making me feel any better, I hope you know."

"I'm not sure I called to make you feel better. But listen, Jonas will kill me if he finds out I'm doing this, but as his brother I'm asking you to please talk to him."

I wrap some of my hair around my fingers and close my eyes. "What can I say?" I have plenty of things to say to Jonas, but in my head I can't think of a way to explain all this without sounding cowardly, and probably ridiculous. And then there is the small piece of me that's still upset with him for lying about Axel. Bottom line, tonight I'm a mess.

"I don't get you, Brita. You tell him that you love him, then leave like it's over, now you won't talk to him?"

"I want to talk to him," I say, a little stronger than before. "But, I just . . . I needed to figure things out."

"What's to figure out?" Playful Axel Olsen sounds like he's nearly growling. It's unnerving. "Do you love him?"

I nod, then remember he can't see me. "Yes."

"Then talk to him. I see no problems. Honestly, I think make up fights turn into some of the best memories, if you know what I mean."

Ah, there is the crass humor coming back out. I sniff, allowing a few tears to finally fall. "I've always pleased people." Why am I admitting this to Axel? "Always done what others wanted. I caved so easily tonight, and I think Jonas deserves more than that. He deserves so much."

Axel is quiet for a long time. For a second I think he hung up. Then he speaks softly, nothing teasing in his voice. "I'm glad you love him, Brit. Figure it out, would you? Because you make him happy."

We end the phone call with Axel finally admitting Jonas is angry, but that's no excuse not to talk (he reminded me of that three times) then with me promising I'd talk with him when tensions die down.

242

I think of what this means, and am ashamed to admit I did take an easy way out. I avoided hurting my family, allowed the feud to weasel between us, I mean come on, how could a Jacobson loving an Olsen actually work?

But I've always done this. Always said what the Swedish bakers wanted or needed to hear, like my future career. Now, I pushed away a man I fell crazy, undeniably in love with.

I'm no Viking. I'm a coward.

And that ends tonight.

Chapter 24

Time heals all wounds.

Pfft, that is what I have to say about that. When Jonas doesn't answer my calls for three days, I start to believe some wounds are too deep to heal.

The first Tuesday after the dinner fiasco, I sit in my lonely corner while Nicholls lectures. My skin heats, and I wonder if Jonas is looking at me. I look up once and he hurriedly shifts in his seat, looking away. When the class ends there is no avoiding each other.

I slip out before the rush of students, and cling to my messenger bag's strap as though it is the only solid thing. Waiting for him feels like hours, yet he's there too soon. Those vibrant blue eyes draw me in, tossing me about, leaving me aching for his hands in my, his lips on my skin.

I don't let the storm inside show. I try to remain flat, afraid of my heart cracking when I've only just started piecing it back together.

He clears his throat and stands maybe a pace away. "So, I—"

"Axel called me." I'm nervous, and blurt things when I'm nervous.

Jonas raises a brow. "What? He called you?" He shakes his head. "I'm going to kill him."

He turns around as though he plans to walk away. *Stop him!* But I stand there, frozen like a marble statue, not knowing how to react. Then Jonas pauses, his hand at the ready to push the door open to leave the building.

"No," he says. "You know what, I have something I need to say to you."

Good, this is happening. An angry make up fight, right here in the English building. I crack my thumb knuckles as Jonas stalks back toward me, my cheeks drain of blood, and I'm likely ghostly pale by the time he stops. Close enough I can touch him.

"Brita," he says. "You believed Logan over me."

"I know . . ." I begin, but Jonas steps closer and I forget how to breathe.

"I've been so mad," he says, but his voice is soft. "But worse is how I've hardly been able to function. I never understood the term heartache, until I watched you drive away the other night." Jonas swallows hard. "Then I realized, when you told me that you thought you were some game with Axel and me, I wasn't upset with you. I was angry at myself."

"Why?" I ask, finding my voice. Everything tumbles into chaos again, but a beautiful chaos.

245

"Because," he says. "If you could think that, then I didn't show you how much you mean to me. So, before I walk out of here, I'm going to tell you. I need you to know how I feel." A tremble comes to his voice. Vulnerable, perfect, and sincere, he meets my eye. "You should know, I started to like you when you got stuck in the trash cans and tried to brush it off as a slip on the ice."

I huff and look out the window. "I *did* slip on ice."

"No, you didn't," he says and takes a heart-stopping inch closer. "But that's not where it ends. I started to fall for you when we jammed out in my car." Another step. Jonas's body brushes against mine now. "And I knew I'd fallen in love with you the night you got sick."

"What? How could that—"

"I'm not finished." Those hands that touch so gently trap my face. My lip quivers when he nudges my chin up. I meet his eye.

"That night," he says. "I knew what I wanted to do for the rest of my life. I want to take care of you; be with you. I want to talk about your obsession with books, and eat gummy worms with you. I should have told you about Axel. I convinced myself I was protecting your feelings, and his, in a way. I'm sorry. Axel isn't malicious, just an idiot, and you weren't a game."

I try to look away, but he won't allow it so I lean into him instead. I love the way Jonas holds my face between his palms, the soft brush of his thumbs on my cheeks.

He drops his smile and looks at me with new intensity. "I was in love with you that night, Brita, and I'm in love with you now. You're not just

246

a girl to pass around. You're the one I want to be with. I need you in my life, and I'm willing to do whatever it takes to prove that to you."

My heart lights on fire, burning a hole in the center of my body. Gently, I draw my hands along his chest before I wrap my arms around his waist. Our bodies melt together.

"You want all this?" I whisper. "The stubborn, overthinking, Jacobson enemy?"

Jonas smiles, his thumb passes over my lips. A touch, barely there, then it moves to my jaw, my chin. I never want it to end. His lips brush mine when he answers. "Every single piece."

I stand on my toes, pull his lips to mine, and I let Jonas kiss me as long as Jonas Olsen wants to kiss me. Fingers in my hair, one hand on the small of my back, pressing me against him. There remains no room between us, yet we're not close enough. I breathe in everything. The time we've spent apart now sparks against our lips as he kisses me.

He smiles against my mouth when we come up for air.

"I love you," I say against his skin. "And that is what I should've said the other night."

Those words are enough to pull me back in for more. I'm not sure how long we stand there, our bags at our feet, kissing as students skirt around us to get to classes, but it doesn't last long enough.

Pulling back, he brushes hair off my brow, resting his forehead on mine. "You know we still have a problem."

"What?" I wrap my arms around his waist.

"I'm in this, Brit, and that means we've got family to tell."

Groaning, my head falls to his chest. He laughs, the rumble of the sound pulses through me, and I think I can forget the drearier truth that we will need to confess to our families, and soon. The way Jonas sends a bright shock through my blood whenever he touches me, avoiding him at home, pretending we are enemies, well, that simply won't be possible.

***

Dreary February drifts to a brighter, warmer March. Jonas is wonderful, have I said that enough yet? When I think how I nearly ran from him, my stomach twists in hard knots.

Midterms are hardly survivable, and I pity Jonas who still has one more test. Working on my capstone paper while he sits next to me studying on a Friday night isn't a glamorous sight. Me in fuzzy socks and an oversized sweatshirt (Jonas looks amazing in his gray sweats and T-shirt, so he is the exception here) and him with headphones, studying Advanced Business Law.

I don't know when I fall asleep, but something stirs me. I have the remote in my hand and the T. V. is on.

"Brit."

Jonas is shaking me, one headphone is out, but his laptop is open. I blink through the fog and sit up.

"Your phone is going crazy."

I roll over the arm of the couch to the small end table where my phone is bright, but then goes dark again with a missed call. Glancing at the clock,

I squint and realize it is just after one in the morning. But when I look at my screen, I'm wide awake.

I've missed fifteen calls.

Some from Inez, some from Dad, two from Oscar. Frantically, I fumble to return Inez's call—when your family calls that many times it usually isn't good news. Jonas watches me cautiously.

I think of Farfar, my heart cramps and my fingers go numb as I wait for my aunt to pick up.

"Brita," she answers, but her voice croaks.

"Inez, what's wrong? What is it? Is it Farfar?"

"No . . . it's Agnes." She starts to cry.

My entire body goes numb now. I pounce to my feet, the blanket slides off and curls around my fluffy socks. Jonas is on his feet too.

"What happened?" My hands tremble.

"She's in the hospital with a bad case of pneumonia, Brit. They have her on oxygen, but she's . . . having a hard time. Sweetie, we just wanted you to know."

"I'm coming, right now. I'll be there soon."

"Brita . . ."

I don't wait to listen to Inez protest. I hang up and rush to grab my shoes in my room. Jonas hasn't said a word, but when I return he has his car keys in hand, is slipping his jacket on, and has me wrapped in his arms in another breath.

I bite against tears, as he presses a kiss to the side of my head. "What's going on?"

"It's Agnes." I hiccup.

At that, he threads his fingers with mine and pulls me to the door. "Come on."

"Jonas," I say, ready to protest him driving me all the way home, but when he shoots me a sharp look, I go quiet.

Leaning against the cold window of his car, silent tears plop down my cheeks. Agnes has been sick before, but never to the point Aunt Inez broke down, or admitted her to the hospital. This time is different. I try not to go there, but occasionally those thoughts—you know, the what ifs—bombard my mind and the tears come.

I draw in a rattling breath when I feel Jonas's hand dig through my folded arms. He links our fingers and glances over at me, his eyes pouring into my very soul. "She's going to be okay," he whispers.

I hold tight to his hand, and close my eyes. I draw comfort from his touch. We don't say much, I don't trust my voice anyway. Soon enough we again pull back into town. The hospital isn't busy when Jonas pulls up in the drop-off lane, but a few nurses and staff shuffle in and out on various shifts. Clearing my throat, I turn to him and gather my bag.

"Want me to go with you?"

I trap his face between my palms and give him a swift, wet kiss, but shake my head. "No, I'd better go alone for now."

"You'll call me as soon as you know how she is, right?"

I hug him tightly. I love him for caring, not just about me, but my family. Even their hatred for his name doesn't stop him from caring. "I'll call you as soon as I know something."

He waits until I disappear through the only open entrance. Inside, the night nurse directs me to the second floor, and I find Aunt Inez and Karl inside Agnes's room. I cover my mouth when I see my little cousin sleeping in the bed. She has an oxygen mask over her mouth, her skin pale has a bluish tint, and monitors, beeps, and sounds wail around her.

"Brita," Inez breathes out. Her eyes are puffy and red as she crosses the room. I hug her tightly, her shoulders shake a bit, before she takes my hand and leads me across the room.

"She's sleeping now. Her oxygen isn't quite where they want it to be," Inez explains, pointing to one of the monitors. "But her cough has died down a bit. They think if she keeps improving she can come home in two days. They just . . . want to monitor her."

Karl holds Agnes's little hand and nods whenever Inez explains something. I squeeze my aunt's shoulders. "She's going to be okay," I whisper the same words Jonas just said to me. With a smile, I lean in a little closer. "What would Farfar say?"

Inez breaks into a tearful smile and chuckles. She nods and rests her head on my shoulder. "We're Vikings."

Chapter 25

When we are satisfied Agnes is sleeping soundly, I drive home with Karl and Inez. The nurse is insistent, in the kindest way, that the parents get some rest, assuring all of us she will be well looked after. Inez's shoulders slump over. I know my aunt is drained as she kisses Agnes's forehead and we quietly creep out of the hospital room.

My dad sits in the kitchen early Saturday morning when I pound down the steps ready to go back and visit Agnes.

"I'm taking the morning shift," I tell him.

Dad nods, rubbing his face. "That'll give Inez and Karl a chance to sleep. Oscar is already there. Want my car?"

I shake my head, and hurry to the front door. "I've got a ride." The text message waiting for me on my phone this morning solved all my transportation troubles.

Jonas: *Hey, I have something for Agnes. Can we go to the hospital tomorrow?*

I take a deep breath and rush outside before my dad can press me. We're doing this, we said we needed to do this. But now that we're here, the thought of tearing away the forbidden curtain on Jonas keeps making my fingertips go numb.

Outside, Jonas pulls up to the bench on the sidewalk. He greets me with a quick kiss, and takes my hand.

"Is she any better this morning?"

I shrug. "She's struggling with keeping her throat clear."

The drive is somber. When we pull up at the hospital, I stare at the doors. I hate that Agnes is here, alone and afraid, but when Jonas takes my hand, I feel like I can breathe again.

"Ready?"

I nod, but I'm not sure I am. To some walking into a building with your boyfriend is not anything to gawk at, but for us, with the chance of being seen this is a defining moment.

Though spring is blooming, the air feels crisp and damp with the last remnants of winter. I embrace the overheated elevator until my fingers have feeling again. Jonas leads the way down the hallway, only speaking when he complains the nurse in charge of buzzing visitors into the wing takes too long to open the doors.

"There's Oscar," I whisper. I see the back of my cousin's head. He's on the phone, probably updating his parents.

253

If Jonas is unsettled, he doesn't let on. He flashes me a quicksilver grin. "We're doing this, right?"

I don't even check to see if Oscar has turned around before I kiss him, slow and sweet. I smile against his mouth and nod. "We're doing this."

Agnes is awake in the room, eyes wide and the oxygen mask from last night is gone, replaced by a nose canula. A nurse checks her vitals, while a lady on the respiratory team creeps around her bed holding a strange looking device that reminds me of the suction tube used at dental visits to suck out moisture. Agnes keeps eyeing the woman with a definite fear of the machine.

"Aggie," I say.

She whips her head around and smiles as best she can. She tilts her head and studies Jonas. I lace my fingers with his. "This is Jonas, he lives across the street."

"I know," she says, her voice a rocky rasp. "The bad bakers."

Heat fills my cheeks, but he chuckles and takes one of the chairs reserved for visitors, I sit next to him. "Well, maybe you won't think I'm so bad in a second." Jonas reaches into the giftbag and pulls out a floppy-eared pink bunny.

My heart swells, and I can't hide my smile, neither can Agnes. She reaches greedily for the stuffed animal, running her fingers over the soft ears.

"I like pink."

"Thought so," he says, bouncing the stuffed toy on her arm.

She giggles, but starts coughing each time, bringing the nurse and her suction contraption closer. "We need to clear her out," the respiratory therapist tells me.

The trouble is, whenever Agnes catches sight of the machine, she winces and clamps her mouth tightly.

I am about to tell her she needs to comply, but Jonas leans forward, tickling her face with the bunny's ears. "It's kind of scary, huh."

"I don't want her to do it," Agnes admits in a small voice.

Jonas flops the ears on the rabbit up and down. "Can I tell you a story?"

Agnes nods, coughing more mucous and secretions into her mouth. She needs to swallow desperately, but can't, or maybe won't.

"I have an older brother."

Agnes's eyes widen, her words hard to understand through the muck in her mouth. "You have an older brother too?"

"Yep, but only by three minutes. Don't let him fool you—he's not even bigger than me."

Both Agnes and I smile.

"Anyway, we had bunk beds when we were kids. And one day, my brother convinced me I could fly. Can you guess what happened? I fell flat on my face and broke my arm. The doctor had to move my arm around a lot, and it hurt. I was so scared, but my dad brought me a little stuffed dog, kind of like this bunny. The dog got a cast just like I did, and I felt like if the dog could do it, I could too."

Agnes glances at the rabbit he's bouncing along her arm, then back at the nurse. Her little cheeks are so full of saliva they puff a bit. Every time she coughs a little spills over her lips and it sounds like it is getting harder for her to draw air back in.

"Do you want your bunny to go first?" he asks.

Agnes nods, and Jonas looks to the therapist who smiles. She sticks the tube next to the bunny's face, never really touches it, but behaves as if the stuffing of the toy is being suctioned and cleaned.

"See, I don't know about you, but I think the bunny feels a lot better. And I think you'll feel better if you let your nice nurse clean out some of the icky stuff inside."

"Will you stay here?" she asks us both.

I brush her sweaty hair off her forehead, and kiss her gently. Agnes coughs, a terrible cough, during the cleaning. Then whimpers as the woman works. Jonas gives my cousin a thumbs up. She squeezes her eyes tight; her little hands grip the folds of her blanket until the procedure is over.

"You did awesome," the nurse praises.

"Very brave," says the therapist and begins gathering her supplies.

"See, you're like Wonder Woman," Jonas adds.

"Thanks for the bunny," Agnes sounds clearer. "You're not so bad."

Jonas laughs. "You're not so bad either."

Agnes focuses on her new toy, hopping the small rabbit along the side of her bed. I tug on Jonas's arm, drawing him to me, stopping when our lips are near enough to touch. "Have I told you that I think you're wonderful?"

He laughs softly and kisses me until a throat clears behind us.

Standing in the center is Oscar, a sly, knowing grin on his face, but my stomach sinks when I see Inez behind him and Farar.

Jonas stands, and I wish I could say I felt better realizing he's nervous, but I feel more like I might throw up.

"Uh, hi," I say, dumbly. We drift to the door since I'm unwilling to let Agnes see what is about to happen.

Jonas slides his fingers into mine, his searching gaze finds me, and it takes all my self-control not to dart down the hall and run away for good. My aunt has tears in her eyes, I'm sure she's heartbroken that I'd do this, bring an enemy to her daughter's bedside. I'm ready for her to lose control, but like the cunning guy he is, Oscar taps his mother's shoulder.

"Hey, Ag wants to show you her rabbit that Brit and *Jonas* gave her."

I could hug the life out of my cousin, how he strategically added Jonas's name. Inez's demeanor shifts. She lifts her glassy eyes to me, there is betrayal there, and something urges me to take a step in front of Jonas. A strange sort of protective instinct overwhelms the need to please my family, and I rather like this new boldness. I love Jonas, and frankly in this moment, I dare someone here to try and tear him down. I feel ready to pounce.

Inez's mouth is tight, but she pastes a smile on her face before striding into Agnes's room. Oscar winks at me and claps Jonas on the shoulder before he follows.

Then we are alone. With Farfar.

His eyes grow darker, his mouth is pressed so tightly I hardly see his lips. Leaning heavily on a cane, knuckles white, he steps up to me, as though he's challenging me.

"You?" he begins, voice a rocky rasp. "Out of anyone, I never thought it would be you who would . . . betray us this way."

"Farfar, stop," I say, my voice trembles, and Jonas squeezes my hand, reassuring me that he's there. "You're not going to mistreat him, and we're not going to argue. Not here, not in front of Aggie."

I've won the miniscule battle; I see it in my grandfather's eyes when he peers into her room. Agnes is a light in this world, and none of us, not even when we're deliriously angry, would want to dim some of that light for her.

He returns his glare to me, makes a sort of grunt, then staggers angrily in the room.

I slump when he's gone, grateful Jonas is there to pull me tightly against him. He cups a palm to the side of my face. "I'm in this."

I adjust, so I can wrap my arms around his waist. "Me too. Even if it's just us in the end."

I feel his arms hold me a little tighter. It's true; I'll choose Jonas, but I think inside we both don't want to turn our backs on our families.

I simply have no idea how the Jacobsons and Olsens will ever find common ground.

***

After we get back, Jonas and I sit in his car in front of my house for a long time. His thumb draws circles over the top of my hand; I watch people stroll the sidewalks.

"I think I should go talk to my parents," Jonas finally says.

I want to be the girl who offers to go with him, but truly I'm terrified. I've never spoken to Sig and Elias personally. I open my mouth to say I'll go with him, but he interrupts.

"It'll probably be better if I do it alone first."

I nod, admittedly relieved. "This is crazy," I say. "I mean, how nervous we are." I try to laugh but it comes out in more a strangled hiccup.

"A little," he says softly. "But I'm so tired of hiding this, Brit. I almost don't care what happens as long as it's out."

Smiling, I urge him to face me. Those diverting blue eyes buoy me against what I feel is coming. "Whatever they say, whatever they do, you've got me in your corner."

He kisses me with meaning. When we break away, he closes his eyes. "I love you. Don't let your family burn the house down before I get the chance to buy those cookies myself."

I laugh, but it's only funny because who knows what might happen today. "I'll do my best."

259

Jonas waits for me to disappear into my house. I hurry to my room, grateful the house sounds empty, but as luck would have it, a knock comes not long after.

"Brit."

I blow out a breath, and open the door to my dad. "Hi."

"So," he says, wiggling his cell phone in front of my face. "Oscar sent me a funny text, warning me the world might implode. Want to tell me what's going on?"

Tears swell over my lashes, embarrassing to cry over such a joyful thing as I found a man who treats me like a queen. Doesn't make sense, but the tears come anyway. My dad lifts a brow and shoves into my room.

"Brita, what is it?" he asks, more deliberately.

"Sit down," I whisper, and he does.

We stare at each other for long moment before I take a breath, and let it all out. And I mean everything. Starting with dating Axel (skimming a few of the steamier kissing nights in his car), moving on to getting to know Jonas during the Christmas Break, becoming friends back at school, and finally to the night I realized I'd fallen for Jonas Olsen, not his brother.

Dad doesn't interrupt, he simply listens. When I wipe my eyes and slump onto my bed, he leans over his knees, staring at his hands. "I'm trying to think of the right way to say what I'm thinking."

"I love Jonas, Dad," I say. "I'm sorry if that—"

"Don't apologize," he says sharply. "Not to me."

260

I'm not sure I remember a time when my father stared at me with such ferocity enough to shut me up, but he is now and it's fascinating.

"Brita, you don't need to apologize to me because you've found a solid guy who treats you well. What else, as your dad, do you think I want for your relationships?"

"Farfar told me I betrayed the family."

Dad rolls his eyes and runs a hand through his hair. "Listen, kid. I don't want you to make the same mistakes I did. Some relationships get hard and I made the mistake of giving up when things got hard. You know that Viggo and your grandpa are locked in this hatred for each other. You know they're not going to be rational, but that means you know what to expect.

"I wish, I'd done something about the fighting when I was growing up, but we all just played into it. Until you, until Jonas. Now, if you really care about him like you say, then you need to decide if you're going to give up like me. Because there are going to be voices that will try to pull you apart."

"You're vaguely talking about Mom, aren't you?"

He chuckles. "We didn't face what you guys are, but I lost sight of what was important. My priorities were misplaced, and when it got hard, I just gave in and didn't fight. Don't get me wrong, your mom is happy, and I'm happy. We care about each other still, and we have you. But I have regrets. That's all I'm saying. The kind of regrets I never want you to live with."

I hug my knees, glancing out my window as though Jonas will be there. "I know this will infuriate everyone—"

Dad clears his throat.

I smile. "Sorry, *almost* everyone. But I'm not going to lie anymore, and I'm not going to deny him."

Dad opens his mouth to say something but pauses when we hear shouts outside. He meets my gaze, there is concern in his pale blue. I hold my breath, my stomach in knots, because I know that voice. I know both voices.

Outside, Philip Jacobson and Viggo Olsen are about to start a war.

Chapter 26

I rush down the stairs, Dad right behind me. I'm met with Oscar peering out the window of the front door. Inez in the living room. My aunt sees me, her eyes look wet. "Brita, don't," she starts.

"Are you kidding me?" I say, ripping open the door. "This is not happening, not like this."

Picture this: Two seventy-something men staggering, one with a cane, the other with a hunch, to the middle of the street, shouting in a salad of English-Scandinavian curse words and words I'm not sure are in either dictionary.

The bell over our door rings cheerily as I tear out of the house after my grandfather. More than this ridiculous sparring match (which is drawing a crowd on the sidewalk) he's so angry that I'm concerned he's going to fall.

"Farfar stop!" I cry out.

He glances over his shoulder, leaving a glare I can feel beneath my skin before he faces Viggo again. "You keep your house out of mine," my grandfather roars. "If I see you or yours near my grand—"

"Philip, if you think I'd let my family mingle with yours, then you've lost your mind. You slimy cheat. You, you *dishonest* fool. I'd rather go to my grave before I see the Olsens embrace a Jacobson."

I cover my mouth, pulse racing as my grandfather into the road. What do they think they're going to do? Have a brawl right here in the middle of the street? Surrounding us are people whipping out cell phones, ready to catch a moment they doubtless find hilarious, between two old men who are about to start swinging.

I see Jonas crash out of Clara's, followed by his parents. He catches my eye, and starts chasing Viggo the same as I'm chasing my grandfather.

Farfar raises his cane. "Keep him away, Viggo. I'm warning you, my granddaughter will no longer be manipulated by—"

"I'm not!" I don't realize how loudly I shout the words until a hush ripples down the street. Both Viggo and Farfar watch me, aghast. My eyes narrow, and I turn away from the stubborn men, and look to Jonas who is a mere ten feet away. "I am not being manipulated, Farfar. This needs to stop. Right now."

"Brita, I don't blame you," he says. "I know how conniving—"

"Stop," I shout again. I'm unnerved by the way I'm speaking to my grandfather. I've never shouted at him. We've always been loving, and tender in our house, but this new, fiery need to stand for Jonas has overtaken me. "I won't let you talk about Jonas, or his family like this anymore."

"Jonas," Viggo hisses, glaring at his grandson when he stalks past him to me.

Jonas ignores him, eyes on me, until he holds out his hand. I swallow past the lump of anxiety in my throat and thread my fingers with his. "Guys," he says to his family. "This is ridiculous. Look what you're doing." He signals to the spectators.

"What are *you* doing?" Viggo grumbles.

Jonas squeezes my hand, gives me one of his shy grins. "I'm choosing her," he says.

I suck in a sharp breath, afraid what will happen to him now, yet my heart burns for this man.

"I fell in love with Brita, and I'm not letting her go just because you two," he says, gesturing to both our grandfathers, "can't get along."

"You'll ruin this family, boy," Viggo says.

I consider for a moment that I might start shouting at him like my own family, but I stop. Elias is moving.

"Dad," Elias says, as though he's exhausted. "That's enough."

Viggo starts spluttering, and I dig the heels of my hands into my eyes to stop the tears when Sigrid lifts her chin and tromps to where Jonas and I are standing in the road. Elias was the one to speak up first, but he hesitates more than his wife. Sig is near us, she looks at me with caution, but smiles and grips Jonas's arm. "I always hoped this would happen.

You're braver than me," she tells him softly, her eyes drifting back to me. "Both of you."

Elias is talking to Viggo. I turn to my side of the street. Farfar looks rather pleased Viggo's family is turning against him, but his face pales when Dad walks past him, toward us, hands shoved into his pockets.

"Nils," Farfar cries out. "Don't you dare."

I blink through the haze in my eyes and wrap my hands around Jonas's arm when my father doesn't stop and joins us. He nods at Jonas's mom.

"Sig," he says. "It's been awhile since we've talked."

She chuckles. "Since ninth grade Biology."

Dad glances at Jonas. For the first time, Jonas looks uneasy. Then again, he just professed love for Nils Jacobson's daughter in the middle of the street. I think my dad enjoys his discomfort a little too much before he finally holds out his hand (Farfar curses a few times in Swedish) and takes Jonas's.

"You have me and Brita's mom behind you guys." A simple thing to say, but it brings some of the color back to Jonas's face.

"And us," Sig says.

I hold my breath. Elias stands next to her now, his eyes on my dad. I can feel the tension, left there to grow between two men who have no reason not to like each other beyond a feud begun by their parents. Then, slowly, and maybe a little awkwardly, my dad and Elias shake hands. They don't say anything, but sort of nod a few times as though there is an unspoken understanding.

266

I'll take what I can get.

"This changes nothing," Farfar says in a bit of a growl. He snaps his eyes back to Viggo. "Nothing. I'll not forget what you did, how you broke Hanna's heart."

"What I did?" Viggo shouts back. "You tried to destroy me. There is scum on the street with more moral fiber than you."

I wrap my arms around Jonas, he tilts my head up with his fingers beneath my chin.

"We knew it would take time," he whispers.

Farfar turns on his heel, storming—as fast as he can—back toward our house. Viggo follows suit. My stomach is in knots. Things changed, we confessed, but I still feel as though we've somehow broken our families. An irreparable wound that we can't fix.

"Hey!" Oscar shouts from the front window. "Bastien! Want to go to the *Burger Room* tonight with Josh? He says Amy Murdock and her friends will be there."

Those of us in the streets whip our head back to *Clara's* where a window is open and Bastien sits behind the mesh screen.

"No way," he calls back. "I'm never showing my face again. How much do you want to bet the entire team is going to see this on YouTube by tomorrow?"

Sig and Elias laugh softly. I feel lighter because it's a little funny. Inside our house, Inez scolds Oscar, Viggo shouts at his youngest grandson in Danish, and Farfar shakes his head, muttering about family loyalty.

I wish, more than I've wished before, that I could find a way to heal the scabrous pustule of a hole that shredded these old men apart.

But I have no idea where to even begin.

***

The cuckoo clock chimes five the next morning. When I come downstairs, my body aches as though I've been running for hours without stopping. I slept like a tense board all night.

Battle raged inside the Jacobson home, only pausing when we received an update call on Agnes from Uncle Karl. We put up the white flag to learn she's breathing without help of extra oxygen now, and should be home by tomorrow night. But after the call ended, peace became a forgotten notion. Farfar and Dad argued after dinner (at least my grandfather is speaking to him), and Oscar began a fight with Inez when he insisted he was going to follow his rogue cousin, and be friends with Bastien. Turns out another Jacobson and Olsen get along well.

We should've gone home last night, but Jonas was dragged into his own family drama. In his text last night, turns out Axel was even forced to sit and argue over the phone. Apparently, Viggo about split his skin when Axel admitted he wholly encouraged this forbidden romance story. Now, I'm simply desperate to escape before a new battle begins.

The bottom stair creaks, as I attempt to leave before the house wakes. I hear a grunt in the front room.

"Sneaking away, I see."

My shoulders slump. "Farfar, I think it's better if I go."

He harrumphs, keeping his eyes locked on the newspaper in his hands. "With him."

"Yes," I say, mouth tight. "And you'll need to get used to it."

"Or?"

My lip trembles, and I'm ashamed when my voice breaks. "You'll lose me."

He doesn't grunt, but he doesn't say anything, the newspaper shudders in his hands. I sigh, and dare to walk over to him as I see Jonas's headlights pull up outside. He has until tonight to take his last midterm; we really need to get back.

I sit stiffly in the rocking chair next to his. "I hate saying that, Farfar, but if you'd simply get to know Jonas, I know you'd see what I do."

"Did you know we were partners?" he snaps.

I assume he means Viggo. "In business?"

"*Jah*. And he took my money, älskling. Because of him, your grandmother and I had to sell our belongings just to pay for our visas to stay here. We lost everything. Because of him. It is a betrayal to me, to your grandmother, associating with that family."

I hesitate, then wipe a rogue tear running down my face. Digging into my purse, I take out the yellowed, creased letter from my grandmother. "I need to go, Farfar, but I think . . . I think you ought to read this. Please do. It's what Farmor wanted me to know, and I think she'd want you to see it right now too."

269

He eyes the letter. I know he recognizes it, but he doesn't take it. Slowly, I set the paper on the table. If anyone can get through to him, it's my grandmother.

"I love you, and I didn't betray you. I simply found happiness. I hope you'll see that someday."

Outside the morning air cuts me to the bone, but Jonas has his car warm; his hand is even warmer when I take it mine.

"You survived," I say.

He cants his head, his thumb brushing a tear I missed on my cheek. "Barely. You okay?"

I shake my head. "I guess I had this dream that it would be smooth, and everyone would be happy for us. I told my grandpa he'd lose me, and . . . I think he's considering it."

Jonas pulls onto the street, pressing a kiss to the back of my hand. "They'll come around, Brit."

"At least our parents are cool," I say with a snort.

"I don't think I've ever been more afraid of your dad than yesterday."

I laugh, the tension melting off my shoulders. "I saved you. We had a talk before the block flipped into a warzone. He was prepared for that delicious bombshell you dropped."

He grins, but I see red tinge the tip of his ears. "Once I started talking it just all fell out."

We go quiet for a few minutes. "Jonas," I say. "My grandpa said that yours was his business partner, and that he took his money. That sounds . . . far-fetched, but what do you think?"

Jonas furrows his brow. "My grandparents were living in a hostel when they started Clara's. They were basically homeless, and he's always blamed their poverty on *your* grandpa."

"If their stories are true then at least one would've had some money to start the bakeries."

Jonas nods, a furrow tugs at his brow. He's thinking.

"I don't know," he finally says. "But I think it might be worth finding out a few things."

I grin. "I like this sly side of you." Pressing my lips against his neck, I enjoy too much when he shudders as I kiss his skin.

"Hey, keep your distance, Jacobson," he tells me. "You keep doing that, and we're going to crash, no other way to put it."

The further we go from home, the more I laugh, the more pressure leaves my chest. By the time we make it back to campus, I know—Jonas makes everything just . . . right.

Chapter 27

"Aren't you going out with Ben?" I ask Jane two days later, when she stomps back into the apartment an hour after leaving.

"No," she snaps, pouring herself a glass of soda. Jane hates soda. "He's a total jerk, and I'm writing him off as a bad memory right . . . now." She tips her glass back and guzzles the whole thing.

I bite my lip. "Want to talk about it?"

"Two girls, Brit. He thought he could juggle two girls and I wouldn't find out. Excuse me. Just who does he think he is?"

"An idiot," I say. "Because you're amazing."

"You have to say that," she says plopping onto the sofa.

"Nope, I don't, but you are, and Ben is dumb. I didn't like him."

Jane snorts and lifts her head. "You didn't?"

"Truly didn't," I say. "Remember, he tried to school me on my capstone. Uh, what's his major again?"

She laughs loudly. "That's right, I forgot he did that. No one messes with you and your lit-nerd stuff."

I nod deliberately. "The day he tried to tell me I didn't know Brönte is the day he lost me."

Jane starts to laugh, but we both jolt when there is a furious knock at the door. When Jane answers, Jonas rushes inside, face flushed.

"What's wrong?" I say, sitting straight.

He kisses me quickly, his lips cold from being outside. Sitting next to me, he slaps a file folder onto our scuffed coffee table. "I found it."

Jane lifts a brow. "Joe did you bring a shiny thing to distract me?"

He glances at me curiously. I pat his arm. "Ben is a jerk."

"Then yes," he says. "I found what our grandpas are talking about. When they lost their business."

My eyes go wide and I lean forward. "You're kidding, what is it?"

Jonas snatches the file folder and goes into a frenzied explanation of his cunning dig through old business sale records, using his mom's connections with the head librarian who also runs the Lindström historical society, and ruffling up a little dirt on some shady business practices, rampant among immigrants at the time.

By the end, Jane is studying the sheets of old document copies Jonas brought with a stick of licorice between her teeth. I slouch against the

273

cushions, entirely overwhelmed. Jonas smiles at me. "Well, how are we going to tell them?"

I shake my head. "Getting them into a room together is one of those impossible things in life."

He scrubs his face and takes one of the papers from Jane. "We've got to though. I mean, they need to know, right?"

Holding his hand, I nod. "Yes, one hundred percent, they need to know."

Viggo and Farfar need to know, but getting them to listen, and forgive. Well, that is an entirely different problem, now isn't it.

***

Friday after classes, Jonas and I make the drive to Lindström, but instead of heading to the bakeries, we go to the high school. Oscar and Bastien's championship game is the perfect place to have our families shoved together on neutral ground.

Music blasts across the gymnasium, the rival school crowd pounds their feet, while Lindström claps and jeers back as the teams are introduced. In the crowd I see Dad sitting next to Agnes who looks like her old self again. Farfar is next to Karl, clapping when Oscar waves from the court. I haven't heard if he read the letter. I hope since he hasn't disowned me yet, that means he's at least scanned it.

Sitting a dozen families away are the Olsens. Clapping along, even though Bastien is on the sidelines with the younger players.

"Which side," I shout at Jonas over the speakers.

274

"Oh, you guys don't want to sit with them; time to make a new united bench."

We both whip around at the reply since Jonas was not the one answer. Axel stands behind us, that white grin back in place as always. My stomach backflips. This is the first time we three have been together, everything out in the open, and thankfully without Logan causing problems.

Jonas eases my discontent when he laughs and claps his brother on the back. "You made it. I didn't think you were coming."

"I wasn't, but then Bass kept sending these whiny texts about how I never support him, like I'm on a vacation. Then he told me there's going to be more family drama." He grins at me. "Since I missed the last one, I couldn't miss this."

Axel has the talent to calm a situation, and by the time we find space at the front of the bleachers I forget this should be awkward, and it's as though Jonas and I have always been. My time with Axel is nothing more than a weird memory.

All through the game, I feel the prickle of steely eyes pinned to our backs. Sometimes I'm brave and peer over my shoulder, and I'll see Inez or Farfar quickly draw their gaze back to the game. Axel watches the Olsens and keeps giving reports in an exaggerated way to keep us smiling. At halftime Agnes plops next to me. She waves her pink bunny at Jonas, smiling.

"Hey, you brought him out," Jonas says. "How's he feeling?"

"Better." She looks at Axel. "Who's he?"

"My mean brother; remember I told you about him," Jonas says, drawing Axel's eyes from his phone.

"Hey, Brit is this your cousin?" Axel's interest is piqued. "Come here," he says to Agnes. "I want you to tell me all about those things you wear in your shoes. I bet they make you go fast."

Agnes seems thrilled and scurries to sit next to Axel. Jonas scoffs. "He's already a physical therapist. Look how excited he is over those shoe inserts."

I laugh, loving everything about this moment. For one thing Axel and Agnes are proudly on our team, for another, Inez knows her daughter is giggling next to an Olsen and, well, she's allowing it. Progress.

When the final buzzer goes off, our team won. I take that as a sign that the fates are smiling on this night. Squeezing Jonas's hand, I give him a tight smile. "Do we have to?"

"Yes," Axel answer for him. "You do. Aggie and I are waiting. We even discussed supplying the popcorn."

"Aggie?" I lift one brow. "She's letting you call her Aggie, now. She only lets me do that."

Axel shrugs, giving Agnes a high-five. "The kid knows a cool person when she's sees one."

"You're going to make grandpa a new friend?" Agnes asks me.

"Well, let's hope," I say, but practically swallow my tongue when Sig and Elias stride past on their way to hug Bastien.

"See you out in the hall," Sig mutters, then turns to her oldest son. "Ax, sweetie, you need a haircut."

He rolls his eyes and says, "Grown man, Mom."

"Always a mother, son."

I hold my breath and smile when my dad waves, and follows Farfar toward the hall. Inez stops to grab Agnes; she politely smiles when my cousin goes on about how 'cool' Axel is and that he knows what her orthotics are supposed to do.

I've never been a schemer, but the idea of ambushing two men with a long overdue intervention is a little thrilling. I lace my fingers with Jonas, Axel following behind us, as we weave through the crowds of people leaving the gym. The lunchroom is our goal. No one goes there after the game, most people shove through the front doors of the school, and it'll give us a little privacy.

"Dad, just hang on, Bass will be out soon."

My insides coil into knots when I hear Elias's voice at the end of the hall, followed by . . .

"Nope, this way Pops, we parked out back."

I hear my grandfather mumble his complaints to my dad about the lighting fiasco in the back parking lot. Pressed against Jonas's hand, my palm is sweaty, but I still laugh when Axel pokes his head between us.

"This is going to be awesome," he whispers.

I wish I shared his enthusiasm.

When we round the corner, Viggo, Sig and Elias are gathered in front of the cafeteria. Jonas's mom gives us a wink, and I feel better knowing she's on our side. According to Jonas, Sig doesn't let Viggo rant too long before she'll give him a piece of her mind. But peace lasts for only a moment before the Jacobson brigade joins.

"Oh, not tonight," Farfar grumbles, beginning to turn around. My dad stops him.

"Wait, Pops, we've got to talk about all this, and there's something you might want to know."

"If I die without seeing his face again," Viggo is telling Elias, "then I will go out with a grin."

Jonas steps in the center of the warring Scandinavians. He clears his throat, and I must say, looks quite sophisticated. He'll be a good attorney. When he's firm on something he knows, a unique confidence bursts from Jonas Olsen. He's addicting.

"Grandpa," he says. "Mr. Jacobson didn't scam you, and he didn't take your investment."

Viggo's brows knit together. "You don't know anything that happened."

"I do. We all do. We took the time to find out, something you both should've done years ago."

"Go Jonas," Axel mutters, not to anyone, but I'm close enough to hear and agree wholeheartedly.

Farfar scoffs. "You think I took money from you? Add liar to your list of things—"

"Oh, my gosh," my dad interrupts through a groan. "Will you just listen for once."

Unexpected, but his insistence gets Farfar to go quiet. Jonas slowly looks to my grandfather, his cracks two knuckles. "Mr. Jacobson."

Farfar narrows his eyes, and I'm ready to jump between them if need be. Truth told, the entire Olsen family seems ready.

"My grandpa didn't take your money either." He backs up so he can see them both. "You were victims of dishonest bankers, a project manager, and a city councilman."

My dad moves in with two file folders. First, he hands one to Farfar, then Viggo. Elias convinces them to sit at one of the cafeteria tables. They put up some resistance at first, but eventually our crowd drifts to the table. Reluctantly, bitterly, they rifle through the pages Jonas, Sig, and my dad arranged for them.

I bite my thumbnail, leaning into Jonas. He wraps one arm around my shoulders and keeps me close while we wait. Farfar grunts as he does, Viggo clicks his tongue, but slowly—ever so slowly—demeanors change.

Sig steps to Viggo's side when he reaches a certain point. "See, Dad," she says softly. "The banker and project manager told you that Philip bought out your half of the lease, but he lied. They manipulated the papers, and took both your investments. Everything appeared very official, and legal, I don't think there's any way you could've known at the time."

"Farfar," I say gently. "The space the city councilman said you could lease, it wasn't even a commercial property, certainly not for something like a bakery." My grandfather looks at me, his blue eyes like glass. "There are more reports of immigrants being taken advantage of like this. You both were taken for, and made out to look like you'd underhanded each other."

"How . . . how do you know this is real?" he asks softly.

"We gathered a few legal records from others who brought suits against these people in the sixties. Looks like they did their scheme from the late forties until the lawsuits." Jonas says. He shows Viggo some of the copies Sig had made from the historical society. "Then we," Jonas gestures to himself and my dad, "reviewed a lot of your old documents; it's all public record. Things just didn't add up."

"But my favorite part is when we found your story," Sig says with a smile, holding up a copy of an old newspaper clipping. "Do you remember doing an interview together?"

Viggo mumbles something under his breath and Farfar glowers at the entire room. Sig goes on anyway. "You never mentioned you met on the ship over here. It talks all about how your upbringing in Denmark, and Philip's in Sweden brought you together. You, Dad," she turns to Viggo. "The son of a pastry chef."

"For the Crown Prince at the time," Viggo adds with a touch of pride, and I think he's subtly informing my family. The Olsens, I'm sure, know the story.

Farfar huffs, and Sigrid turns to him. "And you, Mr. Jacobson. Raised in a bread shop? I can see why you two planned to partner together. And

280

it's impressive how hard you both worked to earn the money for your Scandinavian Market."

"Chimney sweep," Farfar mutters. "Twelve hours a day, sweeping ash."

"Ah, that is nothing to delivering newspapers for a nickel a piece," Viggo says.

I step in before an argument can begin over who suffered the most as young men. "Farfar, Viggo was at your wedding," I say in a breathy voice. I read the article, about the friends, as the reporter put it, who planned to build a new life here. My grandfather schools his haggard gaze to the tabletop. I wonder if he's hiding the emotion we're all feeling. "And my grandparents were at yours and Clara's Mr. Olsen."

"Sounds like you were pretty good friends, Grandpa," Axel chimes in.

"You cared about each other once," I say. "And we've tried to prove that what happened was an awful misunderstanding with the hope that this . . . *fighting* can stop."

No one says anything. Viggo removes his glasses and rubs the bridge of his nose. I hug my middle as my grandfather's chin wrinkles and he ruffles through the file, a faraway expression on his face.

Finally, Farfar clears his throat and closes the file. "As for me, I think too many years have gone by. Too much hurt and unkindness has been done to repair what friendship might have been."

My heart sinks, and I feel a weariness come over the room. Viggo stiffens and gives a firm nod as if he finally agrees with my grandfather on this one, dreary point.

"Did you read my letter?" I ask, my voice hardly more than a whisper.

At that Farfar snaps his eyes to me. He speaks softly, and with a touch of reluctance. "Yes, I did."

"May I have it back then? I know you have it. I'm sure it's tucked inside your wallet behind Farmor's picture."

He snorts, and tries to glare, but grins instead. Probably, because I know him so well. He digs into his tattered leather wallet and pulls out the letter, handing it back to me. I hold it tenderly. Jonas offers me a sad grin, doubtless knowing how important this moment is for me, for my grandmother. Before anyone can protest, I turn on Viggo and hold out the letter. "Maybe you will find more encouragement from this."

"Brita," Farfar snaps. "He does not—"

"It's my letter, and it involves the Olsens," I retort. "Mr. Olsen if you'd like to read what my grandmother wrote about Clara, I would love it."

Viggo looks at me, his gray eyes aren't narrowed in anger against me. As far as I can recall, this is the first time we've stood eye to eye, and I think he truly sees me for the first time. He takes the letter with a nod; Sig and Elias move in, curious.

As he reads, I see Viggo's eyes glisten. He chuckles sometimes. At the end he presses a hand against his chest; his eyes redden. When he folds the letter, he wipes a knobby finger under the rims of his glasses and stares at the floor. Then he laughs. A sound that radiates from somewhere in his belly, growing louder, and louder. He shakes his head and hands me the letter.

"Hair appointments," he says. "That's what she told me. I always wondered why the woman needed two hair appointments each month. Sometimes she came back looking very much the same. I never told her that because I am a man who enjoys breathing."

I laugh and wipe my own eyes, leaning back into Jonas.

Viggo staggers back to his feet and looks at my grandfather. "Philip."

It is the softest I've ever heard Viggo Olsen say Farfar's name.

"I don't know what goes on now," he says, his accent deepening. "Have we been stupid, stubborn men all this time? It would seem so."

Farfar grunts.

"I will not bury grudges tonight," Viggo adds and my stomach sinks. Even Axel scrubs his face and loses his smile. "But," he goes on. "I am making grand plans to do just that."

With a gesture he signals to Elias and Sig that he is ready to leave. I'm left speechless, and thankfully so is Farfar. His face is not curled into a scowl anymore, simply a pensive expression.

"Whoa, what's going on?" Oscar's voice comes from behind us.

"Grandpa is making a new friend," Agnes says from where she's playing with her pink bunny against the wall where Inez and Karl have kept her from overhearing too much.

"What!" Now, Bastien comes up behind Oscar, his mouth open. "We missed it!"

"Sorry, dweeb," Axel says, rustling Bastien's hair. "Better hurry, Mom and Dad are leaving you. Oh, hey good game sitting on the sidelines."

"I played in the third quarter!" Bastien shouts over his shoulder as he chases his parents.

Farfar quietly congratulates Oscar, then tells my dad he wants to go home. The group breaks apart, and I have no idea what happens now. But I grip Jonas's hand and have my answer.

Whatever happens, *he* is there. We've done all we can to change our families. Now, the rest will be up to them.

Chapter 28

Two weeks later I turn on the lights in the bakery display cases as a gray, misty dawn breaks over Lindström. Yawning, I pull out some of the pastries Inez made sinfully early that morning. This week Jonas and I are embracing Spring Break and heading to Michigan, so he can meet Mom officially. I promised to open the shop before we leave, but am excited enough that each step I take kind of bounces. A getaway with Jonas. I'm pathetically giddy.

Stealing a toscabit, a succulent little almond tart that reminds me so much of my grandmother, I flip on all the lights around the tables. Murmurs are coming from the kitchen of the house. Oscar isn't here until later and Aunt Inez left an hour earlier. Dad won't be up for work yet. Odd.

Wiping my hands on the white apron, I go to investigate. We open at seven sharp—I still have thirty minutes.

Rounding the corner, when I see who is seated at my kitchen table, I yelp. Yes, like a little dog that has had its tail stepped on.

"Oh, älskling, I didn't think you could hear us," Farfar says, rising from his seat.

My hand clutches my heart, my eyes wide as I watch Viggo mutter under his breath and shuffle toward the front door.

"Mister Olsen," I gasp. "It's, uh . . . so good to see you. In our home. For the first time. Ever." I speak so slowly, even Farfar seems impatient.

"Morning," Viggo says with a similar accent to Farfar, but a little different. "Philip, consider it all, *jah*? Before we're both dead."

"Oh, get going you miser, or all your customers will leave your empty shop and come discover the superiority of the Swede."

What is happening? The dialogue, the banter, they are playful. Viggo nods, with a smile in my direction. I offer a stiff wave. When the door clicks closed behind old Viggo, I turn and gape at Farfar.

"Oh, don't look at me like that," he says. "It isn't the first time as of late to have that grump in this house."

"When . . . I mean what . . ." I stammer, but Farfar laughs and wraps his arm around my shoulders. "No one has ever said anything." Does Jonas know?

"Because we've been meeting privately. Since we've discovered our families are traitors with the tendency to get too excited, we thought we'd mend a few bridges on our own."

"Farfar . . ." I hardly know what to say. Shaking my head, I meet his eyes. "I'm happy for you, but what was Viggo doing here?"

He pours himself a new cup of tea, peering at me over the rim of his old brown mug. "I thought you'd be pleased."

"I am, of course I am." Is this happening? "It's just, well after the game it didn't seem like anything would change."

"Well, I thought, and he thought. I still think he's a stubborn fool, but we worked well together once. So, we've been discussing combining the shops once again; the reason for our meeting, you see. I'm still not sure how it will all work, but I plan to ask your Jonas and your dad. They seem to have the best business heads."

No, I don't miss how he says *your* Jonas. "You're thinking of doing your market? Wow, that's . . . huge."

He nods and smiles. "We shall see. I feel too old to really think much on it."

The bell dings in the bakery. I stand and kiss Farfar on the cheek. "You're not too old."

"You started all this, älskling," he says patting my cheek. "I hope you'll forgive me for the things I have said to you. You are a light in my life, and I am ashamed at how I hurt you."

"I love you, Farfar." I hug him again. "Always."

He taps my nose the way he used to when I was small. "Alright then, go on. Customers await, and your mother will not want you to be too late for your trip."

My grandfather pats my hand once more before I leave. And all at once, I feel like that last missing piece is finally filled.

Epilogue

"O blessed, blessed night! I am afeard, being in night, all this is but a dream, too flattering-sweet to be substantial."

WILLIAM SHAKESPEARE, *Romeo and Juliet*

Our commencement ceremony is dull and I'm sad saying goodbye to Jane. We make immediate plans to meet at least every three months now that she's taking a job in Pittsburgh. Life has changed, but I sort of like where it's going.

I can hardly believe we are here, two families once at war, huddled around the long restaurant table. Sigrid and Elias sit across from me, and get this, Elias is laughing with my dad about something, I don't know what. Sigrid is asking my mom advice on how to redesign her kitchen. Even Todd fits in. Bastien and Oscar refuse to talk about anything other than their basketball season. We are absent a twin brother, but an internship keeps him out of state. Jonas did receive a rather raunchy graduation gift, and I did too. But I think I've figured out Axel's humor by now.

The strangest part that I'm still getting used to is watching Viggo and Farfar sit by each other, talk, grumble, and return to the friendship they once shared.

Dad asks Jonas about law school. He's applied everywhere and has been accepted almost everywhere. Sigrid votes the University of Minnesota, figures, right? Viggo and Dad suggest LSU in Louisiana, but Jonas always looks to me as though my input matters most. Talk drifts in and out from the new idea for the bakeries that is underway, to Oscar's plans for college, even to Mom's upcoming wedding. That part gets a little weird. Jonas holds my hand under the table, and everything feels right.

When we're set free from the gang of Scandinavians, Jonas and I lean back on the hood of his car, my head on his shoulder, he plays with the curls in my hair. Jane tried to give me decent hair for the ceremony. We look at the lights of the campus, simply being together.

"You did it," he whispers.

I kiss his shoulder. "Did what?"

"What your grandma wanted. I kept thinking it all day, watching everyone act like they've been best friends forever."

I smile and hug his waist. "No, we did it. You found out about those sketchy bankers. I think I had the easy part, I just kissed you a lot. Not that I'm complaining, it is my favorite thing to do."

"I'll dig up hundreds of scams if you keep doing your part." He kisses me quickly to prove his point.

290

My smile fades after a few minutes. I trace his palm. "You know, I almost let the same thing happen with us."

"What do you mean?"

"A misunderstanding almost kept me away from you."

He shifts so he faces me. His palm cups my cheek. "You can't get rid of me that easy, Jacobson. But it's not going to happen to us anyway. You still owe me a winter cabin, where I can fill you with copious amounts of hot chocolate."

I brush his hair off his brow, and snicker. "Not until you go snorkeling with me, and I expect an epic sunburn between us."

He draws my mouth to his. "It's a deal," he says in between kisses.

He curls my head to his chest after a moment, I lace my fingers with his. "I am willing to do anything in life, so long as it's with you," I whisper.

Jonas kisses my brow and holds me tighter. Something tells me this is the way life will be. Brita and Jonas, scheming, eating too much sugar, and loving each other. And that part is by far the most important piece.

Thank You

There are many people who deserve recognition for this book coming to publication. It's been a long road, and many versions of the story. Thank you to my husband and kiddos for always encouraging me to keep writing. Thank you to my sisters, for always reading my books and giving feedback. Thank you to Larissa Rees and Sara Sorensen the best editors and beta readers I could ask for. Thank you to my mom and dad for always embracing our Scandinavian roots, and of course to my grandparent and great-grandparents for keeping the Swede alive throughout the generations. I'm grateful for Fionn at Milktee Covers, and Blue Water Books. Also, thank you to Literary Crush Publishing for first falling in love with Jonas and Brita. I wish you all the best. And of course, thank you to my readers. Without you, these books would grow many layers of dust. Thank you!

Stay up to date with new releases with me at emilycauthor.com. The witty, loud-mouthed Scandinavians aren't finished falling in love yet.

Be kind, and love big,

Em

Made in the USA
Las Vegas, NV
04 February 2023

66915814R00173